the WINTERHOUSE

a novel

Robin McGrath

D1596234

killick press

an imprint of Creative Publishers

St. John's, Newfoundland and Labrador
2009

For my sister Leslie

"The day is short, the task is great, the workers indolent, the reward bountiful, and the master insistent."

Rabbi Tarfon, Ethics of the Fathers

"My father has married me to a mad old man." Rosehannah wrote the words on a slip of onionskin paper and looked at them with something approaching satisfaction. She could never say these words, not to her now-absent father, not to the thin, gloomy stranger who apparently was her husband, nor to the men and women who brought their fish to the premises, but at least she had got them out. It was a great relief.

She picked up the brocade she had been stitching and slipped the piece of paper between the unfinished seams before carefully sewing the collar closed. The letters on the paper were uncharacteristically clumsy, and the small stitches she used to hide them between the layers of cloth a little uneven. She had skinned the knuckle of her index finger to the bone while chopping wood and the wound was stiff and sore.

Rosehannah had bound the finger with a piece of voile, cut from an old dress of her mother's, in the hope that the bandage would escape the mister's attention. She tried to make herself as invisible as possible. The mister made it easy. He rarely looked at her, never commented, spoke only when he had to.

Sitting now in the corner by the fireplace, she could almost convince herself that none of it had happened. The house looked the same—the new mister had changed nothing. She would finish sewing the collar, Papa would come in from the stores for his supper, she would carry a bowl of soup to her mother and settle her for the night, and everything would be as it was before. A coopie, outside under the window, gave a little gurgle of joy as it uncovered a fat bug near the doorstep, sending a flicker of pleasure into the girl. She quickly extinguished it. This was no time for feeling pleasure in anything.

Throughout this last, terrible year, when her mother was dying, Rosehannah had thought nothing could be worse, but now those months seemed idyllic. If her mother was in great pain, she had managed to hide it, but she had become weaker and thinner as the winter wore on. Her father had been uncomfortable with the illness, the inevitability of his wife's death, and had found any excuse he could to be away from the house. When he was at home, he tiptoed around, offering extra goods from the storeroom to a neighbour woman to help Rosehannah with the household chores, longing to escape again.

At first, Rosehannah resented her father's absence, his fear of the silent wraith upstairs, but as her mother withdrew further and further into her own world—the one to come—she began to envy him. He spent most of January, February and part of March back in the woods, at the winterhouses, and by the time he returned, full of tales from the island beyond Thoroughfare, and enthusiastic descriptions of the tight little tilt he had built for them on the far side of Ireland's Eye, Rosehannah was too glad of his company to do anything but throw herself into his arms.

Her mother died at the end of March and they buried the corpse in a deep drift of snow until the last of the storms had been and gone. When a corner of the box showed itself above the snow, they had moved it to a grave on the headland. It was then that her father's grief burst upon the two of them; for a week he sat in his chair in the kitchen and wept, or drank from the keg of brandy stored in the root cellar, or walked up and down the hill between the house and the wharf, doing nothing, carrying nothing, accomplishing nothing except to wear himself out for the deep sleep he escaped into each night.

When the people came back into the settlement from the woods, some were fat and healthy, others gaunt and thin, but all needed provisions and netting, twine and lead, nails and fittings, and a hundred other things to get ready for the coming season. For a day or two, they held off, waiting to see what would happen, who would break first, and then they drifted into the store in ones and twos. Rosehannah had watched it all from the kitchen window and when her father failed to appear, she went in search of him.

2

She found him in the twine loft, sitting with a needle and a bit of net in his hands, as if in a dream. "Come with me, Papa," she had said, and took his large, calloused hand in her own, pulling him towards the door. He had hesitated only a moment and then followed her to the store. Inside, Rosehannah took her mother's place at the desk and her father automatically stepped behind the counter.

Of those assembled, old Toop was the first to come forward. "Well, Mr. Toop," Quint had said, and stopped, not knowing how to go on from there. "Good to see you looking so well after the winter." He pulled the words from the depths of his memory, and looked helplessly around at his daughter.

"I'm tolerable good, thank you, Mr. Quint. Miss Rose. Sorry for your troubles." Toop avoided meeting Quint's eyes, but threw a look of compassion at Rosehannah, who bit her lip and tried to smile. The two men stood staring down at the counter for several moments.

"Papa," Rosehannah murmured. Her father turned and leaned down towards her. "He's in good shape," she whispered, tapping the ledger she had opened in front of her. "Give him whatever you think he needs, and I'll add it up. Then you can negotiate the extras."

The sigh of relief her father gave echoed around the room, escaping from every man and woman in the store. Quint knew what Toop needed, from the first needle to the last hook, but without his wife to interpret the books, he was helpless, for he did not know if Toop could afford to draw the full lot, could have the small luxuries such as sweet oil and cloves they all tried to inveigle out of the merchant's man, or if he was sliding quietly towards a position of debt that only a remarkably lucky year would cure.

The previous autumn, when it was clear that his wife wasn't going to get better, Quint had conveyed word to Trinity to ask that an English youngster be sent out to take care of the accounts, but the boy engaged had been seasick on the voyage and had tumbled overboard two hours before landfall. A message had come from Garland's that they were seeking a replacement, but a literate and numerate youngster was hard to come by in the spring when every community on the shore was looking for help.

Quint looked up at Rosehannah. Poor little scrap. He hadn't given much thought to her through the winter. When she realized what was what, she was going to take it hard. He pushed the thought aside as he noticed Toop sliding a large bar of plug tobacco in among the balls of twine and the strings of fish hooks.

"Still got the taste for the weed, have you, Mr. Toop?" said Rosehannah, with a shy smile.

"Mind your tongue, miss," her father warned. "A man has a right to a bit of a smoke when he works as hard as Toop here." There was a stir of satisfaction in the room. The girl understood the code. When a non-essential item went on the counter, if Mrs. Quint had made a joke, it meant that the account could stand the strain. If she had pretended not to notice, it was over the limit and Quint would silently remove the item and replace it on the shelves. Rosehannah, her nose buried in the account book, felt the change in the room. In those few seconds, she had become a force to reckon with and the knowledge gave her the first undiluted moment of pleasure she had felt in months.

The pleasure hadn't lasted long, she thought as she pressed the voile bandage on her finger. The skinned knuckle burned with pain and she gloomily considered the brocade collar she had just finished. To an unpracticed eye, it would look fine, but she could see the slight discordance of the stitching. She would have to take better care of her hands—swollen and bruised ankles and arms was one thing, but damaged hands would not do. Her sewing skills were all she would have to negotiate with, once the new mister was running the premises.

Hard to believe that she had once enjoyed chopping wood. When the men were away on the boats or in the woods, all the women chopped wood, even her mother had when she was well enough. It gave them some relief from the house, a breath of air. But to be obliged to do it all the time, when there were men and boys present, was humiliating. The medium-weight axe her father had given her the previous year had mysteriously vanished, and she found the small hatchet too light to be effective, while the heavy maul wore her out.

The last time her father had weighed her, setting her on the fish scale down in the store and joking that she was a prize cod, she had tipped the balance at only six stone. Since then, she had grown even thinner but had gained a little in height. She was stronger than she looked, but was still smaller than the few other girls her age on Ireland's Eye. Rosehannah fingered the collar, feeling the slight rustle of paper between the cloth.

Her father had married her off to a mad old man. Well, he wasn't as old as she had first thought. The cropped white hair and the bitter look in his eye had deceived her into thinking him at least as old as Papa, but he was probably closer in age to her than to her father. And mad? Probably not that either, but certainly despairing. For that matter, the legality of the marriage was doubtful, and it seemed that her father, her dearest Papa, was not her real father after all.

Once Mama was properly buried, and her father had got over his fit of crying, things had gone along reasonably well for a few weeks. She kept the books as her mother had done, and looked after the house. Selby was usually nearby to cut wood and carry water, and he hadn't needed to be told, just did it as part of his chores. Then, one morning in early May, the *William and Mary* had arrived from Trinity with the promised youngster on board—only he wasn't a youngster, but a man.

He looked "rode hard and put away wet," Selby had said, and he was right about that. The *Helga*, on which the new man had traveled out from Plymouth, had gone aground in Trinity Bight and while no one was drowned, the passengers and crew had all gotten very cold and the baggage was soaked. Of course, the men from Lester Garland were more concerned with salvaging cargo than coddling passengers, so the man was still in the same clothes he had landed in two days before.

"J. Harris." That was the name on his sea chest. Captain Ryder had only called him "the mister," which gave no clue as to how they were to address him, only hinted that he was a cut above the usual merchant's man. Rosehannah had known right away that he was not there to assist her father, but to take over from him.

Had Triffie Hodder been in the crowd on the wharf when the schooner tied up? Probably. Rosehannah hadn't noticed. She was nearby two hours later, though. While Captain Ryder reluctantly conducted the brief marriage ceremony, she was hovering by the door of the store with her snot-nosed boys hanging off her. When had her father sent the message to Mr. Garland that he wanted to move on to Rise's Harbour? It must have been before her mother died. Yet his grief had been genuine, she was certain of that. And he did love her. He had given her the winterhouse when she asked for it.

Rosehannah had taken all the pieces of the puzzle and twisted and turned them over in her mind a dozen times. As they fell into place, her confusion grew: how could she have had all the facts and not realized what they meant? Fourteen years earlier, like Mr. Harris, her mother had been shipwrecked in Trinity Bight. Her husband had drowned along with most of the crew, her belongings had been lost; Papa was one of the men who had rowed out in the gale to save the few pitiful survivors.

He had plucked Mama off a mast and wrapped her in his own coat, that was what Mama had told her, and then he had married her and brought her to Ireland's Eye. Mama had been a governess back in England, and Papa was only a fisherman, but he was one of Lester Garland's men and an Anglican of course, while she was a Catholic, so she had been lucky to find such a good husband so soon after losing her previous one.

Her mother must have been pregnant when she was widowed, Rosehannah reasoned, and therefore pregnant when she married Papa. She considered for a moment the possibility that there had been no previous husband, that her mother was pregnant by her Papa or some other man who had perhaps abandoned her, but if that were so, why invent a drowned man? Why not just let everybody believe that Nicholas Quint was the father of the baby?

Rosehannah had known about the shipwreck, known about the rescue and the subsequent marriage, yet had never for a moment wondered which of the two husbands was really her father. Nicholas Quint was her Papa. That is what she called him, what he called himself, what he had been to her for fourteen years until that moment when J. Harris stepped off the *William and Mary*.

"I'll be going on to Rise's Harbour with the Captain, Rosie," her Papa had said. "You'd best stay here and give the new mister a hand. Look after the house for him." She had stared at him, uncomprehending, and he had glanced defensively around at the onlookers. "She's a big girl, now. She can fadge for herself." And then, looking at Lester Garland's new man, who clearly wasn't what he had expected him to be, Nicholas Quint had fired over his bows.

"You can take the whole works, but you must take the girl too. You can marry her if you like. She's worth having. She can read and write; sews too. She can keep the books, knows every woman and Christian in the harbour." And seeing the look of incomprehension on J. Harris's face, he looked around at the increasing crowd. "He don't know a thing, do he? He's too green to burn. He won't last the winter here without her to look after him."

That was when Rosehannah had, unaccountably, noticed Tryphenia Hodder by the door. Triffie had walked over from Traytown, and now stood hugging the door post, watching Papa as if she were willing him to speak these words. It was her idea, this ridiculous marriage. Ever since her husband had been killed—fell over a cliff in the fog while out hunting seabirds— Triffie had been breaking her neck looking for a man.

Marry him yourself, if you're so desperate for a wedding, Rosehannah thought, and flung a look of outrage at Triffie.

"I got my man, Rosie. Now you got yours." Tryphenia called over to her, as if reading her thoughts, and grinning broadly, she turned to share the joke with the women hovering behind her. Rosehannah saw it then, saw the swelling belly under her apron, knew now why old Toop had been so sorry for her. They all knew. Papa hadn't waited for Mama to die.

7

Rosehannah sighed and put the collar to one side. Her situation was intolerable. She had no family, no property or income, and was dependent on a total stranger for every bite she put into her mouth. She had been watching J. Harris for the best part of a month, and was convinced he was in a fog of melancholy or despair. She wasn't even sure he really knew what was going on around him, so withdrawn and silent had he been.

At first she had put it down to the shock of the shipwreck. Captain Ryder had told Papa that the *Helga* had suffered a rough voyage over, so the new mister may have already been weak from seasickness when he got dumped into the cold waters of the Bight. Certainly he looked like he'd been dragged from death's doorstep. He'd more stumbled than climbed from the deck of the *William and Mary,* and as soon as his sea chest was unloaded, he'd sunk down on top of it with his head hanging down between his knees as if he were about to heave up.

Rosehannah had studied him closely: here was a strange fish, indeed. He was thin as a gad, with a head of close-cropped, pure white hair. His clothes—trousers, not britches, and a cutaway jacket—were of good quality but wrinkled and crusted with sea salt. His skin was as pale as her own, save for two patches of bright red on his high cheekbones, and his eyes glittered dangerously. Rosehannah suspected he was running a fever.

She had watched the stranger, this J. Harris, all the time her father and Captain Ryder were in the store talking. Had she any idea what they were talking about, she would have abandoned her post at the door of the store quick enough.

It was almost certainly Tryphenia who had come up with the idea of marrying her off. What surer way to get rid of an unwanted step-daughter? And the groom was too sick or too indifferent to stop the formalities of the wedding once the process got underway. He had protested in a half-hearted way, but once he admitted he had no wife at home in England, those protests had been pushed aside.

Lots of people got married on the dock or on the deck of a schooner when they arrived in the colony. Men still outnumbered women here, even in the towns, so a single girl could have her pick, and she had better pick quickly and well if she didn't want to spend her nights sleeping with her back against the door. Rosehannah had not had any problem that way—the mister took no interest in her, not then or now.

As far as she could tell, Mr. Harris had no experience or interest in keeping a store, knew nothing about fish, had not the faintest idea of what to expect from the weather or customs of the country, and was likely to perish of starvation, fatigue or disinterest before the winter had half set in. His sea chest had sat on the wharf leaking water for three days before she finally had Selby haul it up to the house and leave it in its owner's room, next to the bed where Papa and Captain Ryder had deposited J. Harris after pouring half a pannikin of brandy down his throat.

He had taken little interest in anything during those three days, sleeping most of the time, drinking a little of the broth and tea she left just inside the door, and presumably emptying his bladder into the chamber pot under the bed, judging by the increasingly pungent smell coming from the room. On the third morning, when he finally lapsed into something resembling a normal sleep rather than the moaning semi-delirium he had experienced up until then, she slipped into the room, removed the offending vessel, and disposed of its contents off the end of the wharf.

It was almost evening when he stumbled down from the bedroom. Let him be the first to speak was all the plan she could come up with. She did not know what to say to him.

"Who are you?" he asked, his voice raspy and dry. He glanced around the room as if trying to locate something familiar, something to anchor himself to.

This was not what Rosehannah had expected. What to answer? Your wife? Mrs. J. Harris? Perhaps he did not recollect that part of his arrival.

"Rosehannah," she replied after a few moments of hesitation, leaving the question of a last name to be solved later. Leaning forward, she removed a cloth covering a bowl near the hearth and handed the dish to him, gesturing at the chair that was positioned opposite her stool. He sank down as if his legs would no longer hold him up and she rose silently, crossed the room to a dresser and fetched back a spoon. His hand trembled as he ate the salty broth, but some colour returned into his face. When he had finished, she brought him a pannikin of cold water and he drank thirstily. She could almost see the cloud of confusion and illness that had hovered over him dissipate and clear, and she braced herself for what was to come.

"Who are you?" he asked again.

"I'm not sure," she answered, her voice dropping almost to a whisper. "I thought I was Rosehannah Quint." She glanced up at him, to see if he had any idea what she meant. A wry smile twisted his lips for a moment.

"I found this tucked into the bed with me when I woke." Reaching into his vest, he pulled out a rolled sheet of paper and handed it to her. The marriage certificate.

"Jacob Harris of Plymouth," she read aloud. Jacob. That is what the J. stood for.

"It won't stand up in a court," he said. "We are considerably less than fifty miles from a church official or magistrate, and I could hardly have been considered to be of right mind. Besides, you are still a child. What, eleven years old? Twelve?"

"Fourteen," she corrected him. Her mother had told her they got their growth late in her family.

"Nevertheless, the whole thing is ludicrous. There is no marriage, nor is there going to be." The mister sat back in Papa's chair and looked hard at her. Rosehannah shrank under his stare. He had dark eyes in a gaunt, bony face, but was younger than his startling white hair had suggested. "That man Quint, your father—why would he do such a thing to you?"

Rosehannah stared down at the paper in her hand, trying to formulate a reply, for it was a question that had plagued her for days. "I think he meant well," she finally whispered, and then cleared her throat and tried again. "He saw it as an omen, the shipwreck. He met my mother when she was shipwrecked, and they were happy until Mama got sick. Papa's not a bad man, just..." She could hardly bring herself to say it, had not even thought it until the past year.

"Ryder said he was clever with his hands, but remarkably stupid." Rosehannah winced at the blunt words. "He said your mother ran the business, that your father was illiterate and likely to stay that way. But you can read, you read my name on that ridiculous certificate. Why didn't you take over where your mother left off?" He stared relentlessly at her and she squirmed on her stool.

"Trif—Tryphenia Hodder. Her husband fell off a cliff last autumn, hunting sea birds, and she has three small children. Out here, people marry for convenience." Rosehannah stared at her hands in her lap as she said this.

"People everywhere marry for convenience," the mister said dryly. "I did it myself once."

Rosehannah rerolled the paper tightly and pushed it into the pocket of her apron. She looked horrible when she cried, she knew that—her nose got swollen and red and her eyes disappeared into her head, so she tried never to do it. She glanced over at the mister, but he was staring at the ceiling, thinking hard.

"Who do you know in Trinity?" he asked abruptly. "The next boat in, I'll send you back there."

Trinity? Rosehannah had been to Trinity but she knew no one there. What would she do in Trinity? Act as nursemaid to some young matron's family? Scrub chamber pots and cooking pots?

"I can't go to Trinity. I can't leave Ireland's Eye."

"You'll do what you're told," he shot back, and abruptly stood up. The colour drained suddenly from his face and he swayed slightly before grabbing the back of the chair for support. "You'll make yourself useful around here until I can arrange for you to join a family at Trinity, and then you'll go."

Angry as she was with her father, with the whole community who had conspired to put him into Triffie Hodder's bed, the idea of leaving Ireland's Eye had never entered Rosehannah's mind. If anything, she wanted to stay more than ever. With Papa and Triffie away in Rise's Harbour, and the winterhouse waiting, she had every reason to stay.

Mama and Papa had liked going to visit the winter quarters, although they didn't move into the woods themselves. Of all the houses in Ireland's Eye, theirs was the one best suited for the cold season, and the coal allowance that came out from Trinity made winter in the harbour tolerable, so the three of them could stay where they were year round. However, Papa generally visited all his families at the back of the island throughout the cold season, even those across the tickle at Thoroughfare.

Rosehannah and her mother had walked over the hill behind the harbour to view the tilts at Broad Cove one July day; to Rosehannah's eye they did not display much charm in the broad light of the summer sun. The low roofs, dirt floors and small, shuttered windows, most lacking even a pane of glass, looked cramped and sordid. But in winter, on a stormy day, they were cozy, full of life, good company, and games of every sort. Social barriers broke down, quarrels were forgotten, older people slept uninterrupted for days and nights at a time, and young ones played without regard to bedtimes.

If the mister had the marriage annulled, would the winterhouse still belong to her? Papa had transferred it to her in front of everyone, desperate to appease her. Triffie had tried to stop him, but her dead husband's tilt, back from Rise's Harbour, was still in reasonably good repair and everyone knew that. Papa may have been unable to add fifteen shillings to six to make one pound one shilling, but he knew enough to realize that without Rosehannah's mother, he would never have been allowed to act for Lester Garland, nor have all the little extras that went with that position. He owed her a debt.

Rosehannah and Papa had planned the tilt together, arguing about the placement of the cooking fire, the two beds, the one window. They had discussed the best way to construct the chimney, and Rosehannah had measured a nail keg and calculated how many they needed to get the right height. When an old seal skin, too rotten to salvage, had washed up on the rocks, she had spent a pungent afternoon pulling the hair out and drying it on the rocks before stuffing it into a brin sack to be stored in the twine loft. She had also dug out a barrel of clay on the Indian Islands the previous summer, so that Papa could mix it with the hair from the old skin to line the inside of the nail kegs as he strapped them together.

The winterhouse had been his excuse for being away for most of the six months it had taken her mother to die. "Mama will love it, Rosie," he had told her. "She'll fall over herself to come out to the woods, it's so snug and tight." They always spoke as if her mother were going to get better, although both knew she would not: the winterhouse wasn't for Mama, it was for Rosehannah herself, something to make the long death-watch endurable, something for her to look forward to when she and Papa were alone.

She should have known Papa would not be alone for long. Triffie and her children had taken shelter with her sister at Broad Cove, only a gunshot or two from the tilt where Papa was stopping while he built the new tilt across the tickle from Chair Cove Head.

The appearance of the mister was a godsend to Quint. Harris had looked as weak as a kitten when they hauled him from the deck of the *William and Mary,* but Captain Ryder had said he was well connected, that Mr. Garland had personally sent down to see that he was safe after the *Helga* grounded. Triffie had realized right away that he would be useful, could take Rosie and the business off Quint's hands in one fell swoop. He didn't want the business—it frightened him to be in charge of things he did not understand.

"You must look after the new mister," he had told Rosehannah. "He won't be able to manage without you. He needs a housekeeper, someone who knows the people. Selby will have the place stripped to the boards otherwise."

"But where will I sleep, Papa?" she had asked. "I can't sleep down by the fire with a stranger in the house."

"He can take the upstairs, and you can have the linney." Quint looked desperately for Triffie, needing direction. "I'll be moving on. There's a couple of families going over to Rise's Harbour with the Hodders and I can fish with them."

"So I'm to stay here by myself, Papa?" She looked hurt, puzzled and not a little afraid.

Quint suddenly realized that he was leading Rosehannah in the wrong direction with his talk about her sleeping in the linney. He struggled to find the words Triffie had given him. "Not alone, Rosie. The mister will look after you. He's a good catch, and the shipwreck is a sign. He was sent here for you."

This discussion was taking place in the store, behind the counter where they had at least a modicum of privacy. The counter did not prevent the others in the store from hearing what was being said, but courtesy demanded that they pretend not to hear. Captain Ryder glanced her way with concern, as Rosehannah grasped the edge of the counter and leaned forward to look out the door at J. Harris, folded like a dishcloth over his battered sea chest. He looked like an albino crow dying on a longer, like a seagull with a fishhook in its guts, like something used up and wrung out and thrown onto the wharf to dry up and blow away.

She had, of course, thought occasionally of who she might marry eventually, had thrown an egg into the path on Midsummer's Day and tried to discern letters or a token in the spilled liquid, but she had never seen anything even remotely like J. Harris.

"Papa, are you talking about me marrying him?" Rosehannah's voice rose in panic, and everyone in the storeroom turned and looked at her, taking her raised voice as tacit permission to eavesdrop.

That was when J. Harris had seen fit to stagger into the store. There was not the least hint of his taking possession of the place, but Quint acted as if Harris were a challenger, the new mister come to take over.

"You can take the whole works, but you must take the girl too," he had bawled at the newcomer. Harris had swayed on his feet as if he were about to faint. That was when Rosehannah had seen Tryphenia Hodder in the doorway, and understood the deal was done.

Captain Ryder understood it also, and rather than leave Rosehannah entirely to the mercy of the mister, he had bent over the counter of the store and scribbled out something resembling a marriage agreement. Quint produced the cheap, thin ring Rosehannah had removed from his wife's dead finger, and closed Harris's cold hand over it before transferring it to Rosehannah's. It had fallen off and through a crack in the floor minutes later, but everyone present had seen the dull glint of gold and that was all that was necessary.

Make yourself useful, the mister had said. That was her only point of negotiation, and she might use it to her advantage as she had used her father's guilt to gain the winterhouse. If J. Harris really was as helpless as her father had suggested, he might actually need her.

"I must get your clothes dried and cleaned before I leave," she had said. Harris looked down at his jacket and trousers, which were stiff with dirt. "I mean the ones in your sea chest. It's been soaking in water for close to a week and everything will be ruined soon, if it isn't already." He hesitated, as if trying to think the matter through, so she pressed the point. "There are no shirts in the store here, and it could take weeks to bring some from Trinity."

"Yes, I suppose that's true," he allowed. "You'd best come up and have a look."

She followed him up the narrow stair to the room that had been her mother's and father's. She had not really seen it since her mother had died, and she was relieved to find that her father had packed all her mother's things into a basket and put them to one side. At least Tryphenia hadn't gotten them. The sea chest didn't look promising.

"It's been opened," Harris said, fingering the rope that held the lid closed. "Someone broke the lock."

"Captain Ryder said it was like that when it came aboard the *William and Mary*. Whoever salvaged it off the *Helga* must have done it."

Harris sank onto the edge of the bed and a swear word escaped his lips. Rosehannah didn't know what the word was, a foreign language perhaps, but she recognized the tone. What little energy he had left after his illness seemed to have drained out of him and he looked hopelessly at the box.

"If you make a list of what's missing and send it to Mr. Garland, he'll put the word out." She took his sigh for assent and quickly undid the knot in the rope. When she lifted the lid, the contents seemed to be wet but more or less in order.

"My flute is gone. The case was on top," Harris said.

Rosehannah could see a rectangular indentation in the neatly folded clothes. He'd need shirts more than he'd need a flute on Ireland's Eye, she thought. The thief seemed to have left him enough of those. Swiftly she lifted out close to a dozen shirts. She shook several of them out, and aside from being wet, they were sound. No mould, thank goodness. She'd have them washed and dried in no time.

Stockings, underclothes, neck cloths, handkerchiefs and woolen outer clothes soon joined the sodden pile on the floor. The box had been packed so tightly that the inner items were barely damp. Whoever had organized the packing had anticipated the possibility of it getting wet, as a neat bundle of oilcloth lodged at the heart of the trunk, dry as a bone. She lifted it out carefully and placed it on the bed next to him.

"Spare boots, even," she noted aloud.

"My landlady in Plymouth, Mrs. Hart, has a haberdashery. My own things didn't nearly fill the box and she insisted that it wasn't going all the way across the ocean half empty."

"Well, she certainly knew how to pack a box tightly. What shall I do with this?" Rosehannah held up a partial bolt of brocade.

"I don't know." What little interest he'd had in the unpacking had disappeared when he'd realized the flute was gone. "Throw it out, for all I care."

"Oh, no." Rosehannah was shocked at such disregard for his possessions. Clearly, he hadn't the heart of a shopkeeper. "It's beautiful stuff, and there's yards of it." She rolled out a length of the material and ran an admiring hand over it.

"Then take it. It's of no use to me." He pulled the string holding the oilcloth together, opened the bundle and began listlessly spreading the contents across the unmade bed. Paper, quills, a bottle of ink sealed with wax, were evident. He flipped open the lid of a flat tin to reveal neat packets of pigment and several brushes, but snapped it closed before Rosehannah could get a proper look. He rifled through the papers, apparently looking for something that wasn't there, and when he had come to that conclusion himself, he again lost interest.

He began collecting up the papers as Rosehannah bundled up the shirts and the beautiful brocade. From within the folds of the last of the clothes fell a book, unbound but new.

"*Ivanhoe*," she read off the title page, and then glanced up at Harris excitedly. "By the author of *Waverley*."

"Just off the press. All of London is abuzz, or at least the synagogue at Hamborough is." He gave another of his wry smiles, amused by his own irony. "Take it, if you're interested," he added.

"Thank you very much. And for the brocade too." She smiled shyly at him, and for a moment Harris thought she looked quite pretty.

"Get the shirts washed before you start to read it or I might not have a change of clothes before you leave." He scowled, just to remind her that she wasn't his wife, and she wasn't staying on Ireland's Eye.

She dropped the laundry down over the steps, and then turned to open a locker at the bottom of the bed. "Papa's old things, until I get your trousers and coat cleaned up." She laid the clothes on the bed next to the bundle of papers and headed down the stairs. "I'll bring you a bucket of water to wash in. I don't think a basin will do," she added over her shoulder.

Despite the presents and her making herself useful, things with the mister did not improve. If anything, the more she showed how much he needed her—or someone—to run the house and mitigate the errors he made at the store, the less

Harris seemed to appreciate having Rosehannah around. Selby caught the scent of it, and before long was neglecting his chores, being rude to Rosehannah and positioning himself to become assistant to the mister.

She had cooked excellent food that he swallowed without tasting, she had washed and pressed his clothes, even the heavy cutaway coat, so that they looked like new, but he had barely glanced at them, and continued wearing her Papa's old breeches, instead of his own elegant trousers, and he refused to open the store unless someone came pounding on the door. What he did in there all day was anyone's guess.

Three weeks after her wedding day, Rosehannah still knew little or nothing about him. A sly question intended to determine if the generous Mrs. Hart was a lover had elicited the information that she was an old family friend, an ancient widow with a waistline to rival a rain barrel.

Cleaned up, Mr. Harris looked considerably younger than he had with a week's growth of patchy white beard, yet even in breeches, he had a foreign air about him. His English was almost flawless, yet there was a guttural vibration to his Rs that Rosehannah had never heard even Mr. Garland employ. He drank a little wine or beer with his meals if she poured it for him, but he didn't ask for it, and never finished it all.

Selby was the real problem. Mr. Garland would be horrified if he knew the liberties Selby was taking with the stores, and if she got shipped off to Trinity, the whole premises would be in jeopardy.

Rosehannah smoothed the collar she had sewn and admired the pattern of red and gold blackberries on a cream background. The brocade was cotton but it looked like it had silk in it, and she had cut it so as to position a tiny bee on each corner of the collar. She was longing to sew something larger, to give the pattern its full glory, but was afraid to cut it until she'd got her growth, or devised a cut that could be adjusted later if necessary. The collar was a promise to herself that she would one day have a most beautiful dress.

Rosehannah's skinned knuckle had started bleeding again, and she found a scrap of cloth to press against the bandage. Her back ached and her head was swimming. The sodden lump of cloth between her legs bunched uncomfortably, reminding her that it was that nasty time of the month. She saw with something like despair that the fire had burned down again and the wood basket was empty.

She had always liked the hollow knock of a birch billet cleaving in two, and had chopped wood with the best of them, but Selby had used up all the straight, dry wood and left her only knotted, tough junks of juniper. It took six or eight blows of the axe to split one of them, and half the time the pieces bounced back at her. Her ankles and the insides of her arms were covered in bruises.

Pulling herself out of the chair by sheer will power, Rosehannah stepped outside and eyed the chopping stump. One of her hens, Tulip, was clucking around the base, pecking at the small grubs that often fell there from the bark of the wood. Rosehannah reached into her apron pocket and broke a bit of bread from the crust she had there. She sat on the stump and whispered endearments to the hen, who accepted the offering and allowed herself to be picked up and placed in the girl's lap. She did not notice Selby until he had sneaked up to her and lifted the hem of her dress with a long gad he had in his hand.

"Keep back," she scolded him, "or I'll tell the mister on you."

"The mister don't care. Sure, he don't want it hisself." Selby smirked and tried chucking the hen under what would have been her chin if she'd had one. With a loud bawk, the bird flew out from Rosehannah's arms. "Here," he said, dropping the gad into her lap. "Maybe the mister needs the rooster's helper if he's to play thread the needle with a tight little piece like you."

Whether it was the monthlies, the knotty wood he'd been leaving her, or the weeks of tension, Rosehannah was never sure, but without a moment's hesitation she gripped the gad in her hand and whipped it across his face as hard as she could.

"Jesus, you little vixen, you've nearly blinded me," Selby roared, grabbing her by the wrists with one swift lunge. "I'll give you a licking you won't soon forget." Rosehannah struggled to free her hands, but she couldn't escape his grip and he easily lifted her off her feet.

"Let me go. I swear, I'll kill you," she screeched, twisting wildly in the air as he held her arms high over her head.

"Let the child go, immediately," she heard, and with difficulty, turned her head far enough to see the mister pick the axe up from behind the stump.

Selby dumped her unceremoniously on the ground. "I was only making a bloody joke, and she laid into me enough to blind me," he bellowed. "Jesus' blood, I was only making a joke." He clapped his hand over the scarlet welt on his cheek and stormed off.

"Are you all right?" Harris lifted her back onto her feet. In the struggle, her sleeves had pulled up to her elbows and he turned her hands to expose the bruises on her arms. "How did you get these?"

"Selby…" she choked on the words as the fright at what she'd done closed in on her. She began to cry, and he pulled one of Mrs. Hart's lovely handkerchiefs from his pocket.

"I came up to tell you that the schooner from Trinity is here, and you should pack your clothes. You can't go in this condition, though, so I'll send Selby instead. Let Mr. Garland find work for him elsewhere."

"Oh please, I didn't mean…it's just that he hasn't been chopping the wood for me, and the pieces are full of knots so they bounce back at me, and then he said I needed to have a span tied across my back like one of the hens…" Harris had stopped listening.

"It's better this way. I don't trust the man. You can go on the next boat. Now go and wash your face. Apparently, I've let things slide rather badly in the last month, and I have some catching up to do." He pushed her towards the door of the house and headed back down to the wharf.

Rosehannah could feel her nose getting bigger and her eyes getting smaller, so she made no attempt to stop him or follow him. Inside, in the kitchen, she poured a basin of warm water from the kettle over the fire and retreated to the linney where she washed her face, and removed the bloody clouts from under her dress. The flow had lessened and by morning it would have stopped. She lay down on the small cot that served as her bed; her last thought before she fell asleep was that Selby had achieved for her everything she had tried and failed to get from the mister.

Aug. 29, 04

Dear Ms. Hart,

Thank you for your kind words regarding my article in the Royal Philatelist. *Although I never did determine with 100% certainty that Simon Solomon was of Jewish heritage, I found out a good deal more about him than I anticipated when I set about the task of documenting the life of our first postmaster. I think the weight of probability that he was one of the Devon Solomons is such that, eventually, the link will be established. I expect it requires someone with more computer and internet skills than I have, or wish to possess, to really nail it down.*

Now, as to your query about the Jewish Harrises in Newfoundland, I'm afraid there are none. I was, to some extent, flying under false colours when the Philatelist *described me as a member of the Hebrew Congregation of Newfoundland and Labrador. My late wife, who was Jewish, was working on a history of the community when she became ill, and I have been trying to finish what she was unable to complete. The archive consists of two boxes of papers on a shelf in the library cum classroom. I suppose I am a member of the community— I pay my dues and have continued to attend occasional services at the shul since her death, primarily for the sake of our grandchildren.*

And there again I find I am misrepresenting myself to some extent. The grandchildren were hers, not mine, but I am very fond of them, two delightful girls aged nine and eleven, and I have continued my involvement with them and their parents as if they were my own. I am, by birth if not persuasion, a Christian, descended from Harrises who were Christian many generations back. My mother was very attached to the Church of Rome, and for her sake I maintained my ties to that institution during her lifetime, but had no compunction about abandoning it when I married and found myself with an instant family of moderately observant Jews. I confess, I feel more comfortable in the synagogue than I ever did at the Basilica.

I am sorry to disappoint you in your quest for the elusive Jacob. If you were to outline why you think your missing Harris came out to the colony, I could perhaps pursue the matter for you as a sideline to my ongoing research on the Jewish history of the province. I'm afraid I must ask you to reply by what Leah (the eleven-year-old) calls snail mail, as I do not have

22

email. I had an active account at the university when I retired, but they changed the system just about the time my wife died and I never signed up for a new address. Now, I find that I prefer the pace of old-fashioned correspondence, and it gives me a reason to walk to the postbox each day, the only exercise I get unless I am dog-sitting when the children are away.

In reading over this letter, I see that I have given you far more information about myself than you either wanted or needed. That's a risk you run when you pursue genealogy, I suppose. Best of luck with your project.

Sincerely,
John Harris

"Select a master teacher for yourself so that you avoid doubtful decisions; do not make a habit of tithing by estimate."

Rabban Gamliel, Ethics of the Fathers

℞ osehannah woke at first light, having slept through the evening and the night. She had a faint recollection of movement in the kitchen some time after dark the night before, and thought it must have been the mister, foraging for his supper. A pang of guilt brought her out from under the bedclothes before she reasoned that if he had needed her to bring him food, he had only to call through the thin partition to wake her.

She had slept in her clothes, which were wrinkled and not entirely fresh, but they would do for the work she had today. Stepping quietly into the kitchen, she could sense his presence in the room above her. She stopped a moment to listen, and beneath the racket of the crows and the high-pitched, exultant cry of her little bantam cock, she heard a soft snoring.

She quickly examined the kitchen, searching for clues as to what he had eaten and when. The bake-pot she had left cooling when she had fallen asleep was on the table, and she lifted the heavy lid carefully. Half the loaf was gone, and there were tell-tale smudges of jam on the cloth. A puddle of tea in a bowl attested to an uninspired but adequate meal.

She tidied the table, cut the remaining bread into slabs, buttered it and divided the slices into two portions, setting the larger ones aside and wrapping the rest in a scrap of oiled cloth. The day before, she had boiled and shelled all her week-old eggs and immersed them in salted water. From the cupboard she took the heavy clay egg-crock, removed the lid, and put three of the eggs into a bowl. Two more went into a bit of paper rescued from a biscuit box. Two handfuls of raisins, one large and one small, completed her breakfast preparations. A chunk of salt cod put to soak in a large tub of water was her preparation for supper.

Rosehannah turned the empty bake-pot over the mister's meal, and placed her own in the basket of eggs she had been collecting for the last six days. Throughout the week, she had searched out all her missing hens, and three were broody. She had ruthlessly taken the eggs from the largest two and replaced them with a few small beach stones she had warmed in her hands.

From the drawer in the kitchen dresser, she extracted a small wood-framed slate and a lump of hard, yellowed chalk. Licking the chalk, she wrote in her best hand "Gone to Traytown to change the eggs. Back before dark." She propped the slate against the upturned bake-pot, lifted the key to the store from its nail behind the dresser, and slipped out of the house with her basket, closing the door silently behind her.

From the top of the path over the wharf she could see all of Ireland's Eye harbour, its flakes, stores, barrels and buckets, a familiar jumble of chaos and order. A single boat bobbed on the water off Anthony Island, and beyond that she could see Duck Island, dwarfed by an enormous iceberg, almost a mile long the men had said. The morning was clear and bright, but a chill hung in the air, and a light mist hovered over the iceberg as the weak rays of the newly-risen sun began the inexorable process of melting the massive giant.

Rosehannah shivered; the cold air rapidly chilled her skin, and she reminded herself that she would be grateful for the low temperatures once she got up into the woods. Setting her basket to the side of the path, she slipped down to the store and let herself in with the key. The rising sun barely penetrated inside, as she glanced around the gloom.

Her heart ached at the first sight she'd had in a month of the place that had been a part of her home for her entire life. A flicker of resentment against the mister—the interloper—stirred in her and she firmly reminded herself that it wasn't he who had taken her mother from her, nor was it he who had abandoned her. Rather the reverse—he had allowed her to stay, for a time at least: if not for him, she would be wiping the dirty bottoms and faces of other people's children in Trinity.

The store looked much the same, except dustier. She would have to sweep it out one day soon when the mister was busy elsewhere. She looked around for oakum, and her eye settled on an old writing desk that had stood on the shelf as long as she could remember. The boards were warped, so the lid and hinged front no longer closed: no one had bothered to change the date.

She reached up to the shelf and lifted the writing box down. A cheap bit of frippery, she recognized that now, but as a little girl she had been fascinated by it. The box stood tall rather than flat, and the front folded down to make a narrow, impractical writing surface. The lid lifted to reveal several upright slots for holding paper, and a shallow drawer at the bottom had divided compartments intended to hold an inkwell, now missing, and other necessities such as sealing wax and string.

For Rosehannah, the inner front of the box was where the magic lay. Above two upturned brass hooks, intended to hold a quill, were a set of brass knobs that could be turned to scroll a daily calendar framed by cutout openings in the cracked veneer. As soon as she had been able to tell her numbers, it had been Rosehannah's job to turn the knobs ahead each day to change the date, and twelve times a year to change the month.

Mama had taught her to discover the number of days in a month along the knuckles of her hand:

Fourth, eleventh, ninth, sixth,
Thirty days to each affix,
Every other thirty one,
Except the second month alone.

She murmured the rhyme to herself as she scrolled the month ahead from May to June, and then moved the day from the unlucky 13th to the 17th. The year, 1820, she left alone.

She returned the writing desk to its shelf, and stood breathing in the strong scents of the store, the scent also of her papa: tar, fish, linseed, train oil.

Underlying the familiar smells was one not quite so prevalent. She followed her nose to the lowest shelf under the counter and stopped, squatting in the dusty light, to puzzle out what she saw. A small rectangle of canvas, not much more than a foot long, had been stretched over the lid of a biscuit box and tacked into place. On it was the portrait of a woman, richly appointed in a blue dress with a sheer muslin overlay. The box of paints Mrs. Hart had packed into the mister's sea chest lay beside it.

Carefully, Rosehannah pulled the picture out into the light and studied it. The woman was young, perhaps nineteen or twenty, full in the bosom and undeniably beautiful. But there was something petulant about the mouth, a certain slyness around the eyes. It was, to Rosehannah's untrained vision, a very pretty picture of a very pretty woman, but she was glad she did not look like this woman. The portrait was not kind. She slid the canvas back into place, cautiously returning it to exactly the same position on the shelf where she had found it.

Suddenly, Rosehannah was anxious to be out of the store and away. She had not hesitated to enter the premises, but having found the picture she was not at all anxious to have the mister find her. She located the oakum, pulled a few yards of it from the roll, and retreated, locking the door behind her.

Outside on the wharf, she had to will her feet to walk at a normal pace up the path to where her basket of eggs lay. If J. Harris were to emerge from the house at this moment, he must not know she felt anything but confidence about entering what was now his premises. Clearly, the spoiled young beauty, whose portrait he must have laboured over for some weeks after his arrival, was not the barrel-waisted Mrs. Hart. Whoever she was, he did not wish to share this—or any—information with Rosehannah, and would not welcome the intrusion into his personal life.

At the top of the harbour, Rosehannah paused and looked down. The elongated, narrow cove was glass-calm and the first wisps of smoke were rising from the scattered houses around its rim. Out in the bay, the iceberg blinked so brightly it almost hurt her eyes to look at it. A thin fall of water was pouring down from one end of the icy mass; if the sun continued as brightly, by midday it would be a torrent. The beaten path was turning spongy under her feet and stunted trees lay ahead, beckoning her into the woods.

Rosehannah pulled her thin shawl over her head and looped the strands of pungent oakum around her neck over the top of it. The mosquitoes from the woods were already whining around her face, and she braced herself to plunge into the clouds of them amassing in the vegetation. Her heart, which had been beating rapidly from the climb up the path and the fear of discovery, had settled into a rhythm of anticipation. She felt light on her feet and a curious joy spread out from her chest into her limbs.

It had been months since she had been away from the house and store. All through the long, dull winter, she had hovered at her mother's bedside, never going farther than the wood pile or the chicken roost. Through the worst of the dark days, even the store had been outside her purview, locked and shuttered, a drift of snow frozen against the door. After her mother's death, her father had stayed home and slowly her world enlarged again, but she had not liked to leave him for even a few hours and, during the spring, had not even gone into the woods to cut gads for making baskets.

Now, here she was, about to set out on a walk of only a few miles, and she felt as if she had the freedom of the whole world. It is so easy to be happy, she thought. Tears threatened to come into her eyes for a moment and she inhaled the strong scent of the oakum to stop them. She took a deep breath, and picking up her basket, turned to continue her journey, already feeling the burning pull in her leg muscles from the unusual exertion of the climb.

"Good morning, Mrs. Toop," called Rosehannah, as she lifted the latch on the Toop's small house in Traytown. To call it a town was a misnomer, or perhaps a wish for what the inhabitants hoped might come, for the village was even smaller than Ireland's Eye, just a scattered collection of sheds and tilts, housing no more than three or four families at any one time.

"Miss Rose," answered Mrs. Toop, her face lighting up at the sound of the girl's voice. "Or is it Mrs. Harris? I hear everything and I never know what to believe," she added, patting the stool at her knee for the girl to sit down.

"Your guess is as good as mine." Rosehannah dropped down and lay her head in the old woman's lap. The gnarled hands rested on her cheek and she felt the old woman kiss the top of her head. "Oh, it's so good to be here, Mrs. Toop. I feel as if I haven't been out of doors in years."

"I'm sorry about your mother, Miss Rose. And as for your father...well, all men is dogs, and that's just something we women has to live with."

"Surely not Mr. Toop," laughed Rosehannah, lifting her head to see how serious the old woman was.

"Well, he's better than most, but in his young days, he was like that old cock of mine, treading the back of any young hen stupid enough to let him catch up to her." Mrs. Toop smiled broadly at the memory. "I gave him a feed of tongues more than once, I can tell you, and I had my little revenges too. Once I caught him with a girl from Champneys, and the next time he tore his britches, I sewed them up so that they pinched his nunny bag like a carpenter's clamp. The britches looked just the same, so he never figured out what I done—thought he had the French disease." The old woman cackled with pleasure at the memory and Rosehannah gave a small whoop of shock and pleasure.

"It's a good thing Mama's not here, Mrs. Toop. She wouldn't approve of your gossip."

"Oh, you'd be surprised at what your mama approved of. We had more than a few whispers behind the backs of the men in our time. She wasn't so easy upset as you'd think." Mrs. Toop groped blindly around the leg of her chair until she found a string, and gently pulled it towards her. A small chick, tied at the leg, came sleepily out from under the chair and allowed itself to be picked up and coddled.

"How are your eyes now, auntie?" asked Rosehannah, stroking the small downy head.

"Not so good, my dear, but what can't be cured must be endured. And speaking of which, what about that old devil they married you off to? How are you enduring him?" The chick nibbled at Mrs. Toop's fingers and she searched her lap for a crumb to feed it.

"What old devil? Who told you that?" Rosehannah reached into her basket and extracted a bit of crust from her oilcloth bundle. "Mr. Harris is old, but I'm sure he's not nearly as old as people think. I would guess he's only about ten years older than me."

"Has he really got scars on his head where he cut the Jew horns off?" The chick fell off Mrs. Toop's lap and Rosehannah reached to catch it and set it on the floor.

"What are you talking about?" Rosannah was genuinely puzzled now. This wasn't just Mrs. Toop's usual run of scandal and tattle.

"I heard he came out to England from the low country on account of a gambling debt, and then got in trouble with a woman, so Mr. Garland brought him out of London as a favour to Mr. Hart." Mrs. Toop, sensing Rosehannah was genuinely disturbed by this news, paused for a moment. "I got it from Mrs. Whitfield, whose daughter works in the kitchen at Garlands. She heard them talking about it when she was clearing the dishes out of the dining room."

Rosehannah dropped back down onto the stool by Mrs. Toop's knees and took her hands. "What else did you hear?" This was more information that she had extracted from J. Harris in the month or more she had been cooking and cleaning for him.

"That's about all, little maid." Her wrinkled old face looked uncharacteristically serious. "He's not hurting you, is he? Not doing anything unnatural?"

"Heavens, no," Rosehannah assured her. "He hasn't laid a hand on me. He's upstairs in the loft and I sleep out back in the linney. He hardly looks at me, and never says much, either. When he does speak, it's like being barked at." The girl sat, thinking deeply. "He might well be German or Dutch; he's got an odd turn to his speech, but he's not much different from any of the Old English at Trinity." She sat silent for a moment. "How can I tell if he's a Jew?"

"Well, Miss Rose, if you weren't sleeping in the linney, you might be able to look for the sign; let's just say it's not only the horns they cuts off 'em when they're born." Mrs. Toop clucked her tongue and began the slow rise out of her chair. "You give me your hand there, maidy, and I'll go see about those eggs you want. That scrawny little cock of yours is hardly worth his keep when it comes to making chicks." This was an old argument Mrs. Quint and Mrs. Toop had taken up with ritual regularity each year, and Rosehannah knew her part as well as she knew her catechism.

"That big old bird of yours is a brute. He tears the feathers out of the poor hens' backs and bites their necks something dreadful," Rosehannah complained. "My little Jumper is as gentle as a lamb, and he's brave, too. I've only lost one chicken this spring. Why just last week, I was watching them from the window and a hawk came down after Tulip, and Jumper was out in the yard as fast as could be, squawking and showing himself to lure the hawk away from her. He was a regular…a regular Crusader."

The two made their slow way out into the yard, the large old lady leaning companionably against the strong young one for support. Crippled and nearly blind as she was, Mrs. Toop knew exactly where to look for the nests and, in short order, Rosehannah had gathered a dozen large eggs to replace the two dozen small ones she had bedded in the moss of her basket. They were back in the kitchen and sipping tea when Mrs. Toop's granddaughter appeared at the door.

"I ran all the way from Back Cove when I heard you were here, Rosie." Neta was gasping for breath and clutching her side as she came in and collapsed onto the bench at the table. Mrs. Toop pushed the tea kettle towards her and reached a cup down from a hook under the shelf. "I needs a dress, girl, a nice one." She unknotted the corners of her apron and laid a small, folded bundle of cloth on the table. Rosehannah undid several of the folds so as to see the pattern.

"It's not much to work with, Neta," she said dubiously. "It's a bit thin and, well, dull." The cloth was dark blue cotton with no texture to speak of in the weave.

"I know, girl, but it's all I've got. I thought maybe you could line the skirt with some old bit of stuff that wouldn't show, and fancy it up a bit. Maybe some embroidery around the neck or something." She looked at Rosehannah hopefully. "I'm thinking to get married, if Lambeth does well at the fish this summer." Mrs. Toop began rummaging around in a chest at the side of the table and soon pulled out an old dress. Once a colourful tartan, the dye had run and ruined the pattern.

"Think this will do for a lining, Miss Rose?" She held the dress towards Rosehannah, who stretched the skirt out in the light, looking for moth holes or tears.

"It just might. I have a half bolt of brocade, lovely stuff with blackberry leaves on it, and bees. If I used a bit of it in the yoke, it might bring out the blue. You'd have to be careful, though, and take the lining out before you try to wash it or the colour will run all over it."

"Oh, I knew you would have some idea. You can take any old rag and make it special." Neta flung her arms around Rosehannah's neck and kissed her cheek. "Just think, we'll be two old married women, the both of us." Rosehannah rolled her eyes upward but said nothing.

"Now Neta, go and find that old black hen of mine, the one with the yellow feet that's stopped laying. I'll give it to Rose for the sewing. And the young cock with the bloody comb will do for the brocade, but kill it first so she don't have to struggle with it when she gets home."

"Oh, Nan, you're an angel." Neta jumped to her feet and headed out the door.

"Mrs. Toop, that's too much. It's only a dress…" Rosehannah was uncomfortable taking too much from someone who had so much less than she did. "Just the one bird will do."

"Nonsense, child." the old woman retorted. "I can't see your stitching, but I hear from the others that you do beautiful work, and a big pot of soup from that young cock might stir the blood of your old Jew so that you won't have to spend your nights in the linney after all."

Outside they heard a fierce squawk and the thwack of a hatchet as Neta prepared to pay for the brocade.

"I don't know about that, Mrs. Toop. I don't know what I want in that direction."

She arrived back at the premises by mid-day, her legs aching from the hills and her arms aching from the birds, the big old hen, which would have to be caged until she was ready to kill it, and the plucked and gutted young cock, which was twice the weight of any one of Rosehannah's own chickens, even naked and empty as it was.

Her neighbours were not in evidence—the men were probably lying down for an hour's nap before heading out for the long afternoon of work ahead and the women were quieting the babies and watching the sky in case it decided to open up and rain on the fish that had been spread that morning.

In the kitchen, the breakfast things had been tidied to one side, and the basket by the fireplace filled with split wood. She found a box to hold the black hen and after marking them with a bit of waxy black heelball distributed the exchanged eggs among the broody hens. None of the birds objected, and as long as no other hens were allowed to fill the nests with their own eggs, cooling all of them and killing the chicks, they would hatch out a dozen of Mrs. Toop's fat birds, and a few of her own tiny banties within three weeks or so.

Mama had always preferred the small birds because they flew better and could escape the clutches of the rats, dogs and children so much more likely to turn up at their property than at the Toops'. She would change eggs with old Mrs. Toop to grow out some larger birds for the summer, killing one occasionally for a treat for the family. In November, she would set aside a few of the best layers from the previous year, and then hand-rear a couple of small birds to start fresh in the spring.

Rosehannah stopped to watch Jumper do his skittish, little sideways dance for one of the hens and smiled at his splendour. Deep copper-coloured feathers flowed down his neck in a cowl, running into buff and black wings, and then exploding out into iridescent green tailfeathers, two of which were especially long and glorious. Whenever he dropped one of these, Rosehannah would find it and save it, though for what she did not know. Perhaps she could make a fan of them.

In the house, she started up the fire, and as she waited for it to die down, she rubbed the inside of the young cock with salt and herbs and skewered it for the spit. The system of cogs and chains used to turn the bird was faulty, and she had to check it every few minutes, but she had the whole afternoon and nothing more to do except bake a loaf of bread. There was no wood to chop for once. It seemed odd to have time to herself in the middle of the day. When her mother was alive, they had between them turned her father's fish as well as kept the house, but it seemed the mister did not intend to have a boat at all.

The bird was just finished as the mister came into the house. He startled Rosehannah a little, as he had been in the habit of coming in late and eating his supper alone after she had gone to bed, but apparently missing two dinners in a row had made him impatient to eat. He eyed the spit hungrily.

"Have you sacrificed one of your chickens?" he asked, and then without waiting for a reply added, "I haven't had fresh meat in more than three months."

"It might be a bit tough," she warned him. "And there's not much in the way of vegetables." She set the bird on a platter, and put out a plate, knife and fork. He turned to the water bucket, dipped a pannikin into it and quickly rinsed his fingers, tipping water several times over each hand before turning back to the table.

He efficiently carved a slice from the breast and then severed both legs at the joints before helping himself to bread and a few of the rather pathetic root vegetables she had managed to find in the almost-empty root cellar. Rosehannah hovered at the fireplace, not sure what was expected of her. He had swallowed several large chunks of breast meat before he noticed she was not eating.

"Where's your plate?" he asked, and pushed another forkful of food into his mouth before carving two slices of chicken for

34

her. She brought the plate to him and he waved the tip of his knife to indicate that she should sit. They ate in silence for some minutes until he finished what he had on his plate and began to cut away at the bird again. Then, "You've been in the store," he announced. She froze. "How did you get in?" His voice was sharp but she could not tell if he was angry.

"I needed oakum," she said without looking up from her plate. "I thought it was allowed." She held the key out to him. "Papa gave it to me." She lifted her eyes to find him staring hard at her. "I'm sorry. I won't do it again."

Harris said nothing for a moment, and then began slicing once more at the chicken carcass. "Keep it," he said finally. "If I'm going to make a go of this business, I'll need some help from you, at least for a while."

Oct. 6, 04

Dear Ms. Hart,

  Please accept my apology for the delay in answering your letter of Sept.
19th. As soon as I received it, I put in a request to Interlibrary Loans for
a copy of Bernard Susser's history, The Jews of Southwest England.
I am only about a third of the way through, but it is a gold mine of infor-
mation. It has already solved at least one mystery for me (I had no idea
the name Lyon was an English variant of Aryeh) and I suspect it will
solve—and pose—several more.

  I am enclosing a small pamphlet about the town of Trinity, and you
will see in it a picture of the Lester Garland House, reconstructed to the
period of 1819-20. Lester and Garland were the principal fishing mer-
chants of Poole engaged in the salt-fish trade here, their rivals being the
firm of Jeffrey and Street. Thomas Street managed the Newfoundland end
of their business, while Jeffrey lived in England. Perhaps it was Jeffrey
who signed the guarantee for your Jacob Harris, although I suppose it
could just as easily have been Lester or Garland.

  In writing that, I realize I have accepted your premise that when Jacob
Harris left Plymouth, he came out to Newfoundland. I am not usually so
quick to jump to such conclusions, but in reading Susser, I was reminded
of an email my wife received some years ago from a person who signed her-
self simply Sportygirl. Apparently, Sportygirl was looking for Jewish rela-
tives from Trinity by the name of Morris. When Tali (my late wife) asked
why she thought they were Jewish, she got a complicated story about a
Morris who settled in Cuckold's Cove (now Dunfield), who married a
Catherine Clifton. Their daughter married a man from King's Cove,
named King naturally, and after the death of their son James, a friend of
the family told James King's teenaged daughter that the Morrises were
originally Jewish. The daughter confided this to her husband shortly
before her death, and a few years before he died, he told their children.

  I think I've got that straight—I have the file here in front of me.
Anyway, Tali took some trouble to look at the baptism and marriage
records from Trinity and found nothing unusual or indicative of Jewish
background in the Morris entries. The few English Jews she identified in
the course of her research generally had joined the Methodist church
because (I'm on shaky ground here— I'm not sure I've got this right) you

could be a Methodist merely by assenting or asserting you were, without being subjected to baptism. But the Trinity Morrises were Anglican, not Methodist. When Tali tried to get more information from Sportygirl and asked for a street address to send her copies of the church registry, there was simply no reply.

However, Bernard Susser, in his book, identifies quite a number of Jewish Morrises in Southwest England, and in doing a quick scan of the index, I see that at least two-thirds of the first names are matches for the first names Tali found in the church registries for the area of Trinity. Sportygirl may not have been as far off the mark as we thought. Oral history in Newfoundland has as many myths as anywhere, but in my experience it usually also contains a fairly large grain of truth. Around here, Jewish heritage wasn't something everyone wished to advertise, so knowledge of it was often suppressed or simply forgotten. My guess is that if someone says their people were Jewish, they probably were.

When I've finished working my way through The Jews of Southwest England *(I can only keep it for ten days), I will try having another look at the Trinity church records. According to Susser, Jews could and did marry in the Anglican church without becoming Anglican, as long as both the bride and groom were Jewish. Maybe Jacob Harris married a Morris. There were also other Jewish families (Levis in Carbonear and Palmers in Harbour Grace) he might have married into.*

Please stay in touch. I had begun to get thoroughly sick of my own more modest history of the Jews and was beginning to wonder if I was ever going to finish with it. Your input has been as good as a blood transfusion. I confess, I am sometimes lonely since losing my wife and your letters have been a wonderful distraction.

Sincerely
John H.

"Know your origin, your destination, and before Whom you will be required to give an accounting."

Akaviah ben Mahalalel, Ethics of the Fathers

"Do I have to count all of these?" Rosehannah was sitting on the floor, poking wearily at the contents of a paper box. Harris looked up from the account book he had been perusing and leaned over to see what she had in her lap.

"Hmm." He said, stirring the small wooden pegs with the end of his pen. "Just count ten or twenty, and then estimate the number you've got from the size of the box. What are they, anyway?"

"Sprigs," she answered, giving him a look half puzzled and half dismissive. She'd never met any man who knew less about fish, or any woman for that matter, but he seemed to have whole other areas of ignorance that she was yet to discover. He cocked a sarcastic eye at her. "For boots," she added defensively. "You use them to mend the soles of your boots. Or at least most people do." This last was barely whispered, and she bit her tongue. It was easy enough to be mute and invisible to the mister when he was locked away in the store, mooning over that woman, or when she was alone in the house, but harder to remain so when she was with him all day, counting packets of needles and measuring yards of cordage. They were getting along moderately well and this was no time to get saucy.

"Well, there's enough of those little 'doodle-addles' to shoe Pharaoh's army. You say there's twelve families on the island, though I've hardly laid eyes on another human in weeks. Put a fistful of those things into a bit of paper for the store and tie the rest up to go back to Trinity."

Jacob Harris and Rosehannah were doing inventory. It was not a term Rosehannah had been familiar with, but when the mister had decided to make a go of the business, the first thing he said was necessary was an inventory. The store was the repository of the remains of twenty years of stock shipped from Lester Garland, much of it useless, and all of it dusty, disorganized and, worst of all in the mister's opinion, not accounted for on paper.

"How can you know if you're making a profit if you don't know what you have or if you can sell it?" Harris had explained to her. "All these goods are listed at Garland's as being saleable stock in my possession, when clearly they've been using this place as a dumping ground for clerical errors for years. Every time some lazy clerk mistook a one for a seven, or a three for an eight, and ended up with too much of something, they shipped it off to your father and got it off their books and onto his."

"But we always did well enough," protested Rosehannah, whose loyalty to Quint had outlasted his presence in her life.

"Last year, which you say was a good one, the dozen families here had a total catch of about 1500 quintals of made fish. At twelve shillings a quintal that's £900. They also manufactured about twenty-one tuns of cod liver oil, realizing another £360. That's £1,260, a ridiculous figure considering what it costs to run this place. Garland must be out of his mind."

"We knew he wasn't making a lot," Rosehannah conceded, "but having a dealer here prevented other merchants from moving into the area. Besides, we produce other things besides fish."

"You grow a few potatoes and other vegetables, shoot ducks and seabirds, provide your own fuel and building materials from the woods, but you obtain all your other provisions through this store. Not just the salt, lead and twine and other necessities for the fishery, but every shirt and stocking you put on, every dollop of molasses you stir into your tea, every needle and pin you use. It all comes from this store." Harris shook his head at the sheer lunacy of the situation.

He busied himself with his account books again for a time, before pushing them away in frustration. "Selby never should have been allowed near the store. He was worse than a thief—he was an incompetent thief. Why on earth did your father put up with him?"

"He wasn't without abilities, you know. He could make himself useful when he chose to." Rosehannah struggled to find the explanation that would bridge the gap between Harris's world and her own. "He is strong and healthy, and he is not vicious; he just doesn't know when to stop." She could tell from the look on

Harris's face that he wasn't convinced. "There are usually no more than twenty adult men on this island, and Selby is as strong as two good men. He has a feel for the fish, too. He knows just where to look, what bait works best, when the weather is turning. Papa needed him, so Mama put up with the petty thieving and the disrespect."

"And you put up with his ill-treatment?"

Rosehannah looked away. Selby had never treated her badly, until Quint was gone. Then, he took his lead from the mister. "Selby only got saucy towards the end. The worst he ever did until that last day was call me Irish." She glanced at Harris to see how he reacted to this aspersion.

"Why would he call you Irish? Your mother was English, wasn't she?"

"He didn't mean we were from Ireland. He meant it as an insult. Mama was a Roman Catholic. So am I. Everyone else here is Church of England." She sat in silence for a moment. "I never know how to respond to insults like that—just ignore them or...what do you do, Mr. Harris?"

"You mean when they call me 'Christ killer' or 'Jew boy'?" Harris opened a small knife and began mending his pens. "Most of the time, I just ignore it. They want a reaction, so I don't give it to them." He held the blade up towards the light and then began sharpening it on a small stone on his desk. "Occasionally, I have struck back and usually regretted it."

"Why? Don't those who deliberately set out to hurt you deserve to be hurt back?"

"Not necessarily. Once, in Berlin, I was accosted by a whore... You know what a whore is?" He looked at her curiously.

"Yes," she said, with no apparent embarrassment. "It's a woman who goes with a man for money, but without being married to him."

"Yes, that's one way to put it. Well, this whore accosted me in the street. She was drunk and probably had been taking laudanum, and when I politely declined her services—a gentleman is polite, even to whores—she took offence and yelled after me

40

'You can't do this,' and spat at me." Seeing the puzzled look on the girl's face, Harris explained. "There is a belief among some Christians that because a Jew was said to have spit on Christ, we are no longer able to spit, only drool on our chins."

"So what did you do," Rosehannah asked.

"This," Harris replied and, turning, he suddenly hurled a mouthful of spittle against the far wall of the store.

Rosehannah's eyes widened in surprise.

"Only it wasn't a wall I spat at, nor a wall I hit." Harris walked over and wiped the spittle off the wall with his pen rag.

"My goodness, you have a great deal of spleen in you, Mr. Harris. And excellent aim." She smiled in admiration. "I should have liked to do that to Selby, but I doubt I have enough phlegm in me. How did the whore react?"

"Well, there's the rub, you see. She was so startled, she stopped dead in her tracks and then she began to cry. The poor trollop was only doing what she'd been taught to do, by her betters, no doubt. I was obliged to part with several coins to salve my conscience." He dropped the rag back on his desk, sat down and pulled the accounts back towards him with a sigh.

"What next?" Rosehannah asked, forcing herself to her feet and staring into the gloomy pile of barrels and boxes at the back of the store. The massive iceberg in the bay made the dark interior bone-chilling and she longed to get out into the sunshine. She would be counting dabbers and jiggers, kettle ears and fishhooks in her sleep.

"We'll give it up for the day," he said, throwing down his pen. "No chance you'd like me to practice my wood chopping on that old black hen you've got, is there? If I eat any more fish, I'm going to grow gills and fins."

Rosehannah smiled. It was the first joke he'd made that didn't sound hard and angry. "Yes, but I'd have to boil it, because the crooks and crottles don't work properly. You need to turn the spit by hand. Papa tried to fix it, but he can't work metal, only wood." She registered a slight shift in his features which she interpreted as disappointment.

"Pity to waste a bird by boiling it," he said flatly. "I'll have a look at the chain and see if I can fix it. I have my heart set on roast chicken."

She stifled a smile at the idea of his fixing anything, never mind something as difficult as a weighted turning spit. "I have lots of eggs. We could walk over to Jacob's Cove and boil the kettle there." He looked dubious at the prospect, but she thought she'd go mad if she didn't get out into the bright daylight. "Anthony Island will give protection from the wind off the iceberg, and there's a huge bank of wild strawberries that might be ready." He straightened up a little. He liked the thought of strawberries.

"How far is it?" He had, up to this point, shown little interest in Rosehannah's island and had rarely strayed more than a hundred yards from the house and store.

"Nothing here is far," Rosehannah explained. "The whole island is only about three miles long, maybe one mile wide. Of course, you can't go straight from point A to point B, because it's all coves and headlands. Mama said the coast around is probably twenty miles altogether. There's a map…may I?" She gestured toward the drawer under the counter for permission.

"Go ahead, but it isn't very useful." Harris was quite familiar with the contents of the drawer. Rosehannah pulled out a yellow, brittle piece of paper, part of a map of Trinity Bay with geographic notations in a mix of French and English. Ireland's Eye was less than an inch long, about the size and shape of a caterpillar.

Positioning herself so as not to block the sun coming in the small window near the counter, she turned the map over and tapped the paper to get his attention. Drawn neatly on the back was another map, larger in scale and more complex.

"Papa drew it and Mama and I marked the places in. Here, you see, that's where we are, Ireland's Eye. And there's the knob of the hill behind us. If you go southwest along the shore, you come to the entrance to Traytown harbour, which is about three times as long as ours, maybe fourteen fathoms in the first reach, shoaling up to about nine feet in the inner section. Southwest

Ireland's Eye

Ireland's Eye Point

Black Duck Cove

Jacob's Cove

Sheave a Shern

Anthony Island

Broad Cove

Ireland's Eye Hr.

Indian Islands

Tray Town

Back Cove

Round Hr.

The Thoroughfare

Random Island

again is Round Harbour, also about nine feet deep but the entrance is nearly dry at low water and of little use to boats." She glanced up to see if he was taking any interest. He was.

"Does anybody live there?" He leaned forward to study the complex configuration.

"No, though we go there occasionally when the capelin or herring strike, just in case a school has got in and hasn't managed to get out." Rosehannah was warming to her subject. "That's Gunner Rock, you'll want to remember that. It's about three-quarters of a cable from the shore, awash at low water. Now you go west and north, into the Thoroughfare to Back Cove where Papa...where my tilt is. There's one or two other tilts there, just opposite the Baker's Loaf, but they're not very substantial, only thrown up for a season, so there's still plenty of wood.

"Across the tickle is Random Island and Chair Cove Head. North, between the Indian Islands, is Broad Cove to the east. There's a tilt or two there and a few permanent houses, and then Black Duck Cove with a few more families, and then nothing, you just turn east into Smith Sound until you come to Ireland's Eye Point, then south to Jacob's Cove and home. The Point and Jacob's Cove are all cliffs, you can't get at the water there."

"Well, if I'm to be stuck on this island for the foreseeable future, I'd best get to know it a bit better."

"Like Robinson Crusoe," Rosehannah said helpfully.

"Quite the reader, aren't you," he added dryly, and led the way out the door.

"Not really," Rosehannah admitted, and then because she had broken her habitual silence she felt compelled to elaborate. "Mama read *Robinson Crusoe* to me when I was small. They send books over from Garland's when the clerks have finished with them, but we have to send them back at the end of the winter. Summer is the slow time for the clerks because everyone is out fishing, while winter is when the fishing people have time to spare. You're different, of course. Most of the dealers fish, like Papa, because there isn't enough to keep them busy with just a few families to look after. He had to earn our keep."

They were climbing the path to the house as Rosehannah explained this. A sudden, massive *crack* filled the air and before she could turn, the mister had thrown himself on top of her, grinding her face into the dirt and knocking the breath out of her. Seabirds screamed and Rosehannah's hens bawked and bawled in fright. Other than the birds, all was silent again just as suddenly.

Slowly, the two untangled themselves and sat up in the pathway. "Look," she said, and pointed to the south. "It split." Two huge chunks of the iceberg were rocking wildly back and forth on the calm ocean surface, while a scatter-field of smaller bits of ice bobbed for hundreds of yards around.

"*Oybershter in himmel!* I thought it was cannon fire." Birds wheeled and screamed overhead and the hens scrambled to hide themselves under the house.

"It's not grounded any more," Rosehannah observed cheerfully. "If we get a stiff wind this evening, we'll be clear of the ice by morning." She rubbed at her nose and hoped it wasn't as mashed as it felt. Harris dusted himself off and then leaned over to give her his hand.

"Are you all right? I didn't hurt you, did I?" He looked genuinely worried, and Rosehannah felt a small flicker of satisfaction in her heart. For fourteen years, she had been the centre of Mama and Papa's affection, but for months now, no one except Mrs. Toop had expressed even the slightest concern for her well-being. It was nice to be looked after, even if it was only the mister doing the looking.

"I'm grand," she answered, laughing and slapping at her apron. Her breasts, which achieved a rather satisfactory increase in the past month or so, ached a little from the impact but she kept her hands well away from them and concentrated on regaining what little dignity she had. "It will warm up now, once the ice is gone. Just watch, the flowers and shrubs will just fly out of the ground overnight. There will be pitchy paws and darning needles, flags and twinflowers, hundreds of different plants and insects, all in the space of a few weeks. It is so beautiful, you won't think of this as a desert island at all.

"Look," she said, tugging at Harris's sleeve in her enthusiasm. "Just look at that harbour. It's a miracle, so deep and narrow, perfect for the larger boats to lie alongside the fishing stages. Papa used to say, 'You're just as safe here as if you were in God's pocket.' And once you get used to it, learn the ways of the country, you'll find the diet isn't so monotonous either. There's rabbits in the autumn, and ducks and geese too. Sometimes, the men get a caribou deer over on the mainland, and they share it around. Mama and I always let some of the families have a chicken in the autumn, just for a treat, and they always give us back twice in exchange.

"I know you think this is all barren rock and bog, but it isn't. There are dozens of different kinds of berries in among the hollows and cracks; partridgeberries and marshberries, blueberries and plumboys, stinkberries, bakeapples, pin cherries and wild raisins, lots of things that are good to eat. And fish—we don't eat just cod and salmon. There's halibut and mussels and clams, and some people even eat lobsters..." Her voice trailed off. "But Mrs. Toop says you might not care for that sort of thing." Harris was eyeing her with astonishment and she suddenly wished she had kept her tongue still in her mouth.

"Until today, I'd no idea you could string more than three words together at a time," he observed. "Well, find me some of this wonderful food you are so enthusiastic about and we shall go and look at this island of yours. And when we have eaten, you can tell me what else Mrs. Toop had to say about me." He waved his hand to dismiss her and she gratefully scrambled away up the path.

It took Rosehannah no time at all to organize her picnic. She took a taper into the root cellar and searched out the last of the preserved country food her mother had prepared and stored before she became too ill to work in the kitchen. To this she added a bottle of spruce beer she drew off a small keg in the back of the linney, a paper twist of loose tea, half a loaf of bread and a pat of butter. Two forks, a knife, two pannikins and a small pot, narrow and deep, completed the outfit. She carefully lined a large basket with a shawl and a linen cloth, and then packed and padded the crocks and the bottle in case of a fall.

The mister, in the meantime, had been disassembling the fireplace chains and generally making a mess in the kitchen. Rosehannah pulled two pairs of stockings from the drying rack, and just managed to fit them into the basket with the provisions. A shawl tied around her waist, a poke bonnet—old fashioned but practical—and a last glance in the tiny tin mirror in the linney, and she was ready.

By then, the mister was outside the house, so absorbed in the chains and gears of the spit that he did not appear to notice her.

"Mr. Harris," she called. The chill breeze from the water snatched her words away up the hill. Filling her lungs, she shouted as loudly as she could "Jacob Harris!" He looked up, startled.

"I was wondering when you were going to get around to using my name," he said, as he joined her on the path. "I wondered if you'd forgotten it."

"I know your name," she said. "But do you know mine? You never use it." She looked at him with genuine curiosity. He took the basket and they began their journey round the head of the harbour.

"Well," he said, taking her surprisingly seriously, "there's some think you are Rosie Quint, and there's others who would have it that you are Rosehannah Harris…" She held her breath, wondering which he would claim for her. "I think you are Rose Ann Jackman, daughter of the late Captain James Jackman of Newton Abbot and the late Anna Martin Jackman Quint. In fact, I know it,"—he looked at her where she had stopped in the middle of the path, mouth open—"but, I shall call you Rosehannah."

"Mister Harris…" Rosehannah faltered, and for a long moment wondered if she was going to faint or if the ground was really sinking beneath her feet. "Mr. Harris, this is not a matter for jesting."

"No, indeed it isn't, Rosehannah. And I'm not jesting. We'll speak about it when we get to wherever it is you are leading me." He made to step around her but she blocked his way.

"We'll speak of it here, sir. And directly." The ground, which a moment before had felt soft and unsteady, now felt flat and hard, and she was rooted into it like an oak. She pushed the cloth brim of her bonnet back upon itself and tipped her head up to stare defiantly at him. He matched her gaze, his face impassive.

"Very well," he conceded after a moment. "I wrote to Mr. Garland, to see if he knew of relatives who might help you out of here. He said he had looked into the matter long ago, in consultation with your mother.

"Your father was a widower, retired from the army after the Napoleonic wars ended, and considerably older than your mother. He had a small property, entailed of course, and when he married your mother, he turned it over to his only son by his first wife. Almost everything else he sold and left in trust with this son for the care of his daughter, a girl grossly deformed in the face. Your parents then came out to the colony to begin new lives."

"So I have a sister and brother?" Rosehannah lifted her hand up as if to touch his sleeve again, but she did not.

"No. I'm sorry. Garland says the son lost the money, all of it, and hung himself in despair. The girl was taken in by one of the neighbours and died some years later. There is nothing left, no money, no estate, no sister or brother, not even a locket or a tin spoon for a keepsake—it was all dispersed by the time your mother learned of it. Apparently, your mother felt there was no advantage in your knowing—thought it might only make you dissatisfied with the life you had."

"I liked the life I had." Rosehannah pulled her bonnet forward again, hiding her face almost entirely. And then, wistfully, "I wish I had it back."

"I'm sorry, Rosehannah. Truly I am." He wished he could say or do something to ease the ache she so obviously felt, but the desire to help only made his face look angry and bitter and his words sounded false, even to his own ears. Surprisingly, it was she who reached out to him.

"Of course you are," she assured him, and placing her small hand over the one he had wrapped around the handle of the basket, she pressed it briefly and then turned briskly back to the path. "We'll lose the sun if we don't hurry. The weather can

48

change in minutes around here so we must 'seize the hour,' as Mama used to say." She set out at a determined clip over the hills towards Jacob's Cove.

Even with his land legs, Harris had a job to keep up with Rosehannah when she was on a randy. The rough path got rougher, and the basket he carried grew heavier, but she skipped from one rock to another, dodging around boulders and calling to warn him when they hit a marshy bit. Occasionally, she stooped to pluck a bit of vegetation, which she presented to him with instruction as to its eventual usefulness, because it produced an edible berry, root or leaf. They stayed near the shore, venturing only occasionally into the little clumps of stunted var and spruce that made up the tuckamore.

Near Jacob's Cove, they climbed a high hill and emerged at the top of a cliff overlooking Anthony Island. The temperature had improved considerably as they worked away from the masses of ice and further into the protection of the island offshore. By the time Rosehannah dropped down onto a carpet of moss and lichen, she was pink with exertion and Harris was winded and damp through his shirt to his waistcoat.

After catching her breath the girl sat up, and pulled away clumps of moss and browse to reveal a small, well-used fireplace. "Here," she instructed. She emptied the contents of a pocket attached to her waist into his hands. "You start a fire, and I'll find a bit of blasty bough." She was gone before he could protest, so he set to work, using the hardened steel and flint to catch alight the nest of birch bark they were bedded in. She was back just in time with her apron full of dead spruce twigs and hard, grey starrigans, which he took to feed the tiny flames he had produced. Then she was gone again, swinging the pot as she ran.

Her return was more sedate, as she was careful not to spill the water she carried. Harris was unpacking the basket, having purloined a corner crust of bread. "Mind the tea," she warned, and rescued the paper packet from his curious fingers. The two settled in to watch the kettle boil, and if Harris had not known how shaken she was by his unexpected revelation of half an hou

earlier, he would not have guessed Rosehannah was anything but a happy, ignorant housemaid on her day off.

A whale offshore spouted, dived, and resurfaced, slapping the water with his fins. "I've always wondered why they do that," she observed, looking over at him from the shade of her poke bonnet. "Papa thought it was to stun the capelin and other fish so it could more easily catch them. Mama thought it was a signal of some sort, to other whales."

"You've got a curious mind, haven't you," he replied, "always wondering, and always taking in more than you give out." He sounded more resentful than admiring as he offered up this opinion.

"And today I'm wondering why you told me about my real father when my mother and Mr. Garland had decided not to."

Harris shrugged. "You're a bright girl. You've a right to know where you came from. It won't change your circumstances, but it might change how you choose to deal with them."

"And what of your circumstances and where you come from? Has one changed the other?"

"History had made me what I am, and history has changed my circumstances. I'm afraid there are an extraordinary number of similarities between me and your late half-brother, except that I chose not to hang myself."

"And did you, too, abandon a helpless woman to the kindness of strangers?" She was speaking ruthlessly, with all the ignorance and sauce of a girl of fourteen.

"No, *danken Got*! I had no sister, no dependents at all. If anything, the shoe was on the other foot. I have nobody to blame me, and nobody to blame but myself for my present situation." He broke off a larger crust of bread and smeared it with a bit of the butter. Rosehannah pulled the top off a pint-sized crock and dug through a layer of fat with one of the forks. She held out a lump of greasy meat to him and he allowed her to place it on the bread.

"Is your current situation all that terrible?" she asked, as he bit into the rather unattractive morsel of food. Ninety-nine percent of the men and women in Newfoundland would have regarded his

circumstances as ideal—a secure position with an honest merchant, not too much work expected of him, a capable girl to wait on his needs, and the potential for a long and prosperous life in a quiet and out-of-the-way country. Yet he saw himself as alone among savages.

Harris, who was pondering his present situation as he bit into the meat, abandoned the intellectual effort as soon as his tongue savoured the gastronomic delight that is *confit d'oie*. He almost choked in his haste to take a second mouthful.

"Is this goose?" he demanded as soon as he could form the words.

"I hope so," ceded Rosehannah. "Mama and I spent two weeks worrying about it when it was in the salt. The weather was uncooperative and we kept thinking it was getting too warm and the fat would go rancid before we could cook it. That's almost the last of it."

Harris leaned over and took the brown stoneware jar from her hands and began rooting around in it with the tip of his knife. "To think I've been eating salt cod, fresh cod, cod boiled and baked and beaten to a pulp, every day for two months, and you had this little treasure hidden away in that mysterious cellar of yours." He glared at her over his fork. "Women have been beaten for less. What else have you been holding back?"

"Not too much, really; Mama was too sick last autumn to do the usual preserving." Rosehannah pulled the waxed linen cover off another small jar and handed it to him. "Try this."

Harris probed the jar carefully, extracted another meaty chunk, and tasted it. "*Hasenpfeffer*," he declared with pleasure.

"Papa called it 'rabbit jam,'" replied Rosehannah. Harris was waving his fork at the third jar, which she opened a little reluctantly. "Pickled mussels," she explained. "I wasn't sure…"

"No more or less kosher than hare, I assure you. As well to be hanged for a swine as a shrimp, I always say." By now he was smiling broadly, and she smiled back, although she didn't get the joke. "Can you make all these things without your mother to direct you?" he asked, waving at the picnic food.

"I think so," she answered, slicing the bread to try and impose a somewhat more civilized air on the meal. "I might not get it perfectly right every time, but I watched her do it every year since I could walk, and I've helped with every stage of the process at some point. Papa did the hunting, but I think you could arrange to get game from the Toops, or even from Captain Ryder. And of course, I have my own rabbit slips."

"Well," he said, settling into a more leisurely pace of eating, "you have some very attractive talents, my dear. I wonder what else you can do to make yourself useful?"

Rosehannah took the question at face value. "I can sew, of course, and embroider and crochet. I'm sewing a dress for Neta Toop, in exchange for that old black hen and the young cock you already ate. I can make baskets—I made that one there," she added, nudging the picnic basket with the toe of her boot. "I can read, write, add, subtract and multiply, but you know that already." The girl lay back in the moss and closed her eyes against the sun. "I can cut hair, too." This with a pointed edge to her voice.

"I cut it off on board ship because of the lice. Don't you like it longer?"

"Cropped hair makes you look a little sinister, so people are afraid of you. Until you find your feet, that is probably a good thing."

"Then you shall cut it off again, as soon as possible. Continue enumerating your accomplishments." Harris helped himself to more mussels, dipping them out of the vinegar with his fingers.

"I can raise chickens, and kill and clean them," she acknowledged in a sleepy voice. "I'm a prodigious berry picker, and I can make confit and relish and wine from what I gather. I know several of the soliloquies of Shakespeare by heart, as well as a number of psalms, the ten commandments, the seven deadly sins, in English of course, and the *credo*, the *pater noster*, and the *magnificat* in Latin." She was silent for a moment, and he thought she had fallen asleep in the sun, but then she added "And I can juggle four beach stones in the air for as long as it takes to hard boil an egg." This last declaration was smothered by a gigantic yawn; after which Rosehannah tossed the hem of her apron over her face and entered the arms of Morpheus.

Harris laughed silently. The girl was welcome to sleep, as long as it left him free to pursue the jugged hare and the goose. He spread a slice of bread with a thick layer of the salty goose fat and then dug into the jar of hare, which seemed to have been preserved with some remarkably tasty berries, like very superior cranberries.

He moved the boiling pot from the fire and set it to one side to stay warm. The food was delicious, the view was magnificent, the weather seemed to have passed through at least two seasons in two hours, and it was high summer in one of the most beautiful places he had ever seen. He looked at the sleeping girl, the coarse cloth of her apron moving up and down with her breath. She was a rather obliging little thing, he thought, and clever with it, but before he could formulate any more positive response, he forced his mind onto other subjects. He had erred in that particular direction too often in the past.

Dear Dr. Hart,

If you are going to insist upon calling me Dr. Harris, I shall have to give you your proper title also. I confess, Leah googled you. It was not my idea, but she wanted to know why I was so anxious to get to the mailbox each day, and when I told her about your most interesting letters, she suggested we look you up. Initially, she had some trouble locating you, as I had told her your first name was Brina, that being your signature, but clever girl that she is, she eventually realized it was short for Sabrina. I was more than a little intimidated by the list of honours and awards she came up with. I myself have only a very modest teaching award and my medal from the philatelists to boast of, having always been more of a teacher than an academic.

Oh dear. I notice that in among your numerous awards for scholarly publications are several teaching awards also. Leah says not to mind, as you are probably a rotten piddly player, while I am (modesty forbids me to use her exact words) not half bad. Shibby, her younger sister, insists that I tell you I am also a very good cook. The two girls (and Culhoon, their dog) are spending the day out here in the country with me, getting roses in their cheeks and staying out of their parents' hair, while they repaint their kitchen. They are each leaning over a shoulder as I write this and they say I must tell you the dog is actually called Fionn McCool the Hound of Culhoon, Culhoon for short. I am sending them out to the garden to look for eggs, since Culhoon has managed to chase the chickens into the bushes, so hopefully there will be fewer interruptions to this missive, which up until now has been all interruptions.

I have found no Harrises, Anglican or otherwise, in the Trinity registry, but have been thinking it might be worth having a look at the ships' records for the White family. Captain Street was originally an agent for the Whites. I am sending you a copy of an old map of the Trinity area. You will see that there are numerous outpost stations (we call them outports or outharbours) that would have been supplied by, and trading through, Trinity. It is possible Jacob Harris went out to one of the more isolated settlements to act on behalf of a Trinity merchant.

The more I dig into the early trading history of the Trinity and Harbour Grace-Carbonear areas, the more covert Jews I seem to find.

I was making inquiries at the library the other day and a man working at one of the microfilm readers overheard me. He told me that the Noftals of Broad Cove (near Carbonear) were really Navratalis or Naftalis, Jews from the Channel Islands, found in the Plantation Book for the 1770s. I've tried to confirm this, but the library's microfilm copy of the Plantation Book is unreadable and the original is under lock and key at the Provincial Archives, which is temporarily closed to accommodate a move to a new building. This fellow at the library said that when he was a boy, he and the other children used to "chase the Nofties" with a pointed stick, which had a chunk of fatback pork stuck on the end.

I'm not sure what that was all about, but there is a saying here, "Nofty was forty when he lost the pork." That means, "Don't count your chickens before they're hatched," or "There's many a slip 'twixt cup and lip." Nofty was said to be a man called Noftal, who was forty points up in a game of Forty-fives (a popular card game), but unexpectedly lost. "The pork" in a church-sponsored card game is the prize, often a shoulder of pork or a ham, but sometimes anything from a box of chocolates to a load of birch billets. Do you suppose Nofty didn't want to win the pork because he was Jewish?

I was gratified to hear that you can't cook. Shibby says my blintzes and halupchas are as good as her Bubby Riteman's.

FYI: Piddly is an ancient game—a cross between hurley and cricket—that was played here in my youth. I taught it to a group of Leah's friends the year they started school and it has experienced a bit of a revival. Its great advantage is that it requires nothing more than two bricks or stones, and an old broom handle sawed in two—no profit for Nike in that.

I note that your husband died just a year ago— I think the unveiling must have been within the last month. My sympathy for your loss. I think you will find that the worst is over, or at least that was my experience, having been through it myself not so very long ago. I was rather long-in-the-tooth when I married Tali, and losing her so suddenly was a terrible blow, but her son Harry, and Harry's wife Judith, took me on as their own personal restoration project and Leah and Shibby did the rest. I still miss my wife very much, of course, but it no longer interferes entirely with my enjoyment of life and I sometimes go for whole days without thinking of her, although I rarely go for even a few hours without thinking about the children.

Speaking of which, there is a most unholy racket coming from the hen house. If they have tried to put Culhoon into one of the nesting boxes again, there will be words.

All the best,

John

"Do not disdain any person; do not underrate the importance of any-thing—for there is no person who does not have his hour and there is no thing without its place in the sun."

Ben Zoma, Ethics of the Fathers

"Do we have any coal?" Harris had been rooting around behind the house for the best part of an hour, while Rosehannah was scrubbing out the kitchen, particularly the area around the fireplace, which Harris had stripped of its old turnspit.

"A little," she answered, wiping soot from her hands with her second apron. It had always struck Harris as odd that women wore aprons to keep their dresses clean, and then wore aprons to keep their aprons clean. However, watching Rosehannah scrub the linen each week had given him a new appreciation for the labour of laundering. "We get a coal allowance from Lester Garland's each year, and we generally tried to save it for an emergency, but last winter was all emergencies." She disappeared into the linney and emerged again a few minutes later pulling a wooden box behind her.

"More than enough," he pronounced, and lifted the box effortlessly onto his shoulder. She followed him out the door and around the end of the house.

"Can I help with anything, Mr. Harris?" she asked, curious to see what project had finally broken through his listlessness and boredom.

"Soon," he replied. "I'll need you to supply the air for the fire." Scattered around him on the ground were odds and ends of scrap iron, salvaged from the long mound of rocks that served as midden and retaining wall. Harris had positioned a large shard of metal from a shattered barking pot on a bed of stones. In the hollow of this, he had built a small fire with splits and shavings of wood, and dropping the box onto the ground, he carefully began adding lumps of coal around the edge of the flames. A bucket of water stood nearby.

An odd assortment of rusty tools was laid out on a large boulder to one side of the assemblage. Rosehannah could identify a hammer, chisel and tongs. Harris produced a long, thin tube of brass, and began hammering one end flat. Before it was quite pinched together, he inserted a thick nail into the end, flattened the tube on either side of it, and then wiggled the nail out. He put the tube to his lips and tentatively blew down the pipe, testing the other end against the palm of his hand.

"Here," he said, handing her the tube. "Blow into this." Rosehannah gingerly placed her mouth against the round end of the tube and huffed into it. "Gently and slowly," he instructed. "I need a thin, steady supply of air to get the fire hot enough."

"It's not a very big fire," Rosehannah observed, looking dubiously at the small conflagration.

"Doesn't need to be. A fire the size of your fist is about right, but it has to be hot and it has to be constant, so I'll feed it coal and you'll feed it air." Harris placed more coal around the edge of the fire, and positioned the kitchen poker ready to push the pieces into the centre of the makeshift forge. He took the pipe from her and began blowing gently on the fire, catching the coals alight and nudging them in to the centre to create a small, glowing heart of heat.

"Your father, or whoever tried to mend the chain last time, used a link from something else—it jammed in the pulley. Also, the wheel has come loose from the skewer, so we just need to tighten it up a bit." This explanation was offered in between steady puffs into the air pipe. When the small fire was cherry red in the centre, he handed the pipe to her and gestured for her to keep supplying air, while he set to with the tools.

Rosehannah found it hard to concentrate on keeping the fire a constant heat while watching him work, but he seemed to know exactly what he was doing, and within minutes, he had turned a large nail into a perfectly formed link, using the boulder as an anvil. He twisted the hot metal with the tongs, hammered the sides flat to match the chain from the turnspit, and cut the nail head off with the chisel before plunging it into the bucket to cool.

"Now comes the tricky bit," he explained. "It's often easier to make a new piece than it is to mend an old one, but I don't think this outfit is up to the job." The air pipe was becoming uncomfortably hot, but he seemed to realize this without having to be told and, pinching the pipe in his tongs, he dunked it in the water bucket before returning it to her willing hands.

"Pay attention, Rosehannah," he warned in a sharp voice. She had turned her head to watch him, twisting the stream of air away from the centre of the fire. She focused her eye and her breath on the fire again, and contented herself with an occasional glimpse of his face, intent and animated, as he mended the turnspit.

After he had plunged the wheel of the spit into the water to cool, Harris gestured for Rosehannah to stop and she sat back on her heels, dizzy from blowing.

"You have to control your breath," he explained. "Bring it right up from below your ribs and don't gulp so much. Like playing the flute," he added, and lifted the blowing pipe side on to his mouth to demonstrate. She felt a long, slow, steady stream of air stir the strands of hair that had come loose from under her cap as he leaned in towards her.

"I'm very impressed," she said. "I'd no idea you could do anything useful." He turned the pipe, and blew a hard puff of air up her nose, causing her to tip back on her heels onto the ground.

"No man is a hero to his valet, but that is a particularly unflattering remark," Harris said. "I have any number of skills, though they do not include snaring rabbits or juggling beach stones."

"What do they include, besides playing the invisible flute?" Rosehannah fished into her pocket for a bit of bread and began coaxing the old black hen towards her with it.

"Given the appropriate tools, I can work gold, silver and brass. I can dress a boil, pull a tooth, compound sedatives, stimulants, laxatives and ointments, and set bones. I can produce an ace of spades from a deck of cards, even when there is none in it," he intoned, "and I can catch a hen quicker than you."

At the last phrase, he had turned, snatched the old hen by the wing, and wrung its neck in one quick twist. "You dress it while I put the turnspit together again," he said, dropping the dead bird into her lap.

The chicken was browning nicely when Mahala Sevier came scrambling in at the door. "Rosie, the mister says to tell you the schooner's coming from Trinity, and he thinks Mr. Garland's on board. You've got half an hour to have dinner on the table."

The child had turned and was heading back down to the wharf when Rosehannah caught her by the strings of her pinafore. "Back you come, young one. I need water, and you've got to mind the bird while I make a pudding. You can scrape the bowl after." Mahala reluctantly turned back into the house, torn between the promise of the pudding and the much more immediate gratification of seeing the schooner come in.

The table was set, the pudding was steaming in the pot, and the plump old hen was resting on the platter under an overturned bowl when Harris led Mr. Garland into the door.

"Rose, my dear, you've grown at least a foot since I last saw you," Mr. Garland greeted her. She smiled shyly as she curtsied, and he leaned forward to take her hand briefly. "So very sorry about your mother, my dear. She was a charming lady."

"Thank you, sir," Rosehannah answered, genuinely grateful to hear a kind word about her dear mama.

"You look more like her every day," Mr. Garland added, although there was no truth in the remark at all. Mrs. Quint had been short and plump with reddish hair and a ruddy complexion, while Rosehannah was dark-haired, pale and thin as a whippet. "Now, we badly need to scrub our hands before we eat, as we have been investigating the mysterious properties of cod oil."

Rosehannah stepped back and gestured towards a basin on a bench by the water barrel. Next to it was a chunk of soft, brown soap and two gleaming white linen cloths. Lifting the steaming kettle, she tipped a small amount over her fingers to test the heat, and then poured, first for Mr. Garland and then for Jacob Harris. By the time they had dried their hands, she had the soup in the bowls and wine in the glasses. The bread lay under a clean cloth on the table.

"Well, this is very nice, indeed it is. Wouldn't you agree, Mr. Harris?" Garland was known to be a trencherman, and never turned his nose up at even a simple meal if it was properly prepared. Harris murmured something that could have been assent. "And a proper loaf of bread. Not easy to do well without an oven," Garland asserted, peering round at the chimney. "Some of my dealers complain that they eat nothing but hard tack from one end of the year to the other."

The barley soup disappeared quickly and Rosehannah removed the low bowls and replaced them with dinner plates. Mr. Garland's eyes lit up when she uncovered the platter and placed the chicken on the table in front of him.

"Shall I carve, Harris?" he asked, taking the knife and fork without waiting for an answer. "Fresh meat in the middle of the week—you do yourself well, I must say. Not that you shouldn't, come to that. There are some who live on cod, but anyone used to the tables of Berlin and London would have a hard job to do that." Garland laughed, and Harris sighed and cast a baleful eye at Rosehannah.

The two men devoured most of the bird, while Garland quizzed Harris on his knowledge of the local fishery. Rosehannah was surprised at how much he had apparently absorbed in the short time he had been active in the store. During the week it had taken them to complete the inventory, Harris had peppered her with questions. What was the difference between dry salt and bulk, pickle and brine, Madeira and West Indie? What distinguished a dapper and a jigger, an anchor and a grapnel, a clumper and a ballycatter? What was the difference between summer fish and winter fish? Which bait was better, squid or capelin?

When she admitted ignorance on a matter, as was frequent as soon as the topic moved offshore into the boats, Harris made a note of the query so that he might later ask Mr. Toop or one of the other fishermen. That he had taken in a good deal was evident as he conversed with Mr. Garland, who appreciated that he made no attempt to bluff his way when he got out of his depth.

By the time they had reached the pudding—stewed dried fruit with a hot rum sauce—both men were speaking comfortably in one another's company. Rosehannah was already aware that Harris was a cut above the common, but seeing him conversing with Mr. Garland, particularly when she recalled the torturous interviews she had observed between her father and the merchant, made her think he either had some mysterious hold over the man or he simply didn't care what the outcome of the interview was.

Garland was the first to push himself back from the table and light his pipe. "So tell me, Harris, you've had a good opportunity to look the place over, and by the sounds of it, you've got a handle on the business. What do you propose I do here?"

Harris signaled for Rosehannah to remove the dishes while he prepared his response. She silently came forward, afraid that if she made herself too conspicuous, she would be sent from the house, thereby missing all the talk.

"I've sorted out the accounts, sir, and copied them, so you can take those back with you and come to your own conclusion. But it's no secret that you are losing money on the operation and will lose more if you leave me here, as I'm not adept at…rabbit slips and such." He smiled at his own shortcomings, and Garland joined him.

"I realize that. However, I have to keep in mind the larger scheme of things. This part of the bay is known to be careless and barbarous, but it has some of the best summer fishing in the colony. These small-boat men bring in excellent fish, and the light-salted, shore-dried cod brings a better price than when it's been kept in salt bulk. If I don't maintain a presence here, someone else will move into the area to pick up the trade."

"But a dozen families—that's not much fish." Harris pulled a paper from his pocket and studied it.

"There'll be more moving in over the next few years. This island can maintain four times that number easily, and they supplement their living with hunting and such. I notice there are already a few small gardens here in the harbour. Under the circumstances, I'm willing to carry you through until spring and see what you can make of the place, if you're willing to winter here." The two men sat in silence and Rosehannah held her breath. Harris slowly slid the paper across the table to Mr. Garland.

"If you can see your way to taking the useless stock off the inventory, and letting me have these basic supplies for myself and for trade, I might be able to break even within the year."

"Hmm. One hundred and thirty bags of hard tack, eight casks of beef…raisins, suet, peas, vinegar. There's not much to spare here. If the hunting is bad, you might find things a bit tight." Garland tapped his pipe on his teeth. "It can get pretty dismal out here on the islands. Are you sure you're up to it? I didn't think you'd take to the business, especially given your background. I hope you know what you're getting into, Harris."

Harris gave one of his ironic smiles. "Someone once wrote that trade has all the fascination of gambling, without the moral guilt. I don't think I've ever encountered a commodity that so allows for speculation and a gambler's chance for profit as cod."

"Well, I'm not one for reading, I'm afraid—I leave that to the ladies—but in this case, I think the author is right." Garland glanced at the paper again before pocketing it. "There's Toop, coming to fetch me. The tide must have turned."

The two men headed to the door. Harris stepped back to allow the merchant to pass through first, but Garland waved him on ahead and then hesitated in the doorway.

"Everything all right, Rose? Mr. Harris is…" He hesitated, encouraging her to finish the sentence.

"A gentleman, sir, always," Rosehannah answered, blushing slightly.

"Stay in touch with Mrs. Garland, when you get the opportunity. Perhaps write her a letter when you send over the smoked salmon. She takes a great interest in you."

"Thank you, sir. I will." Rosehannah curtsied. She watched him set off down the path to the wharf, and when the schooner finally cast off, she collapsed into a chair with relief. She was hungrily gnawing at the remains of the chicken when Harris returned.

"So, it seems we're both on the collar for the foreseeable future," he remarked in an offhanded way.

"*In* collar, Mr. Harris," Rosehannah corrected him. "*On* the collar is when you anchor a boat offshore. Is it true that the station loses money for Mr. Garland? People here work awfully hard. I know Papa did, and Mama too."

"Over time it might make money, if the fishery goes well. Things slid a bit everywhere in the years after the wars, but it's picking up again now and, if we can get enough seals to increase the production of oil, it's possible he might turn a good profit." He sat and idly watched her eat. "You think this place is a bread-basket, because you've never seen anywhere else. But believe me, that little scrap of a garden and those scrawny chickens of yours would not even be worth bothering with in Hamburg or Devon."

"You shouldn't insult my chickens when you've just eaten one. Considering her age, I think she tastes remarkably good." Rosehannah felt the insult was more towards herself than to her chickens, but she didn't say so.

"Yes, of course," Harris said, but he didn't actually apologize. "The trouble is, the fishery is so time-consuming, there's no way for people here to feed and clothe themselves without an advance from the merchant. Everything has to be brought into the country ready-made—flour, cordage, clothing. Even the salt comes from England or Spain. It's almost impossible to get ahead."

"Mama said that it is much the same back home for most people, but people back home have other burdens as well. Here, the work is backbreaking, but the place is our own, and we have no ministers or government officials to make our lives worse. Mrs. Toop says that at home, if a woman should mistakenly take a yard of ribbon from a shop, she will likely rot in gaol for years, at the mercy of brutal guards and the whim of the court."

"And here?" Harris pulled the chicken carcass apart, searching for a last tender morsel.

"It depends. There are no shops here, only our store, but if a woman takes a yard of ribbon and someone knows of it, it goes on her family's account. If she takes it and no one knows, but we see her with new ribbon on her dress, she might be shunned, or her family might be denied credit and have to go elsewhere the next season. However, if she's a good midwife or generous with the produce from her garden, we might just turn a blind eye and chalk it up as the price of doing business with her. But to put her in gaol, where she can do no one any good, while her children starve, her man breaks his back catching fish that rot in the sun, and the garden goes to weed, all for a yard of ribbon, is too foolish to think about." Rosehannah dumped the remains of the chicken into the kettle and added water to make soup for their supper.

"And might Mrs. Toop have once taken a yard of ribbon by mistake?"

"Perhaps." Rosehannah lifted the kettle and hooked it onto the crook in the fireplace but didn't turn back to the table. "And perhaps Mr. Sevier had debts he couldn't pay, and perhaps someone else was caught cheating at cards and had to be hurried out of the country by his friends." The silence that followed this pronouncement hung in the air of the tiny house.

"I only cheated when I was sure he was already swindling me," Harris responded indignantly. "Unfortunately, my opponent was so wealthy and powerful that, as you put it, people had accepted it as 'the cost of doing business' with him. I'm being punished for not turning Nelson's eye on him." She remained with her back to him. "Oh, for God's sake, Rosehannah, at least have the civility to look at me when I'm speaking to you."

Meekly, Rosehannah returned to the table. "I'm sorry I mentioned it, sir. Mrs. Toop said Mr. Garland wouldn't have had anything to do with you if you were what she called a 'thimble rigger.' But you see what I mean about this place. Over there, we have to be what we were born, but here, we can be what we are. At home, I would have nothing but shame. Here, I have a comfortable life, a place in the community, a tilt in the woods. Even without you, sir, I'd have my choice of husbands and the hope of a good life. Out here, there's two men for every woman, so we females aren't obliged to take what's offered us but can wait to find a good man."

"And I'm keeping you from that, Rosehannah? It's my fault that you haven't got a real husband and the hope of a good life?"

65

"Heavens, no, sir." Rosehannah laughed and stood up to clear the rest of the table. "My hope of a good life is right here, on Ireland's Eye. And, as for the good husband, I'm not ready for him yet. Mama said I shouldn't choose a husband 'til I'm hungry for one, and it so happens that at this moment, I'm plimmed right up to the waterline."

Rosehannah's cheerful mood seemed to be the last straw for Harris, who would have much preferred a fierce argument, and he slammed the door on his way out, which didn't stop him from hearing a peal of laughter behind him as he headed down to the wharf.

Mr. Garland's visit marked the end of Harris's leisurely days. The familes of Ireland's Eye—the Toops, Seviers and Mayhews, the Raymonds, McGraths and Nichols, and all their relatives and sharemen, many of whom had suddenly found it necessary to be in or around the Lester Garland store, while the schooner from Trinity was at the dock—understood without being told that Mr. Garland was going to hold on for another season. Work that had been tackled half-heartedly, when it still seemed possible that Lester Garland's dealer would be withdrawn, suddenly came to the fore.

Shy men who had, up to this time, barely raised their voices above a whisper when addressing Harris, turned up on the doorstep at four in the morning, demanding that he open the store and issue them cordage to repair a torn net or hooks for lost hand lines. Rosehannah didn't turn them away, as he expected, but called him from his bed in the loft to attend to them, as if this were the most normal thing in the world. Once, when he was less than expeditious, she took her key, ran down the narrow path in the dark dawn, and measured off the cordage herself, marking the length on a birch shake with a sharp nail for him to enter in the account book later that morning.

"They cannot wait," she explained to him sternly over the bread and tea she later provided for his breakfast. "When the fish strike, they have only a few hours to get them. One exceptionally good morning can make or break their season. Have you seen how they work? And the women, they have to make the fish as well as look after the gardens and cook if they can find the time, though often as not they can't and the men go to work with little more than cold water and hard bread in their stomachs." She pushed the jam pot towards him, as if daring him to spoon the sweet mess onto the soft and sweet bread on his plate.

Determined to avoid her scolding tongue and accusing looks, Harris kept to the store as much as possible throughout August and September, yet even through his window he could see that what she had said was true. Every soul on the island seemed engaged in a mad dash from the first faint rays of light in the early morning to the last reflection off the water at night. Life was an endless string of chores to be accomplished. The men caught, split and salted an infinite number of fish, which the women drained, stacked, turned, restacked, spread, turned, stacked, gathered and covered as many as a dozen times a day.

Small children staggered from the flakes to the sheds with one or two fish at a time, while older girls carried burdens that would have been difficult for many adults. Babies stood and screamed from the safety of empty barrels until their harried mothers could stop for a moment to nurse them. Sundays were supposed to be days of rest, but the strain of doing nothing when there was so much crying out to be done made those days a torture. While the men were napping, some of the women slipped away to the headlands and came home with berry-stained hands but no berries, although a quick traipse through the same meadows on Monday often produced an inordinate number.

"Young Raymond asked me if I was going to sort the fish before it was picked up by Garland's collector boat," said Harris to Rosehannah one day over his dinner. "He seemed mightily amused by the prospect."

"Oh, pay him no mind, sir. He'd probably got some bet on with one of the other boys. Nobody expects you to cull the fish. Papa used to do an initial cull, just to save time, but Mr. Garland will send a culler." Seeing the look of interest on his face, she went on. "You see, if the dealer does the cull, he might be accused of favouritism, or of holding a scunner against someone he doesn't get along with. It can cause a lot of bitterness. So, Lester Garland sends along his own culler and the fish is sorted on the dock as it goes into the boat.

"Papa would take out all the worst, the stuff with bloodspots or gashes or slivers..." And seeing his look of incomprehension, she took his dinner knife and tried to demonstrate on the remains of a loaf of bread. "After you've cut the gills from the body, you introduce the knife between and under the lug bones, and then rip the belly from this point straight to the vent, but not beyond. If the rip continues, it tends to carry the knife up the side at the last, so part of the flesh is left attached alongside the fin when the splitting is done, instead of going to the side to which it belongs.

"It's hard to make a fish properly. There's bleeding, throating, ripping, cutting, beheading and trimming, splitting, washing, whitenaping, salting and drying"—she counted the steps off on her fingers—"and, at any stage, a dozen things can go wrong that will affect the cull. If the weather is warm in July and August, the fish can become soft and sour. Usually, you can spot this when you're splitting it, but sometimes it seems all right and then it opens up when it's being handled. The man will think he's got number one Spanish Choice, but the surface will appear rough when it's dry. The experienced culler will notice.

"If the fish isn't salted properly, it can result in putty fish. We don't get putty fish here much, because there's usually a breeze to keep things cool. You have to put more salt on a thick area of the fish, less on the thin parts, so it is evenly distributed."

"You're quite the expert," Harris observed, salvaging what was left of the bread and using it to sop up the remains of the rabbit gravy in his dish.

"Oh no, Mr. Harris," said Rosehannah solemnly. "What I know about fish, you could fit in your eye. And you have to know the salt as well. There's salt that's obtained from evaporation of the sun— some of it has impurities that form a rough deposit on the fish, although other types whiten it nicely. Mined salt can have clay in it. Evaporated salt is best, I think, but it's also the most expensive and it can be too fine. Fine salt tends to become solid or caked in damp weather, while very coarse salt may strike slowly and mark the surface. Best is a mix of the two, Papa always said."

"And was your papa such a very good fisherman, Rosehannah?"

"Not as good as Mr. Toop, I think, for Mr. Toop has luck with him. But I believe Papa could think like a fish…" Seeing Harris try to suppress a smile, she smiled too. "I know that sounds disrespectful, but if you live on water, it's best to think like a fish. Papa is suited to this place. He can turn his hand to anything."

"If he could think like a fish, why did he become a dealer? Surely he should have stuck with what he knew and understood." Harris absently took a pinch of salt from the saucer on the table and sprinkled it on the remains of his bread.

"It was the only way to get ahead. You can be a good fisherman, and even a lucky one, but you will never do more than break even. The profit goes to the merchant. The fisherman who is also a dealer is the merchant's man and might get a little ahead if he works hard and is lucky and if his merchant's ship doesn't go on the rocks or his warehouse doesn't burn down." Rosehannah swept the last of the bread crusts into her apron to give the hens. "You'll never be a fisherman, Mr. Harris. You haven't the nerve for it. But you might be a dealer, and a very good one, if you put your mind to it. There's a thousand honest and capable fishermen on this coast, but I can count on the fingers of one hand the number of honest and capable dealers there are." With that, she ducked out of the small house and he could hear her calling *coop, coop* to her hens.

It was something to think about. In the various trades he'd tried his hand at, Harris had always preferred those aspects that were inherently practical and useful. As an apprentice, he had taken more pride in a well-made brass compass than in a finely wrought gold brooch or snuff box. It was hard to think of salt fish as something to be proud of, but watching Rosehannah choose a fish to put in to soak for his breakfast, it was clear that she had a very exacting standard.

Harris pushed himself away from the table and headed for the wooden settle by the fireplace to smoke a pipe before going back to his store. Unlike the fishermen, he wasn't up at four in the morning, but since all the men took a short nap before going out for the last haul in late afternoon, he had gotten into the habit of taking a rest at that time. Generally, the women were out on the flakes turning the fish or stacking them into piles to let the fluids drain from them, and it was probably the only time the cooking areas and kitchens were quiet.

There was no rest for him this day, however. Rosehannah was soon back with a stack of dried fish in her apron, and within moments she had them spread at his feet for examination.

"Look at this one. You can see from a mile away that it's poor quality." Rosehannah jerked a dismissive chin at the offending split cod. "My guess is this is some youngster trying his hand at it himself, without any help from his mother. Martin Raymond, perhaps.

"See that black on the napses? That's belly skin. You have to peel it off. It's not hard to do, but you have to have the knack of it. And look here." Rosehannah demanded his attention. "The neck isn't trimmed, there's a gouge in the spinal cord, there's a couple of folds in the flesh, and where that blood spot is, you can see the backbone is broken off when it should be cut. And remember I showed you about the sliver with the loaf of bread? You can see, the fish is uneven as you move down towards the tail. And the bottom part of the tail is left rounded when it should be flat and symmetrical, like the rest of the fish." She sat back on her heels. "That's a really bad fish, the worst kind of West Indie you'll likely see on this island, and thank God for that, because if there were many more, you'd be out of business by spring.

"Compare it with the other three," she continued. "What do you notice about them?"

Harris considered ignoring the girl, but the faults she had indicated were so obvious once she'd pointed them out, that he found he was interested despite himself.

"Well, for one thing, they've all got white napes, not black."

"Right. Taking off that little film of skin is really more for appearance than quality, but it sets the scene, you might say. Do you see any blood spots?"

"Here?" he ventured, feeling a little foolish. The mark from the liver on one of the fish was obvious.

"Right. That's caused by belly burn, when the stomach juices start to 'eat' the cod after it's been caught. But also, check at the neck and at the end of the backbone. That's where blood's usually overlooked, so of course that's exactly where the culler checks for it."

"This fish isn't as symmetrical as those two," Harris continued, shuffling the fish around as if they were items in a shell game.

"Right again. And what about the surface?" Rosehannah sat cross-legged on the floor with her hands in her lap and looked up at him with a slight flush of pleasure in her cheeks.

"The surface of this one is a little uneven," he guessed, lifting the fish and shuffling them into a new order.

"So far, you've only used your eyes. How else can you judge a fish?" She was by this time suppressing a smile, as if he were a prize pupil on examination day.

"Well, when I was thinking of being a doctor, I went about with an old gentleman who said little but taught me a great deal. He always held the hand of a patient, claiming that he could judge from the hand how the rest of the patient was. Depending on how wet or dry it was, how hot or cold, how the fingers clung to his or lay apathetically in his palm, he judged whether the patient was likely to recover." Harris lifted and turned each fish as he explained the method of his old master, and Rosehannah grinned in approval. Laying the best fish to his left and the worst to his right, Harris picked up the other two and studied them carefully. "This one has a small, shallow gash, but is otherwise wholesome and smells well. The other, likewise, smells good and is without a gash, but it has a slight discolouration at the neck. I'd say they are both of equal worth, but..." and at this he grasped the two fish by their tails and weighed them in his hands. "This fellow is a slight bit heavier, though it looks the same size, and I suspect that, by the time it reaches Spain, it might be a little fousty."

"Very good, Mr. Harris," Rosehannah said, collecting the fish back into her apron. "There are probably fifteen other factors to be taken into consideration when culling fish, but you show some aptitude for the business. We might turn you into a dealer yet." She rose to return the fish to the sheds, and barely caught Harris's words as she pushed the door closed.

"Praise, like gold and diamonds, owes its value only to its scarcity around here."

Early one afternoon, towards the end of October, Mahala Sevier came running into the store. "Miss Rose says you're to come over to Black Duck Cove, Mr. Harris." She was holding her side and gasping for breath.

"She's not hurt, is she?" Harris grabbed his hat off a peg, lifted the child into his arms and headed out the door. At the top of the hill going down from the height of land into Black Duck Cove, a group of women and children were gathered in a tight, worried knot.

Out in the Thoroughfare, he saw a small boat sailing clumsily towards the shore. The vessel listed severely to one side, so much so that the gunnels were almost in the water. A slight lop on the surface of the tickle threatened to turn the craft over at any moment.

"Who is it?" Harris strained to make out the two figures in the boat, but they were just dark shapes hunched beneath the ochred sail.

"Young Mrs. Toop and her daughter," Rosehannah answered. "They went blueberry picking on Bird Island this morning, taking Mr. Mayhew's punt. Mrs. Mayhew sent for me when they didn't get back in time for their dinner."

"Where are the men?" Harris didn't see any boys older than eight in the group, and there were no other boats on the water.

"A schooner came over from Random with word there was mackerel in Smith Sound." Mrs. Mayhew had dropped to her knees and was praying loudly. Most of the other women and girls joined her. One of the babies began to howl.

"Is there no other boat we can take out?" Harris tried to ignore the racket that was rising around him and hardly dared take his eye off the curiously lopsided vessel.

"There's one in Traytown but it would take us hours to bring it round to this side of the island. And besides, few of the women know how to sail a boat. Papa always gave the order and I just did what I was told." Rosehannah moved away from the praying women and Harris followed her. They stood together awkwardly for a few minutes, both staring at the slowly approaching boat, willing it to remain on top of the water.

Mahala Sevier came and buried her face in Rosehannah's apron, wrapping her arms around her waist. "Go and join your mama, maidey," she told the child. "Say a prayer with her. God might listen to a good little girl like you." Mahala reluctantly disengaged herself from the older girl and went to pray with the women. "I'm afraid I'm what Mr. Garland calls a 'shirttail Catholic,'" she commented to Harris. "I don't think my prayers would do much good."

Harris continued to study the boat. "You know, it looks odd, the way it sits all over to one side, but I think that Mrs. Toop knows what she's doing. For the life of me though, I can't think what makes it lay on its side like that."

"You said you were married once, Mr. Harris," Rosehannah replied. "Would the woman in the blue dress happen to be your wife?" Harris looked startled at the turn the conversation had suddenly taken, but Rosehannah kept her eyes fixed on the lopsided punt out on the water.

"Not my wife, no." And after a moment's silence, he added, "My wife was a good deal older than me."

"She died?"

"No, she divorced me, or rather I divorced her, as that's the way we Jews do things. It was all part of the arrangement between my uncle and her father. She needed a husband with residency papers for Berlin, and I needed to buy my way out of the family business. It was a satisfactory transaction for both sides."

As the boat came closer to safety, the prayers of the women petered out. There was a quiet, collective whoop when young Mrs. Toop dropped the sail as they came towards the beach, and the boat rocked in response. Rosehannah and several of the older women ran down into the water and caught the gunnel to pull the boat up onto the shingle; after a moment, Harris joined them. Together they hauled the boat out onto the landwash, and the rest of the women and girls gathered as they pulled it further up beyond the tide line. Hands reached in to haul Mrs. Toop out of the boat as Neta stepped on the gunnel and jumped to the ground.

"There was a big wave came and dropped us down on top of a rock," Neta explained excitedly, wringing water from the hem of her soaked skirt. "Mam loaded rocks into the boat to make her list with the hole side up, and we sailed home."

"Mind you don't spill them berries," warned Mrs. Toop as Mahala and the other children lifted out the pails of fruit. "Do you suppose we can get the boat fixed before the men get home?" She looked doubtfully at Mr. Harris.

"I'm not much good with wood, I'm afraid, Mrs. Toop," Harris conceded. "Best wait until Mr. Toop or Mr. Mayhew have a look at it, but it doesn't look too bad, just a plank or two gone."

"Selby could fix that with one hand tied behind his back," one of the Raymond women noted sourly.

"Yes, and steal the pennies off your eyes with the other one while he was doing it," answered Rosehannah. "We'd best get back to work or the men will have more than a stove-in boat to complain about when they return." The women obediently began to move off, and Rosehannah turned back up the hill towards the main harbour. She and Harris quickly found themselves alone.

"Don't mind her complaints, Mr. Harris. She was just frightened. At this time of year, the loss of a boat would have been almost as bad as the loss of the two women. They're all exhausted from the work and Sundays drive them mad—at least I get to spread the work out over seven days instead of six."

"I haven't been much help, I suppose," Harris conceded. "Is there anything I can do?"

"Well, we need hooks for the smokehouse. The ones we had disappeared about the time Selby left. You could make me some more, perhaps, if Mahala did the blowing for you. I can't take the time—I've got the vegetables to see to and Mr. Raymond gave me half a dozen ducks that are in salt and need to be potted, and I've got to cut and dry some meadow grass and browse for the few chickens I'll keep over the winter, and…oh, there's just such a lot to do before winter sets in.

"Maybe you could do the smoking too," she added. Rosehannah looked cheered at the prospect. "There's a dozen barrels of salmon in brine and they'll get too salty if they aren't smoked soon. It's not hard, but it requires you to be nearby all the time to check the fire and the vents."

"But what if I spoiled it?" Harris was dismayed at the thought of having to take responsibility for such a large quantity of fish.

"Oh, you probably *will* spoil the first few batches," Rosehannah assured him. "We'll have to eat your mistakes, but you'll catch on pretty quickly, I'm sure. After all, you can make hooks and mend chains, and smoking salmon isn't as hard as that. It isn't nearly as hard as making dried cod, either. You can control the fire—you can't control the sun and the wind." They had reached the height of land again and she had stopped to catch her breath. "I'm not much of a gambler, Mr. Harris, but I'm willing to wager that you will get tired of eating badly smoked salmon very quickly."

Dear Brina,

Your recollection of the rhyme *"Get a bit of pork,/Put it on a fork,"* sent me to my classroom copy of the Opies' Dictionary of Nursery Rhymes. They trace it to Jew-taunting at least as far back as 1792, and probably earlier. I expect this is where the "Nofty" taunt originated. It may not be proof that the Noftals were Jewish, but it certainly confirms that people believed they were.

Your *"Get a bit of pork"* rhyme reminds me of something a retired colleague told me with reference to the last line of the rhyme: *"Give it to a Jew boy, Jew."* This man, when he was eighteen years old, was the principal teacher in a two-room outport school. He boarded with a woman who took a great interest in visitors to their isolated community. One day, a Jewish peddler appeared in town, and as he walked by the house, the landlady called out, *"How you getting on, Jew b'y?"* The peddler kept going, barely glancing at the old woman, but as he returned on the road, she called again, *"Business good, is it, Jew b'y?"* This time, the peddler made it abundantly clear that he didn't appreciate the appellation. My friend intervened at this point and explained that his landlady thought the man's name was Ju, for Julius, and the "b'y" was simply a common form of address in the region. The encounter ended pleasantly with the peddler stopping for supper and developing fast friends in the region.

The more I think about it, the more sense it makes that Jews came out to Newfoundland from Plymouth and surrounding areas. Susser documents a significant out-migration of Jews from the 1820s on, to South Africa, America and Australia, so why not to Newfoundland? There were ships constantly leaving Plymouth for Newfoundland, and thousands of seasonal fishers and traders going back and forth, so it would be only logical that at least a few of these outmigrating Jews would follow that route.

When Tali began her work on the history of this community, she thought the first Jews came to St. John's in the 1890s when her family, the Rosenblums, arrived. The only mention of Jewish settlers prior to that time was my old friend the postmaster, Simon Solomon, and a rather questionable reference to another watchmaker, Benjamin Bowring, the scion of an old merchant family here. She never did prove that Solomon was Jewish (though I think I have pretty well convinced the philatelic world he was) *and, if anything, she proved Bowring wasn't, but that was it. She looked no further back, assuming there was nothing to find.*

Perhaps because my people have been hundreds of years in this place, I wasn't quite so comfortable with that conclusion. There is an old family story, which in brief is that a Jewish coastal trader went to peddle over the side of his schooner at Red Island where he was entertained by my grand-father's father-in-law (no blood relation—the old man was married three times). This fellow—McCarthy was his name—claimed to be a direct descendent of the kings of Ireland, and bragged of it to the Jew. Not to be outdone, the peddler reminded McCarthy that he was a direct descendent of the patriarch Abraham, and further offended his host by claiming kin-ship, since they were both descendents of Noah, who was the only one to sur-vive The Flood. McCarthy roundly denounced the peddler for his deep ignorance and informed him in high tones that "The McCarthys of Red Island always had a boat of their own."

I first heard this story when I was a boy of eight or ten, and jokingly used to claim that the trader was Tali's great-grandfather. Later, I did a bit of genealogical mathematics and figured out that if this was, indeed, a true story, the trader had to have visited Red Island in the early 1880s, so the Perlins and Rosenblums were not the first Jews in Newfoundland.

Since then, I have identified a number of nineteenth-century families of possible Jewish heritage: The Ezekiels and the La Cours of Harbour Main, the Morrises of Trinity, the Dancys of Burin, the Palmers of Shoal Harbour, the Tocques and Levis of Carbonear, the Coens and Cohens of St. John's and Harbour Grace (some of them may be Irish Aucoins), the Lyon brothers of St. John's, and possibly some of the Leamons, Webbers, Roses and Gills of various other communities. None of which gets you any closer to your Jacob Harris, but all of which improves the odds that he came here.

Susser says intermarriages and apprenticeships were common between Jewish families in the Wessex region (we have adopted the Thomas Hardy nomenclature for the three counties of Southwest England where most of our forefathers originated) and in looking through his list of nineteenth-century apprentices, I find Philip Ezekiel apprenticed to silversmith Aaron Levi, Henry Jacob apprenticed to his shoemaker father, George Morris apprenticed to his jeweler father

William, and Henry Rosenberg apprenticed to his pawnbroker father. All but one of those names are found in Newfoundland at the same time.

I was reminded by your observation of your late husband's aversion to rural life of a Hebrew teacher we had here some years ago. He claimed that, until he came to St. John's, he had never even once walked on ground that was not either paved or artificially planted. Needless to say, he did not last long here—about four months, I think. His most extraordinary accomplishment in that time was to avoid actually seeing the Atlantic Ocean, a feat I would have considered impossible given the geography of the city.

I assure you that I did not take your remarks about my interest in nursery rhymes to be in any way denigrating. I long ago accepted the fact that my own scholarship, primarily focused on the domestic and folk tradition, will never be viewed with the respect accorded work such as your own. How can I argue for the importance of Minnie White's accordion repertoire or Mildred Dohey's Jack tales over the works of Thomas Mann or Hannah Arendt? I can't and don't. All I can say is that they are important to me. I would rather read a transcription of a fine old Newfoundland sea ballad than one of the plays of Shakespeare any day. I appreciate Shakespeare, I have taught his work and enjoyed doing so, but he is not directly a part of my life, and Minnie and Mildred are.

I think, perhaps, that is why I keep chickens and a small garden. They keep me closer to the lives of the people, both living and dead, who are the focus of my studies and research, ordinary Newfoundlanders who caught fish and cut wood by day and whiled away their winter evenings with playing cards, hooking mats and making up riddles. These are my people, my ancestors, just as Rahel Varnhagen and Henriette Herz are yours.

I am a great believer in instinctive truth, and am thus convinced that, if you think Jacob Harris was indeed the husband of your Berlin Jewess, and that he went out to Newfoundland after being banished to England, you are more likely to find him by assuming he was, than if you constantly back off because you do not know the facts for certain. The libraries of Berlin and Poole are stuffed to the rafters with papers and documents—the libraries and archives of Newfoundland are not. Until recently, my people as a whole were virtually illiterate, and record-keeping was rudimentary at best. If Jacob Harris came here, there might be a letter or a ship's list in England, but there will likely be no documentation at this end. The most you can

78

hope for is a trace in the oral tradition—a nursery rhyme or a song—or perhaps initials on a powder horn or crook knife.

Thank you for your kind inquiries as to my hens. Rest assured, they have suffered no lasting injury from the Hound of Culhoon's unwelcome attention. Hens are remarkably resilient creatures, rather like children, I suppose.

All the best,

John

"The property of others should be as precious to you as your own."
Rabbi Yose, Ethics of the Fathers

he smokehouse for Ireland's Eye sat above the store and wharves, below and to the right of the dealer's house. It was constructed of upright studs with two hinged vents and a low door, and the smoke was supplied by way of a small, ten-foot tunnel lined with slate that was dug into the peaty soil of a large fissure in the rock outcrop leading up to the Nob. A slow-burning fire in a pit at the lower end of the tunnel supplied smoke that was pushed upward by the prevailing winds from off the water.

After discovering that Mahala had far better breath-control than Rosehannah, Harris needed only one morning to make the hooks on which to hang the slabs of salmon. Another morning was dedicated to cleaning and mending the smokehouse and the tunnel, which had collapsed at its lowest point. By the time Harris had assembled a supply of oak barrel staves, and the small quantity of cherry and apple wood that Mr. Garland had sent over to fuel the fire, the weather had turned from cool and dry to cold and wet.

Rosehannah had little sympathy for him. "If you wait for good weather, it might never come," she explained. "Mama always said never put a chore off for the weather, because by the time the conditions are perfect, there will be other chores to do. Papa says there is no such thing as bad weather, just bad outfitting." She handed him her father's old oiled jacket. "I shall help you build a bough-whiffen and I'll bring you tea, but I have my own chores to see to today. You're not made of sugar. You won't melt," she added in a more kindly tone when she saw the look of dismay on his face. Bad enough to tackle a new chore, without trying to do it while cold and damp.

The bough-whiffen was soon assembled from a couple of longers and numerous armloads of spruce branches held in place with a bit of old netting. An upturned puncheon tub made a fine seat and soon Harris was ensconced with a pannikin of tea in one hand and the blowing pipe in the other.

"Just see that you move the fish around occasionally, and keep an eye on the smoke. If it turns from white to blue, you are running low on fuel. Add some damp shavings of the applewood on top of the fire every hour." Rosehannah's directions were distracted and abrupt. She was potting up various meats in the house, and trying to clean berries for preserves at the same time. "Stay away from the softwoods—the resins are ruinous to the fish." She seemed not to notice that Harris's mood had gone beyond glum into full-blown self-pity.

He hunkered down out of the drizzle, and not for the first time, wondered how he had ever landed himself in a situation where he was little more than a day labourer. True, he made better wages than, and was deferred to by, the dozen or twenty men he had dealings with, but he was expected to hew wood and draw water with the rest of them, and when he failed to do it, he was both pitied and scorned.

He picked out a large splinter of barrel stave and began shaving bits off it with his pen knife. Unlike metal, which he enjoyed working, wood had an inconsistent density and his blade often turned away from the grain for lack of pressure, or dug in too deeply. He began to rough-carve a netting needle. He did not know how to use one, but the shape was pleasingly simple and lent itself to an amateur's hand. The light rain kept the fire appropriately damp without entirely dousing it, and after a time, Harris forgot his discomfort and began to enjoy himself.

The bough-whiffen put him in mind of a *sukkah*, and he smiled as he remembered his uncle, holding him up to tie flowers and apples to the roof of the harvest booth. When Sukkot fell early in the autumn, they had taken their meals in the *sukkah*, lavish picnics of stuffed vegetables and braided breads, sweet honey cakes and grapes. Occasionally, they had made up beds in the carpeted enclosure, and he and his cousins had slept in the makeshift structure.

That was as close to living rough as Harris had ever come—sleeping in the garden of his uncle's home in Berlin, where if a few drops of rain made their way through the lacy roof of leaves and vines of the *sukkah*, they would immediately abandon their temporary cots and retreat, laughing, to their comfortable beds indoors. He was eighteen years old before he ever walked on earth that was not a groomed path; twenty-two before he climbed through a meadow that took him out of the sight of houses. He recalled little of his arrival on Ireland's Eye, but he did remember sailing down the shore towards Trinity, passing nothing but dark, uninhabited shorelines for mile upon mile. It had terrified him.

The bough-whiffen shed the light rain without difficulty and the heat from the small fire was sufficient to keep Harris dry, so he was soon able to abandon the oiled jacket, pulling it back on only to go up the few steps to the smokehouse itself to rearrange the rods of salmon on their hooks. He worked quickly, so as to maintain the heat and smoke in the small structure, and this is how he was occupied when the rock slide happened.

Rosehannah was in the kitchen, moving a large and very hot kettle of duck breasts in fat, when the slide occurred, so that except for the hens' noise, she might have missed it entirely. Tulip, the least timid of the birds, not only bawked loudly, she came skittering into the house through the partly open door and flew up to perch on the ladder to the loft. Rosehannah quickly covered the kettle, for fear the chicken should decide to investigate the pot more closely and be burned, and tossed her coarse apron over the bird's head. Outside, the other hens were still clucking and calling out and the little bantam cock, Jumper, was in a state of high alert. Rosehannah released Tulip into the flock and returned to her kettle of duck.

Several minutes later, when she went outside to empty a bucket of slops water, the hens had quieted down again, and so had the rest of the world. There was not so much as the peep of a junko or jay to be heard. Rosehannah turned her hot face up to catch the cool, misty drizzle and took in a lungful of fresh air. Somewhere, not far off, she heard a thumping like a wooden mallet on a stake, and her first thought was that the mister had abandoned his smokehouse duties. Exasperated, she marched over to the bough-whiffen, ready to give him a feed of tongues.

The large boulder that had slammed shut the door of the smokehouse sat, immutable and content, snugly against the latch. Rosehannah could hear faint thumps from inside, and smoke continued to filter out from the vents. She made a quick and unsuccessful attempt to roll the rock away, then ran to rake out the fire. Grabbing the net, she pulled the bough-whiffen apart and released one of the longers to serve as a lever. She and the longer were insufficiently strong to shift the huge boulder, which had rumbled down from the Nob in a slurry of smaller stones and mud, until it came to the smokehouse that had been built especially to take advantage of the fissure in the rock. The thumping had stopped.

As she ran down towards the store, Rosehannah fleetingly wished she had asked Mr. Harris to teach her some of his foreign swear words, because she was greatly in need of a good, strong one just then. The store was, blessedly, unlocked and she hauled out the box of rusty tools she had assembled in the hope that the mister would one day take an interest in simple carpentry. She rapidly located a pry bar and a hammer, and ran back to the smokehouse with both. It took less than a minute for her to break the bottom foot or so off several of the upright and horizontal studs on the back wall, and reach in to feel the wool of his trousers leg. She grabbed Harris by the foot and pulled, but it only served to jam him between the upright studs that framed the structure.

"Oh Mama, what am I to do," she wailed, yanking in frustration at the boot, which was all she could see. For some reason, the image of Mahala Sevier's foot came into her mind, and she seized upon it. Her mother had "found" Mahala, a difficult delivery because of the baby's position; young Mrs. Toop had taken great delight in describing the breech birth, and how Mrs. Quint had tucked the baby's foot back into the womb, and turned the tiny infant so that she came out head first.

Rosehannah stopped yanking on the boot, and furiously pushed it the other way, shoving it well into the confined space of the floor of the smokehouse. The smoke, by this time, was pouring out of the opening in the wall, directly into the girl's eyes, and she coughed and choked as she thrust her arm in as far as the shoulder and felt for the sleeve of her father's old jacket. Her groping fingers finally found it, and gripping it with determination, she pulled until she had the mister's head in the broken gap. Tucking his chin down, she grabbed the back of his collar and slowly hauled him through the hole, turning his shoulders to ease him through the narrow space.

Once she had him outside, she rolled him over and tried to sit him up, but he slipped from her hands and fell backwards, hitting the ground with a grunt and a gasp. Well, at least he was breathing. She ran to the house, fetched a pan of water, and by the time she was back he was sitting up, gagging and coughing. She held the water to his lips and he sucked at it gratefully between bouts of coughing.

"Are you all right, Mr. Harris?" Rosehannah was soaked and covered in mud. He nodded and coughed again, deep, wrenching coughs that were painful to listen to. Eventually, he indicated that she should help him to his feet and she did, leading him towards the house, where he collapsed into a chair. White-faced and frightened, she helped him out of his jacket, and then put it on herself and headed to the door.

"Where are you going," he asked, his voice so harsh and raw it was barely decipherable.

"To the smokehouse. I'll have to repair it, or the salmon will be ruined. When Mr. Sevier comes in for the evening, I'll ask him to help me move the boulder."

"It never ends, does it?" he observed, raising his bloodshot eyes to hers.

"The work? No, it doesn't. But thank God you've been spared." She turned to go but looked back again as he attempted to speak and was wracked with coughs.

"It's you I need to thank, not God. He would have let me die there if you hadn't intervened," Harris said when he could speak again. "You have your work to do here. I'll fix the smokehouse." Wearily, he held his hand out for the jacket, and she reluctantly took it off and gave it to him.

By the end of the week, Harris had finished smoking the salmon, and aside from an occasional bout of coughing, he seemed to have recovered from his ordeal.

"Cold smoked like a haddock," Old Mrs. Toop said when she heard the story. "That'll toughen him up. I never eat haddock meself, it's the divil's fish. Ye know, now, the marks on the haddock were caused by the divil's thumb and forefinger. 'Ah, haddock, I've got thee,' said the divil, grabbing the fish, and 'No, divil, thou hasn't,' the haddock replied, wriggling away."

"We don't eat haddock because they aren't plentiful around here," grumbled Rosehannah, when Mrs. Toop had finished.

Perhaps it was the intermittent rain, or the after-effects of the smoke inhalation they had both suffered, but by the time the salmon was packed away, Rosehannah and the mister were grating on each other's nerves.

"What is that bird doing in the house?" Harris demanded, as he came in for his dinner. A plump little hen, which was tied by a string to the leg of a stool, had been busy pecking away at the straw Rosehannah had scattered on the floor; it flapped its wings ineffectually when he pushed it roughly out of his way with the toe of his boot.

"It's almost time to kill the hens. I'm going to keep Jumper and Tulip, as I'll need them for new chicks in the spring." Rosehannah lifted the pot of white bean stew off the crook and set it on the floor by the hearth. "They can't survive the cold in the roost when there's only two of them. She needs to get used to being inside with us when I bring them to the winterhouse. The cock will go wherever she goes."

"If you think I'm going to live with two stinking chickens all winter, you need to think again. And besides, we aren't going to the winterhouse. This house is perfectly adequate, and Mr. Garland is sending out extra coal to supplement the wood Raymond and Sevier are cutting for me."

"That's ridiculous, Mr. Harris," Rosehannah answered sharply. "There'll be nobody here but us, and besides, when the wind comes off the water, it melts the snow all along the shore.

Without snow to keep the drafts out, you might just as well live in a barn as live here. I know—I did it every winter." She laid the pot with a thump upon the table, rattling the dishes and sending the chicken into squawking, aborted flight again.

"That bird has to go," Harris said, pointing at Tulip with his table knife. "You can get more chickens in the spring."

"Not birds like Tulip, I can't. Tulip lays an egg every day, right into November. Find me another chicken who will do *that*. And she hatched three clutches of eggs this past summer, more than half of them female, even the first brood." This last was said triumphantly, but since Harris didn't know enough about poultry to realize the significance of such an accomplishment, he remained unimpressed. "If you want to eat eggs and chickens," said Rosehannah, "you must look after the cocks and hens. Mama used to say, 'You can't take out of a bag what you didn't put into it.'"

"It's only a stupid bird, for God's sake. Mr. Garland will send out replacements from Trinity."

"Papa always warned me, there's a slippery stone at a gentleman's door. I wouldn't like to rely too much on Mr. Garland, or Mrs. Garland either, for that matter, especially in the matter of chickens." Rosehannah looked fondly at Tulip, who unfortunately chose that moment to produce something that was definitely not an egg.

"'Mama always said.' 'Papa used to tell me.' If I had a penny for every aphorism you have heaped on my head in the last six months, I'd be a rich man. As it is, I'm a man who can't eat his dinner without chickens defecating on his boots, or you telling me what your precious mama or papa used to say. Your mother is dead and gone, Rosehannah, and your father is making the beast with two backs with Triffie Hodder in Rise's Harbour, so you'll do what I say and get that damn chicken out of here." Harris slammed his fork onto his half-empty plate, pushed back his chair and was out the door, stepping squarely into the hen's droppings and raising another *bawk* out of Tulip as he went.

My dear Brina,

What can I say? The beautiful little hanukkiah you sent the children, and the accompanying story of how it was redeemed out of Poland so many years ago, moved them deeply. I did not see how I could accept, on their behalf, such a gift, but I also was not capable of withholding it and sending it back.

They will have written to you by now, I am sure (their mother is a firm believer in matters of etiquette) but I wanted you to hear from me how very magical the evening was when they lit the first candle.

You are probably not aware that, like Gibraltar, Newfoundland is affectionately called "The Rock" by its citizens. It happens that the Jewish children of this community discovered early on that the "Maoz Tzur" could be sung to the tune of "The Ode to Newfoundland," our old anthem. My wife Tali always found the intertwining threads of her heritage in this particular song to be very moving and I do not recall that she ever once got through the first night of Hanukkah without tears. When I heard Leah and Shibby and their parents sing "Rock of Ages" this year, I too was highly affected.

Shibby, in particular, loves the little silver bear climbing up the branches of the tree, past the bees, to the honey pot. She thinks the children at the bottom of the tree need only a dog called Culhoon to achieve perfect contentment. I know that it was a gift, freely given with no expectation of return, but I shall do my best to find your Jacob Harris for you. If necessary, I will go to Trinity in the spring and beat the bushes to locate him.

May your dreidel always come up gimmel!

Have a gut yontev!

John

87

"An ill-tempered person cannot teach."

Hillel, Ethics of the Fathers

*R*osehannah looked up from her book and suddenly realized that the day was almost gone. Between the longest days of summer and the shortest days of winter, they lost about eight hours of light; at this time of year it still took her by surprise when, at mid-afternoon, the gloom of night began descending.

Looking out towards the bay, she saw a dark flurry of cloud moving across the water. "Snow," she thought, and tightened her shawl around her shoulders. She moved towards the small side window and smiled as she saw her chickens rapidly running up the path towards their perch in the roost. They hated snow and, when obliged through greed or necessity to go outdoors in winter, they minced through the drifts like fussy old ladies, or flew in erratic bursts from fencepost to rain barrel to outcrop of rock, anything to avoid getting their yellow stockings wet.

She hurried outside to secure the door to the roost, automatically counting the birds as she did. Nine only! The hen with the grey-blue tail, the one she had promised to Mahala Sevier, was missing. She looked towards the Sevier's house and realized that they had gone. She had not expected a light in their house—they rarely lit the lamp—but the smell of smoke coming from their chimney usually drifted over in the direction of the store. Now, their chimney was cold and empty.

The dwigh of snow was moving on the water with considerable speed and Rosehannah could see white caps in the bay. They would soon be in the harbour, as the wind picked up. She had not seen the mister all day and the empty feel of the small collection of houses that made up the village unsettled her.

She secured the door to the roost extra carefully and headed down the path to the store. The door was locked, and she had left her key on its nail in the kitchen, so she peered through the window into the gloomy interior. She could just make out the date on the writing-box calendar, December 4th. He had not been in the store since the previous day. Quickly, she checked the salt house, the cooperage, and then the smokehouse. Empty.

The first flurries were swirling around her head and sticking to the rocks as she headed back to the house. It was not particularly cold and the flakes half melted as they fell, but the wind was erupting in ragged bursts around her. It did not feel like there was a lot of snow in the air, but there was a gale of wind brewing which could be considerably worse.

In the house, she moved about, securing windows, fixing quilts over the doorways and shoveling out the fireplace. There was already a fine layer of ash on everything in the room where an aberrant gust of wind had forced its way down the chimney. Rosehannah replenished the water and wood and then slipped into the linney, where she pulled one of her mother's old wool dresses over the one she already wore before bundling herself up in the oiled jacket that Quint had left behind.

She was tying her shawl over her head and around her neck when a particularly sharp blast of wind hit the house, shaking it so that it creaked. The painted sailcloth that served for a carpet in the main room lifted around the edges several inches from the floor before settling back down. Without snow to chinch them up, the boughs she and the Sevier children had placed around the foundation offered little protection to the house.

Outside, the wind was blinding and wet snow whipped her eyes. Rosehannah was just struggling up the path towards Traytown when she saw Harris come slipping down the rock face of the Nob. He was wearing an overcoat but had little else in the way of protection from the vicious weather. They met at the line of trees and, without attempting conversation, which was impossible given the wind, she linked her arm into his and led him down the slippery path. He seemed stiff and awkward, and his sleeve felt wet through her mittens.

With their faces to the water, the wind seemed worse; at times, they leaned downhill into it but were unable to progress. Rosehannah turned the two of them facing back to the Nob and waited until it let up. Snow was still falling, but as they got closer to the harbour, the wet salt spray coming off the whitecaps turned the air into a cold, soupy sish. Snow clung to the grass and shrubs but melted on the beaten path, and they could see their way easily along the dark ribbon to the door.

Inside, they both had to lean their shoulders against the door to close it. The relative still and silence after the latch clicked into place was almost shocking. Rosehannah pulled her soaking shawl off her head.

"That was a bit of an adventure, wasn't it," she laughed, and shook the wet hair from her eyes. When Harris didn't answer, she fumbled for a dry cloth near the chimney and wiped her face on one end before holding out the other end to him. Her smile faded. "Are you all right?" She took him by the arm and led him to his chair by the smoldering fire. He looked as bad as he had the day he'd arrived.

"You're soaked through," she said, as she began to pry his sodden coat off. He didn't answer, just looked at her, barely registering her presence. Rosehannah dropped her own oiled coat into a corner and quickly took the quilt she had intended for the door and wrapped it around the mister's shoulders. Turning to the fire, she used the poker to pry a large rock from the hot flankers and, wrapping it in an old bit of sailcloth, she pulled it towards his feet.

"I have to get your boots and stockings off," she urged him. "You must help me if you can." With a supreme effort, Harris bent first one leg at the knee and then the other, allowing her to extricate his feet from the drenched wool and leather encasing them. She vigorously rubbed them dry with the cloth and then placed his two feet flat on the hot rock. Looking around the room, she spotted a small hearth mat, which she wrapped around his ankles and feet to trap the heat.

Taking his hands in her own, she began rubbing them as hard as she could, but they still felt like two blocks of ice between her fingers. It hadn't been that cold a day, and wasn't even below freezing now, so how could he have gotten so chilled? When Harris finally began to respond, she pulled the quilt tight around him, trapping his arms around his waist, and got up to tend to the fire.

"I don't know what you've been up to, Mr. Harris," Rosehannah admonished as she worked, "but you manage to get into more difficulty than half a dozen youngsters." She stuffed several rolls of bark under the dying embers and anchored them with a thick, heavy birch junk. The water in the kettle was still hot, and she quickly made tea, to which she added a dollop of molasses and two fingers of spirits. "Open up," she urged and then spooned half of it into him, the metal utensil clinking against his teeth.

"Your feet aren't scorching, are they?" Rosehannah asked, and slid her hands under the tablecloth to feel if they had gone beyond thawing and were now cooking. The rock was still giving off prodigious heat. She ran up the ladder to the loft and came back with dry stockings and the spare boots Mrs. Hart had so generously provided, as well as the elegant clothes he had arrived in. Gently, she took the canvas-wrapped rock and slid it under the quilt into his arms and with his feet in her lap, she proceeded to pull his stockings on. There was a large bruise on the left foot, which was swelling up, but he didn't wince when she handled it so he had not broken any bones.

"You have to eat something, and then you have to get out of those wet clothes," she instructed him. He hugged the rock and refused to open his eyes. The absurdity of the situation suddenly struck her and she lost patience. "For goodness sake, Mr. Harris, you're a grown man. It's a nasty night out, but it wasn't that bad. Where on earth have you been all day?" He didn't answer, only made a gagging noise. She got a bowl under his chin just in time.

There was no way to dispose of the mess until morning, so she covered the bowl and shoved it under the dresser. A grumbling and heaving in her own stomach was only hunger, she realized, so she pulled the lid off the bake-pot with a dull clang. The beans and barley she had left simmering had dried out so she stirred in some water and scraped the crusted bottom with a wooden spoon. She served a portion out into a bowl and gulped down the glutinous mess with her back to the mister. After she had eaten, she became aware of her own damp clothing and hair. She pulled her mother's dress off and hung it back from the fire. The skirts of her own dress and petticoat were also wet.

"I'm going to change my clothes, Mr. Harris. You should at least put on dry trousers," she announced, disappearing into the linney. The wind coming through the floorboards slammed the door behind her.

Rosehannah fumbled around in the dark room, having forgotten to take a taper or lamp with her. This was the second time the mister had managed to almost kill himself just as she was about to leave for the tilts. Surely he wasn't doing it on purpose, but it certainly seemed like an extraordinary coincidence.

She pulled her damp clothes off and searched in the box at the foot of her cot for dry clothes. Her worn shift was still serviceable but her old dress was too small for her, so she found another of her mother's and pulled it on, shivering in the cold. She could hear Mr. Harris moving around in the outer room, so although she longed to be back by the fire, she took her time, combing and pinning up her hair in the dark and covering it with a clean cap.

At the bottom of the box, she found her mother's old green cloak. As she wrapped it around herself, it released a faint scent of orange peel and cloves from a pomander she had once made. Standing alone in the cold, dark, little lean-to, Rosehannah made up her mind. She could not bear a whole winter of this, when the cozy tilt was out there waiting for her. She would go as soon as the weather was cold enough.

When Rosehannah returned to the main room, it was empty. The old clothes Mr. Harris had been wearing, her papa's clothes, were draped over the back of the chair. He had taken the hot rock with him to the loft. She replaced the mat by the hearth, spread the clothes out to dry, scraped another helping of grains off the bottom of the bake pot and settled in on the bench by the fire. The unbound pages of *Ivanhoe* stirred in the draft of the room; she picked it up and began reading again.

In the morning when she woke, a dull, grey light suffused the room. For a moment, she thought she must have slept to mid-morning, but then realized that it was barely dawn. A profound silence met her ears, and when she heard the little cock crow, she felt like crowing herself. Snow. Lots of it. In the early hours of the morning, after the winds of the previous night had blown themselves inland, the temperature had dropped and the snow, soft and silent, had come tumbling from the sky and smothered the entire house.

Rosehannah shivered in her quilt, and slid off the bench to coopy down near the ashes of the fire. When she stirred them with a stick, a few faint embers glowed and winked at her; within minutes, she had coaxed them into a cheery blaze. She filled the kettle and, as much to warm herself up with movement as to restore order to the room, she began moving about, wiping the layer of ash and dust from the table and dresser. Snow had filled every crack in the house and under it, and the heat of the fire soon radiated out into the room.

By mid morning, the place had been put to rights, bread was cooking under a fine layer of coals in the bake-pot, and a kettle of beans with salt pork was simmering its way towards the dinner table. Rosehannah had settled herself back in her quilt and was deeply immersed in the adventures of Gurth, son of Beowulph, and Wamba, son of Witless, when the mister appeared from the loft.

"Do you suppose the author meant us to dislike the Abbot and admire the Jew?" she asked as she looked up, having become so embroiled in the world of twelfth-century England that she had forgotten their own adventures of the previous day. "I mean, presumably, we are supposed to admire the Christian who has dedicated his life to God, and despise the Jew who thinks of little but his daughter and his pocketbook, but the author makes it very hard."

"Why do you think he disapproves of the Abbot?" asked Harris, drawing near the fire and checking the teapot, which was mercifully full and hot.

"Well, he's supposed to have renounced wealth and honour, but he wears very rich clothes and jewelry, and he seems unusually absorbed with his dogs and his dinner." Rosehannah leaned forward to feed the fire and continued mustering her argument. "I am fond of my chickens, especially Tulip, and I get very cranky if I have to miss a meal, but this holy Abbot seems entirely too worldly."

"And what of the Jew? Why do you like him?" Harris seemed to have recovered his appetite as well as his equanimity and was showing an anticipatory interest in the bean pot.

"I'm not sure," admitted Rosehannah. "Probably because he *does* show affection for his daughter and his pocketbook, in that order. He puts Rebecca's well-being ahead of his money and even his own life, and of course I must admire that. But he also realizes that money is security, that it can buy him out of dangerous situations." She just prevented herself from swatting Harris's hand away from the beans and fetched him a handful of raisins from a jar on the dresser instead.

"We have no money here, of course," she continued. "I don't think most of us see two shillings in cash in the course of a year, and when we do, it's somebody else's. But fish is money and we take good care that, once we've acquired it, we protect it while it's in our possession and we sell it for the best price we can get." She looked at him very solemnly, as if she had given this great thought. "That's not avarice, that's common sense."

"And you, miss, are an uncommonly sensible young woman." Harris washed down the raisins with the last of his tea and poured himself more. As an afterthought, he filled the cup that she had been drinking from and handed it to her. "I was incredibly stupid yesterday, and it almost cost me my life."

Rosehannah looked into her teacup, into her apron, anywhere but at Harris, so that he would not see how wholeheartedly she agreed with him, for once.

"For months now, I've been relying on you for everything— meals, water, wood, clothing, whatever I needed, you had to hand. You've been nursing me along like I'm a reckless two-year-old who must be watched and cosseted for fear of tantrums.

"Suddenly, I thought I'd like to prove I am well able to look after myself, so I set off to see this place in which I've landed. I began by climbing the Nob, and when I saw how small the island really is, I got careless. I got into a copse and couldn't find the path and it might have been only half a mile from the coast, but it might as well have been a hundred miles because I couldn't find my way out.

"Finally, I made my way up a slope to a large tree, and I thought if I climbed the tree, I would be able to see where I was. The damn thing was a lot harder to get up than I had expected, and then just as I was nearing the top, I think it must have broken off, because the next thing I know I was on the ground, half frozen, with a lump the size of an egg on the back of my head. I have the most cracking headache now."

Rosehannah went round to the back of his chair and peered at his scalp. Through the short, white hair, she could see a huge blood blister.

"It looks awful. You might have been killed. I could have showed you the paths, if you'd wanted."

Harris shook his head ruefully. "I know. I shouldn't have gone off without telling someone where I was going, but there are precious few people around here to tell anything to, and I was annoyed with you because of our disagreement yesterday."

"I haven't changed my mind, Mr. Harris. I think we should go to the tilts, and if you won't come, I will go alone."

"That is your right, Rosehannah. But do you think it is safe, a young woman alone like that in the woods?"

"There is no chance of my being alone, Mr. Harris," she answered. "As soon as the others know I have two square inches to spare in my tilt, they will send a child or two to live with me. It makes a little more room in their own over-crowded tilts, and it keeps the young men and even the not-so-young ones from deciding to keep me company of an evening. I assure you, I will not have more than a few minutes in a row to myself from the moment I arrive until we all leave in the spring. But are you sure you won't come with me? It will be bitterly cold out here by the water, and lonely, too."

"No, Rosehannah, I'd rather stay here. I think I can manage, and I will be much more careful in future. No climbing ladders without checking the rungs, no explorations, no candles left alight on the table at night. I shall have nobody to blame if things go wrong, so I shall be much more careful of how I conduct myself."

Harris got up and wandered to the window, breathing on the glass and scraping the frost away with a fingernail

"It's beautiful, isn't it," Rosehannah said, not needing to look out at the blanketed landscape to know what it looked like in the strengthening sun.

"It is," Harris answered. "Like a world made of lamb's wool or goose feathers, and lit from within like a lamp. I've seen bowls full of diamonds that didn't look as beautiful as this."

"Well, just don't be surprised if you wake up tomorrow and it's all gone," warned Rosehannah. "It's unlikely to stay on the ground this early in the season and, out here by the water, it has to be very cold for the snow to stay, even in February or March. The salt spray and the wind will wash it away, even in the depth of winter. But it's wonderfully cozy when it is here." Leaning forward, she lifted the lid of the bake-pot and ascertained that the bread was done by tipping the loaf out into a clean cloth and knocking the crust with a knuckle.

"I'm famished," Harris declared. "I suppose I shall have to learn to make bread or do with hard tack for the rest of the winter."

"I'll come over once a week, Mr. Harris, on Sunday. I can do your shirts and make you a meal and bread for the week."

"I thought you Christians didn't work on your Sabbath?" Harris still had no clear idea of the differences between the various sects of Christianity and tended to assume they were all the same.

"I'm 'Irish,' don't forget," Rosehannah said with a smile, as she put the kettle of beans onto the table. "We Papists work or not, as we choose, any day of the week at all. Unfortunately, as the only Catholic in a sea of Protestants, I'm inevitably asked to do their work for them on Sundays. If someone runs out of sticks to put on the fire, it's 'Rosie, come and give me a hand with this, as you're going to burn in hell anyway.' Around here, Sunday is a good day for me to be out of the way. I can do for you instead of for half the island."

"So I'm to have my very own *Shabbos goyeh*," Harris laughed. "I shall save up all my questions and problems for you, then." And going to the table, he seemed greatly cheered. Rosehannah was light-headed with relief.

January 11, 05

Brina,

    I have found, through the kind efforts of John Griffin (a very capable librarian I have reason to consult frequently), an advertisement in the Royal Newfoundland Gazette, *April 1820, for a "German flute, lost or stolen" when the brig* Helga *ran ashore in Trinity Bight. Anyone having information or desirous of returning the instrument is asked to contact Jas. Harris or his agent, George Garland of Trinity. I cannot give you the exact wording, as no copy of the paper itself has survived, but a reference to the advertisement is made in an article written by J.W. Withers in 1907 and published by H.M. Mosdell in 1923. Mosdell was notoriously casual with first names, often rendering Theo. as Thos., Jasp. as Jas, etc.*

    Brina, I think it is your Jacob. I cannot find any James Harris who fits the bill. There is a James at Bonavista in 1810—but I have eliminated him, as he died in 1812—and another at Brigus in 1822, but he is only twelve years old at that time, and would have been a mere ten when the Helga *got into trouble, too young to have an agent, or an expensive German flute.*

    The weather here is filthy; snow up to the top of the hen house, roads iced over and every corner blind from the work of the plow. Harry says I'm not even to think of heading for Trinity until the worst of the winter is over. He is right, I know that, but I am aching to get out there to snoop around.

    What was it Sherlock Holmes used to say? "Come, Watson. The game's afoot!" If only it were so. I shall plug away at the archive and my millstone of a history and hope for an early spring. Your frequent and so welcome letters are all that make the delay tolerable.

    Affectionately,

    John

    P.S. I am enclosing a portrait of myself that Shibby rendered after dinner last night. She says to tell you that I am much better looking than this and I am inclined to agree, but I think she has been a bit too generous in the hair department.

    P.P.S. I do have some hair, honestly, just not quite the mop she has endowed me with here. I think she was getting me mixed up with Culhoon.

"Do not judge your fellow human being until you stand in his situation."

Hillel, Ethics of the Fathers

The snow was gone within two days and it was a week before the temperature dropped again and the ground was hard enough for Rosehannah to carry the first load of bedding and utensils over to the new tilt at the back of the island. There were two tilts completed in the untried winterhouse area, and signs that two more were under construction. A thin line of smoke rose from one of the shelters. She made for the other and quietly let herself in; it was just as she had imagined, only better.

Like the house she had left back in the harbour, the tilt consisted of just one room, but was smaller and lower so there was no loft. A small window, opposite the chimney, had been set into the upright studs. It consisted of only one pane of glass, hardly wider than the span of her hand, but peering out, Rosehannah saw that her father had positioned it so that she would be able to see both the Seviers' tilt and the water. The room was about sixteen feet by fourteen, larger than necessary, perhaps, but built tightly so that it could retain heat, while also being large enough to clear the air of smoke from the small fireplace.

On either side of the hearth were two rough frames butted into the walls which, when fitted with small, flexible sticks, would serve as beds. Rosehannah noticed that the larger, directly behind the door, was generously long to allow her father to straighten out when he slept, and she felt a stab of pain as she thought that he would probably never sleep there. The shorter, narrow structure was to have been hers. The fireplace and the two bed frames took up approximately half the tilt. The rest was simply furnished with a rough table and two benches.

The door had swung shut behind her, and the dim light from the single window barely cut through the gloom of the tiny space. Rosehannah deposited her bundles on the table and, turning, propped the door open again. The floor had been laid with round logs, dubbed to form a near-level surface. As her eyes adjusted to the light, she saw that the seams between the studs needed chinching, but there was time enough to do that once she had collected and dried the moss. She knelt to examine the fireplace, and putting her hand up into the chimney space, felt a small stir of air lifting upward from the floor. It would draw beautifully, she thought. Her father had made the lower part of the fireplace out of flat slabs of slate from Nut Cove, and had formed the upper part from lined nail kegs, butting the two parts together to make a compact and tidy hearth. The fireplace would be the envy of every woman on the island, some of whom were obliged to manage with little more than a hole in the roof to let out the smoke.

Turning back to the room, she was surprised to find that the light striking the back wall from the door revealed a deep recess in the studs. Stepping outside, she walked around the tilt to discover that a small linney, perhaps eight feet square, had been added to the structure. A low hatch on leather hinges gave access to the bottom of the addition, and another smaller one, was set above it, up under the eave of the roof. Sliding the top hatch to one side, Rosehannah could see into the cabin. This was a puzzle. She entered the tilt once again and studied the linney from the inside. It was divided into two. The lower section, like a cupboard, was obviously intended for passing wood into the house without allowing the weather in. The upper section, also accessible from the outside, was perhaps intended for storing food, but if so, why did it have a tiny hatch leading to the outside?

Rosehannah stood on her toes and peered into the upper level of this curious cupboard. A wooden pole had been set into the interior, much as the iron bar had been set into the fireplace for hanging pots, but its purpose was not so readily evident. She examined the enclosure closely and quickly discovered an old piece of net gathered like a curtain at the top of the opening. She dropped the curtain down, stood back, and burst into tears. Papa had made a roost for her hens. He had devised a clever, tidy, safe, warm place for her birds, where he would not be stepping on them all the time and where they needn't be tied on. He really had been planning to live with her here. He had *not* spent the whole of last winter thinking of Triffie Hodder and sneaking into her bed.

Rosehannah's storm of tears was brief. She did a quick inventory of what she would need from the store and, picking up Mahala's dollymop, which the child had left under the table, she prepared to visit Mrs. Sevier. Why her father's kindness brought her so quickly to tears, when she had accepted his abandonment months before, was something she would have to think through. Perhaps love was more dangerous than hate, attention more insidious than neglect.

Leaving her things bundled on the table, Rosehannah made her way over to the Seviers' tilt and let herself in. Mahala was there alone, drawing a pattern into the newly cleaned floor with a sharp stick. The child looked up from her occupation and flung herself into Rosehannah's arms.

"Oofh! Mind how you go, Mahala. You're getting too big for this. You almost knocked me over. You left your doll under my table." She handed the worn, limp, little figure to Mahala and stood back to admire the child's work. "I used to love making the Walls of Troy when I was your age," she observed, "but it's better to have a proper floor. My tilt is planched."

"Me and Mam went in to have a look when we first arrived. It's beautiful, and so big. It's like a castle."

Rosehannah laughed. Mahala had never seen anything even remotely like a castle, not even the Lester Garland house, which was Rosehannah's idea of what a castle might be like. She looked around the Seviers' tilt, which was packed to the rafters with bedding, clothes, tools and dishes enough for six people. There was only one bed, all along one wall.

"I think your house is the same size as mine, only there are more of you than me, and I haven't moved my things in yet."

"And you have a bed all your own…" The child hesitated. "Unless you might be sharing one with the mister, like Mam said."

"No, I don't think the mister will be coming into winter quarters. And if he did, I'd have a curtain or a little partition for my cot to make a cubby hole." She looked at the cozy disorder of the room and wasn't sure if she was relieved not to be part of it, or jealous of the companionable squalor. "You'll be a lot warmer than me, with all of you in the one big bed, than if you slept by yourself every night."

The two girls turned as they heard a fumbling at the wooden latch of the door, and Mahala's older sister, Missy, came in carrying a brace of rabbits. Her sleeves were pulled up to her elbows and her hands were still streaked with blood where she'd skinned and gutted the pair.

"Get me a damp cloth, Mahala, and the basin for these." She held the rabbits out, a forefinger hooked in under the ribs. The smaller girl brought her a battered tin bowl and then went to dampen a rag for her sister to wipe her hands. "Nice to see you, Rosie. We was wondering if you was coming." Missy reached up and, with the tips of a finger and thumb, pulled the shawl off her head, revealing a bristle of short, straight hair, sticking up like a tuft of marsh grass.

"My Lord, Missy, whatever have you done to yourself?" Rosehannah was too taken aback by the peculiar hairstyle to laugh.

"Pap was wanting to use the space here to best advantage, so when he was building the bed, he was particular to make it no longer than the longest one of us, which of course is me." Missy spoke with amused resignation. "He had me lie down on the floor, and straighten out with my feet to the wall, and then he laid a measuring stick by the top of my head. When he went to notch the stick with his axe, he cut all the hair from the top of my head."

"Well, it's a blessing he wasn't measuring you the other way around or you'd be hobbling around with no toes now." She waited to see if Missy grinned at that, and then laughed. "You're a real sight."

"Yes. Bad enough that I'm head and shoulders taller than every man in the harbour now Selby's gone, but I got to look like one of them red savages they tell of from over Exploits River way." She held up her blood-stained hands and Mahala gave her the damp rag. "Mister's not comin'?"

102

"No, at least I don't think so. He plans to spend the winter out by the water."

"No loss, I'd say. He's not the most sociable creature God put on earth. I thought a Jew would be interesting, like having the devil for dinner, but he's just as glum and sour as a Methodist preacher." Missy cracked the rabbits at the hips and shoulders and then used a small knife to disjoint them. "You want neighbours that are a bit friendly when you're in the woods, someone with a sense of revelment in 'em."

"Well, I can't say he's amusing, but he is interesting at times. Things sort of slip out of him by accident, as if he didn't mean to say them, and then he has to explain himself, and it's like a journey to a foreign land." Missy threw Rosehannah a dubious look. "No, really, Missy, he's not a bad fellow, just poisoned with himself."

"Poison to those who have to live with him, more like," countered Missy. "We're well rid of him, I say. Mam will send Mahala over to you, probably, and when those big galoots she also gave birth to get to be too much, perhaps you'll have me in along with you as well."

"And who else will there be here? I see there's two more tilts going up."

"There's a Methodist family from Shilling Harbour, name of Coutts, but they're hardly Methodists at all, really, for he smokes a pipe and she's been known to take a drop of wine. And Joe Ganny's got the one furthest out. The men are all in the woods over at Thoroughfare now cutting the ridgepoles and such to get 'em framed in." Missy seared the pieces of rabbit in the frying pan that had been heating on the fire, and Rosehannah stepped back so as not to have the fat spit on her clothing.

"Is Mr. Ganny bringing his wife or Eliol?"

"His wife's took the twins to her parents at Trinity. She's got no use for the winterhouses, and Joe Ganny's got no use for her when Eliol is around." She turned the rabbit with a toasting fork and looked round to see if Mahala was listening. "They say they live like brother and sister ever since she got the twins. She's upstairs and he's down, and they only meet on the fish flakes."

103

"Maybe she's afraid of having more babies." Rosehannah was a little intimidated by the idea of giving birth herself.

"It's not having 'em she minds, it's the making of them." Missy grinned, showing two big front teeth like pickets in a fence. "There's no torn blankets in that house, I'll tell you. Now Eliol, he might be a nancy boy but I'll wager he could make the blankets fly, judging by the way he can kick up his heels in the dance." And, whispering into Rosehannah's ear, she confided "There's some say 'twas him what fathered those two little devils on Mrs. Ganny, not old Joe."

"It's none of our business, Missy," whispered back Rosehannah, who had heard all this before, and from more reliable sources than Missy Sevier. "Besides, you can't have it both ways. If he's Mr. Ganny's nancy boy, he can't be Mrs. Ganny's lover. And if he was, he'd be in Trinity with her, not out in the winterhouses with him."

Mahala, noticing the whispering, was suddenly all ears. "Mrs. Raymond says it's not natural, two men living together like that."

"Mrs. Raymond is a scurryfunging old misery," retorted Missy. "We spent a winter with the Raymonds the year you was born, Mahala, and it's a wonder any of us was speaking to each other by the time we came out of the woods, she'd put such a curse on us all with her whispering and her backbiting." Missy poked the rabbit viciously with the fork.

"You and Miss Rose were whispering just now," Mahala reminded her sister.

"That's different," retorted Missy. "We was whispering to save you hearing something you might misunderstand, while she was whispering to make trouble."

Rosehannah shook her head at the logic of that one. "Seems to me Mrs. Ganny has two men to look out for her and the twins, two men working hard to see those boys are brought up properly, for Eliol dotes on them just as much as Mr. Ganny. I find it hard to feel sorry for her and I've never heard she feels sorry for herself. In fact, I'd say she's got it scald."

"You're right about that, Rosie," agreed the older girl. "It's a real treat to see them two men hop when she says 'come.' It's usually the other way around. I've been waiting on men all my life. I'm thinking of taking a man myself some time soon, because I'd rather do for one of my own than for those two brothers of mine."

"Oh, Missy, who do you fancy?" Mahala clutched her doll in excitement.

"I can think of three or four who'd come at the gallop," Rosehannah said seriously. "You'd just have to give them the nod."

"Yes, now, I could have me pick," said Missy sardonically, and jumping up from the fire she lifted a small cracked looking glass from the wall and tried to flatten down her tuft of cropped hair before giving up. "Touch me not, for I am temptation," she drawled comically, and then cackled like an old hen at her own wit.

"I'll sew you a cap, Missy, to cover your hair until it grows back. I've a beautiful bit of brocade the mister gave me."

"Can you sew me some shorter legs while you're at it?"

"Your husband, whoever he is, will be glad enough of your long legs when it's time to make the fish or go running after the babies." Rosehannah cocked her head at Missy and gave her an appraising look. "You've got a fine bosom, which I'm never going to have, and you've a much more cheerful disposition. Have you anyone in mind?"

"No, to tell the truth, I don't. It's only lately I've been thinking on it. But one thing I do know, I want someone who's taller than me. I can't stand to see a woman going around with a little maneen under her arm, like Mahala's doll there. It would make me feel like such a big lump."

"Well, if I find a big, tall man floating in the harbour on a grindstone, I'll fish him out and send him over to you." Both young women laughed, and Missy took a light from the fire and touched it to the wick of the old lamp to take the edges off the increasing gloom in the tilt. "I'd better head back, if I'm to get home before dark," Rosehannah said, and pulled Mahala to her for a parting kiss on the cheek. "I'll make a cap for your dolly, too."

"There's another brace of rabbits hanging on a tree by the wood pile, Rosie. Take 'em for the mister's supper."

"Thank you, Missy, I'll do that. He'd eat meat every day of the week, if he could."

"And I'll have the boys cut some gads for your bed frames. Best do it soon in case the snow comes down." Missy gave her another good-natured, gap-toothed smile and turned back to her cooking.

"I'll be back with another load in two days, if the frost holds," Rosehannah replied, and slipped out of the tilt into the open air. The rabbits were tied by the feet, hanging up well beyond her reach, so she rolled a section of log over, climbed up and unhooked them. They were larger than the two Missy already had in the pan, but compared to the heavy pack she'd carried over the Nob, they were a featherweight. She slung the pair around her neck and set off for the harbour.

Feb. 13, 05

Dear Brina,

I'm so pleased that your article on the daughters of the Haskalah movement has been so promptly accepted for publication. My articles on Newfoundland folklore were easy to place in popular journals, and while this precluded them from being taken seriously as academic publications, it allowed me to move on to new material without the frustration of having months of work sitting in a drawer. Your own area of study is so esoteric that it must be difficult to find exactly the right place to send your work. I've always felt that scholars working in obscure areas, Medievalists for instance, should be given tenure for having published three articles in seven years, that being about the most any reasonable person could expect to find homes for. Nowadays, however, young scholars are expected to publish that many pieces in a year, and they can't even think of tenure if they haven't a book under their belt.

But down to business. I have been in touch with the Trinity Historical Society and, as I suspected, most of the papers related to that town are in England, presumably at the archives in Poole. I am enclosing a list of names and addresses from the Wessex Society, which has members on both sides of the water, and I think you will find them a pleasant and co-operative crowd, should you have the time to pursue the matter. In the meantime, I will do what I can at this end. I write a column on folk arts for a monthly magazine here, and I may be able to work an appeal for information into it for one of the spring issues.

Trinity is an odd little town now, "neither fowl nor flesh nor good red herring" as my mother used to say. It was once a rich and bustling place, full of clapboard castles and busy wharfs, but it went into a decline in the twentieth century and, for a time, was rather shabby and dispirited, with buildings boarded up and streets in disrepair. In recent years, it has become a tourist centre—some would say a tourist trap—featuring a historical pageant performed outdoors, as well as contemporary plays done in a theatre, built to look like a fishing premises.

All the lawyers in St. John's vie to own a piece of the place, so it seems the people who actually come from Trinity have to live on the edges or in nearby communities. It's overrun in the summer and dead as a doornail in winter. I haven't been there in a couple of years, but last I heard there were a couple of small boatyards still on the go, but barely enough children to keep the school and the health clinic open. The locals must have a real love-hate relationship with the theatre crowd.

I believe that if Jacob Harris had settled in Trinity, even for a short time, there would be some trace of him there. I think we should be looking further afield, to Old Perlican or Little Heart's Ease or one of the outlying islands off Random. Trinity supplied dozens of small outlying fishing stations, even then.

We are still "bogged in the snow," but Judith came to my rescue this afternoon between Leah's ballet lesson and Shibby's swimming. She arrived on my doorstep bearing gifts of fresh vegetables and another of those videos with Helen Mirren as the lady police inspector. Judith says it is one of the Questions that Plague the Universe why the English can make such good television programs when they can't make a decent sandwich. She carried away a fresh loaf of bread and a jar of blackcurrant jam, and apparently considered herself well rewarded.

Have you really no domestic skills at all? I cannot imagine eating most of my meals in restaurants. Aside from the expense, I would die of boredom, but then I didn't grow up on a kibbutz. When I was a boy, my mother insisted that my brother and I take turns helping with the cooking. My brother quickly learned that if he burned the toast or left lumps in the gravy, he was off the hook. When I tried the same trick, Mother would say that I obviously needed more practice and I would have to do it over again. Perhaps she had some instinctive knowledge that I would spend much of my life fading for myself. My brother is married to a woman who has been his devoted slave for close to fifty years now. She's as dumb as a post and he's grossly overweight, so I am not the least envious of him.

Must dig my way out to the chickens and see how they are surviving the snow.

À bientôt.

John

"One who stays awake at night, or one who travels alone and turns his thought to trivial matters, endangers his life."

Rabbi Hananiah ben Hakhinai, Ethics of the Fathers

A hot spill of blood flicked through the cold air, and the last of the chickens jerked and shuddered under Rosehannah's hand. She felt a warm, wet trickle as a drop that had landed in the open neck of her dress ran down and soaked into the edge of her shift. She bit the inside of her cheek to remind herself to put the cloth to soak in cold water when she went to bed, and upon tasting the salty heat of her own blood, heaved a huge sigh of relief that the task was over.

She had slaughtered all the birds except Tulip and Jumper, extracting each from the roost where she had left them that morning and taking them one by one across to the chopping block. She had often seen her mother chop the heads off the hens but, despite what she had told Harris, had rarely done it herself. Her hands shook slightly as she drove a nail into the side of the stump and tied a string to it, but by the time she had to dispatch the first chicken, she had steeled herself to do the job. Animals could sense fear and would take it onto themselves, so she handled them with a firm confidence she did not entirely feel.

Quickly, she wrapped the bit of string around the neck of each bird and pulled it by the feet until it was stretched tightly across the chopping block. The first one caught her by surprise, its beheaded body wriggling and kicking its way out of her hands and escaping half a dozen yards away before she knew it. The rest she controlled by the simple expedient of placing her foot firmly across the tail and holding them in place until the birds went limp. By the time she had finished, there was a dark pool of blood at the foot of the stump and she felt she would never eat roast chicken again.

Leaving the pile of feathered corpses, she almost ran down to the wharf and stripped off the old oiled clothes she had worn for the butchering. She had just finished rinsing them in sea water and hung them to dry when the mister came out of his store. One look at her pale face and he knew what she had been doing.

"All over, is it?" he asked. "I would have taken care of them for you if you'd asked."

"Have you ever killed an animal, Mr. Harris?" Rosehannah dropped the bucket over the side of the wharf again and allowed it to fill before she pulled it back up.

"No, but I've seen it done a hundred times."

"So have I. And I've killed more rabbits than you've ever eaten, but it still isn't easy." She plunged her arms into the sea water and scrubbed them to the elbows.

"It isn't supposed to be. That's why we have a *shochet*, a trained slaughterer, to kill our chickens." Harris dropped down onto an upturned puncheon tub and slipped into the curious, melodic voice he adopted when talking of his home. "The *hahamim* believed that killing animals could make you hard-hearted and violent if you didn't approach it the right way, so they developed a system of sanctification and reverence for life that meant only persons of great piety were eligibile to slaughter animals. Women could be trained in the practice of *shechitah*, but it was thought they would have an untoward emotional reaction to the act of killing, so they rarely did."

Rosehannah emptied the water out of the bucket and pulled her sleeves down. She turned the bucket over, settled herself down next to him, and tucked her chilly hands underneath her arms to warm her fingers. She looked in anticipation at Harris, who seemed to be gathering his thoughts.

"You know how you rhymed off the steps for cleaning a codfish a little while ago? Beheading, trimming, splitting, washing and so on? Well, the Talmud has similar rules for killing a chicken with a knife: *shehiyah, derasah, haladah, hagramah* and *aquirah*. The blade must be drawn across the neck of the bird without pause, the knife must not be used to chop or strike but must go in a to-and-fro motion, it must not be used with an upward thrust or inserted under the skin, it must be made below the larynx, and the trachea and esophagus must be cut out, not torn or ripped in any way.

"When the bird is slaughtered, the blood must be allowed to pour out onto a bed of dust, and you say a special blessing while you do it, because there is no more obvious symbol of life than blood. Blood must be covered up, just as you would cover a dead body out of reverence for the life it once had." Harris paused and looked out toward the mouth of the harbour.

Rosehannah pulled her hands out from her armpits and blew on her chilly fingers. "You must think we are a rough lot, the way we kill and kill and kill, without even so much as a word of thanks to God, never mind a prayer every time we haul a fish from the sea."

"Well, maybe it's just as well your ways are different. You'd be praying half the day if you had a blessing for every cod that came over the side." Harris laughed. "We have a prayer for just about everything we do: put on a new shirt—pray, see a scholar—pray, smell a flower—pray. Prayer is the one thing we've always had plenty of."

"So why don't you ever say grace before you eat your meal?" Rosehannah's mother had rarely said grace before meals but had at least taught her how.

"Well, you called yourself—what? A shirttail Catholic? I guess I'm something of a shirttail Jew. And besides, we don't say our thanks until after the meal, just in case some Cossack comes along and does us in before we actually get to eat it." Harris stood up and Rosehannah followed suit.

"I'd better get back to those birds before they cool. And I'll cover the blood." She turned to go, but stopped, shyly. "Thank you for telling me about the Jewish butchers. I feel a bit better now."

Harris watched her climb up the path towards the yard. What an odd little creature he was sharing his days with, and what curious subjects she got him talking about. He hadn't thought about ritual slaughter since he'd left Berlin, and not often before that.

Up at the yard, Rosehannah got a rake and carefully covered the pool of blood by the stump before chopping a half dozen birch junks into splits for the fire. She would have to pluck the chickens out of doors, and the chopping warmed her up for the task. By the time she went to gather the carcasses, she had composed a dignified, little prayer that she whispered under her breath, thanking the coopies for being such fat, little birds and for going to their deaths with a minimum of fuss and noise. When she had finished the plucking, she gathered all the feathers in a brin sack, discarding any that had blood on them, and set them aside for augmenting the bedding in preparation for winter.

In the two previous weeks, the girl had made four more trips to the winterhouses at the back of the island. Now, as soon as the weather turned for good and there was a little snow down, she would load the tiny sledge Quint had made for her and man-haul it up the hill and through the woods for the last time that year. Of course, with the mister out on the coast, she would have to tramp back to the harbour as often as possible, but she would be eating, sleeping and living in the winterhouse and that would be home. Pity the mister wouldn't come with her—he was going to be cold, uncomfortable and possibly even lonely in the coming months.

True, he didn't pretend he had friends among the fishermen of Ireland's Eye, but he had been forced to interact with them more when they were bringing in their autumn fish, and he seemed to have an unusual ability to see past exterior characteristics and assess a man for what he was really worth. This was brought home to her later in the morning when Mr. Ganny and Eliol brought their boat around to the harbour to collect flour and molasses for all the winterhouse people. The mister saw past Mr. Ganny's unassuming demeanor in no time.

Eliol had come up to the house to arrange for Rosehannah to sew him a fancy waistcoat, using the by-now infamous bolt of brocade for the front, and by the time they got back down to the shop, Mr. Harris had taught Mr. Ganny the basic moves for a game of chess, and the two were deeply involved in a discussion of Catholic emancipation. There being no other business or work to do that day, Rosehannah discreetly drew off a jug of squatum from the cask in the cellar for them before she and Eliol withdrew to the house for tea and gossip for the duration of the morning.

When she went down to call the men to their supper, Harris looked surprised that the day had slipped by so pleasantly and quickly. Rosehannah saw him suppress even more surprise when he asked Ganny—a Lester Garland man but on the books in Trinity—to sign for his goods, and got only an X.

"I could swear that man is one of the most intelligent fellows I've encountered since coming here," he observed later over his pipe, "yet he could not even sign his name. Why, a four-year-old could learn to sign his name within half an hour, even if he never learned to read or write another word."

"The people here are not encouraged to learn, Mr. Harris," Rosehannah explained. "They are told that reading and writing are very difficult, so they expect not to understand. The few children who are in a position to attend school are beaten for their stupidity even before they open their mouths, so it's little wonder so few of them try. The Methodists like their people to know the Bible, so some of them can read, but many people can't."

"It's the social convention, I suppose," Harris responded. "Among my people, the lowest rag picker or sponge seller can puzzle out at least a few words in the Hebrew script." He pulled several times at his pipe, which was threatening to go out, and Rosehannah picked up her sewing and sat on the small stool by the fire. She was finishing off a snug little cap for Missy Sevier, and had inserted a slip of paper into the seam which read "A fine leg for a skin boot."

"When I was three years old," he began, "my uncle came and fetched me from the nursery and brought me into his library. With him, he had a young fellow of about fourteen, who was to be a clerk in his offices, and he had decided this boy would do very nicely to teach me my *aleph-bet*, in preparation for my beginning studies at the *cheder*. On his desk, he had a china plate and a pot of honey.

"This boy, the clerk, he sat me on his knee and using the handle of a spoon, he drew out each of the letters: *aleph, bet, gimmel, daleth*, and so on, all the way through to *taf*, and as he finished writing each letter in honey on the plate, I was allowed to put my face down and lick the letter off. As I finished off each letter, my uncle said a blessing...I don't remember it, but it was probably something like: 'May it be Thy will, Lord our God and God of our ancestors, to make learning an occasion of sweetness and happiness.' When I got older, of course, the teachers at the *cheder* were inclined to be more generous with the strap than with the honey. And that night, I threw up my supper from too much sweet stuff, but at least I got off on the right foot when it came time for school."

"You must have been a good student." Rosehannah's reply was wistful. "Mama said I was a good student but I'm not so sure any more. Even your English is better than mine."

Harris considered this for a moment. "I'm not sure about that. I have a wider vocabulary because I'm drawing not only on Hebrew and German, but also French and scraps of half a dozen other languages. Also, I've been exposed to various levels of society, while you've only had the company of a couple of dozen people, all of them from the same background. I've noticed that you are very good at adjusting yourself to the needs and expectations of other people. You're as comfortable with Mr. Garland as you are with Old Mrs. Toop."

"I have a funny story to tell you about the Toops," Rosehannah interjected, not so very comfortable after all when the conversation turned in her direction. "One time, when Mama was visiting Trinity, Papa had to look after the store by himself. He used to draw little pictures to remind himself of what he'd given out, and then Mama would write them in the ledger when she got home. She was going over the accounts with Mr. Toop later that season, and listed on his debits was a round of cheese.

"'I never had no round of cheese,' he said, 'and I'm not payin' for it.'" Rosehannah did a credible imitation of Mr. Toop's little swagger when she said this, which brought on one of Harris's rare smiles. "Well, Mama was beside herself. There it was, written in her own hand, and a round of cheese is a big item,

114

but barring the odd bit of ribbon, the Toops are honest people so she didn't want to go accusing Mr. Toop of deceit.

"Well, later that morning, Papa got in from the fishing grounds, and she asked him about the round of cheese, and they realized that the debit was dated for when Mama had been in Trinity, so Papa goes foraging around in the wood pile until he finds the shingle where he drew up the debts while she was gone. And there was the circle, next to the letter T for Toop. 'Oh,' he said, 'I forgot to put the hole in Toop's new grindstone.'"

Harris laughed, and leaned forward to knock his pipe out on the hearth. "He sounds like one of the wise men of Helm." He said "Helm" as if he were clearing his throat. "Our old nursemaid used to tell me and my brother and my cousin stories of a place in the country called Helm, where the people were incredibly stupid. They worried about robbers breaking down their doors when they were away from home, so they used to take their doors with them when they went out. And, once, they gave a pair of gold shoes to the wisest man in Helm so everyone would know who he was—but they covered the shoes in leather so they wouldn't get dirty."

"People tell a lot of stories in the winterhouses," Rosehannah responded. "Jack stories, often, about a boy who is the youngest of three brothers. He's always getting into trouble, but he's so clever he usually manages to get out of it. He goes out into the world, seeking his fortune, and meets some creature, a cat or a unicorn or even the devil, and in the end, he tricks his way into getting a pot of gold or a shoulder of beef or even the king's daughter if he's lucky, and goes home to show his two brothers how successful he is."

"I think I know that story," Harris said, with an odd look. "Only in my version, one brother dies of fever, the other is killed by a debtor, and Jack meets the devil and gets lost in the wilderness."

Thinking back on that conversation, Rosehannah wished more than ever that the mister would come to the winterhouse with her, but that moment of sociability wasn't repeated. He had retreated once more into his store, and came in late to bed smelling of paint and spirit of turpentine, with an underlying scent of squatum. He held his liquor well and was neither rude nor mawkish, but he went to the loft immediately and slept late the next day.

That night, the temperature dropped and the snowfall was heavy. Harris was still asleep the next morning, as she was tidying up prior to leaving. The sled was ready when she went to the store to fetch the empty squatum jug. It was sitting on his desk next to the small oil painting of the pretty blonde girl. Careful not to touch the surface, Rosehannah turned the canvas towards her and caught her breath. Harris had altered the portrait so that two wisps of hair curled up on each side of the fair head like stubby horns. From between his subject's lips peeked a little, pink, forked tongue.

The effect was grotesque and frightening and Rosehannah's first instinct was to reposition the picture and back out of the store empty-handed. On second thought, however, she propped the portrait up against a shelf, doused the paint-caked brush with turpentine and wrapped it in the pen wiper to soften, and took the squatum jug on her way out the door.

Up above at the house, she rinsed the jug and left it on the table with the mister's breakfast before going out to the roost to capture Tulip and the cock, Jumper. With the two birds tied carefully in a bag on top of her sled load, she set off over the Nob to the winterhouses. Tucked in under the rope was the blowing pipe.

March 29, 05

Brina, my friend,

The talk at the shul *is all about presents these days. One of our young Arivim volunteers is getting married and the community naturally wishes to send her a present. I should explain that the Arivim girls come out from Israel to teach the children, usually for just eight months, but this one stayed two years, so we got to know her quite well. Anyway, someone suggested silver candlesticks, and some of the congregation thought this was perfect, while others felt it was too intimate a gift, more suitable coming from her parents than from us. Another faction said that the candlesticks should come from the husband-to-be, because of their association with establishing a home and family and the Friday night rituals.*

Around here, in the gentile community at least, a gift of a prayer book from a lover is thought to bring bad luck, and one must never give a knife or scissors without receiving a coin, even a penny, in exchange, or it might cut the recipient, so the art of gift-giving is like negotiating through reefs and shoals.

But you, my dear, have a gift for giving gifts. The mechanical chicken was perfect. It laid its tin eggs all over the carpet, bawked each time, and best of all, it sent the Hound of Culhoon howling off to the attic, thereby sparing me his attentions and his shedding coat for the remainder of the evening. How did you know it was my birthday? The internet, I suppose. We will have no secrets at all soon. Leah and Shibby insisted upon all seventy candles, instead of the token seven, so Judith used two big boxes of Shabbat candles propped up in saucers and eggcups and bottles all over the room and we dined in style, which was just as well, as the electricity went out half-way through and I had to stay the night.

I spent all of yesterday at my lawyer's office, not for any sinister purpose but because he has a rather good collection of law books and it is more comfortable than the public library. I don't know why I hadn't thought of it before, but it occurred to me that while the Provincial Archives might be closed, there are the published decisions of the Supreme Court available elsewhere and I should have a look at them for any cases related to the Jewish community. When I asked my attorney where I might find them, he volunteered his own firm's library. He also gave me access to a copy machine, which he might regret when he sees the accounting at the end of the month.

His secretary actually brought me a biscuit and a glass of sherry at three in the afternoon, which I think is a very civilized way to do business.

I had no idea our small Jewish community was so litigious or so downright devious. There are cases of peddling without licenses, mutiny, smuggling, postal fraud, marital disputes, trespass, disputed wills, sale of defective goods, and one particularly nasty sexual assault. I don't really know what to do with this information, particularly the last which goes back a hundred years and involves the patriarch of one of our leading families. In some cases, it is clear that these people were simply the victims of prejudice, in the courts, as well as elsewhere. But some were rather dodgy characters, taking the "geographic cure" by heading for the most isolated, obscure place they could think of to avoid prosecution closer to home.

You have suggested that Jacob Harris was a remittance man, paid to get out of the way so that his wife could divorce him and marry up, but surely England was far enough away from Berlin to accomplish that. Why did he leave England? Do you suppose he was on the lam from some other problem? What little you've been able to tell me about him doesn't suggest a criminal type. In fact, I've begun to feel rather sorry for the fellow if your speculation is correct that he was in an arranged marriage with a "salon woman."

Imagine him growing up in Berlin, surrounded by a small coterie of rich Jews with sophisticated tastes, married to an older, accomplished woman who subsequently dumps him, forced out of the country, and then on to a backwater like Newfoundland with its bad weather, few books, lack of theatre, diet of salt pork and biscuit—and no way out for six months of the year. What would he have been playing on that German flute in 1820? Not sea ballads, you can bet. It would be as if someone hauled you out of your cozy London flat and dumped you in the wilds of Maddox Cove with no car and the nearest restaurant a fish and chip shop three miles away.

Oh dear, I don't think I like that comparison. I actually thought you'd like it here if you ever decided to come for a visit, but perhaps not. I am going to stop writing and walk this to the mailbox, while I think about that.

Yours,

John

"Do not look at the flask but at its contents. You can find a new flask with old wine and an old flask which does not hold even new wine."

Rabbi Meir, Ethics of the Fathers

*T*welfth Night marked the beginning of the real winter. Missy Sevier had dressed herself and Mahala in their brothers' clothes, and Eliol had donned Missy's dress to go mummering over at the Coutts' tilt. Only the youngest Coutts child did not know immediately who the mummers were, and cried when the big mummer with the tree-moss beard tried to dance with him. Rosehannah had whispered to Eliol that she had brought a small cask of squatum laced with brandy on her last trip from the harbour, so he collected Mr. Joe, the Couttses, and the rest of the Seviers, and they saw the season out at her tilt, which was not just the snuggest but also the roomiest, having very little in the way of gear to fill it up.

Eliol, who was still wearing Missy's dress, entertained them with comic songs, which he did in the guise of a penny-gaff clown he had once seen at the Albion Saloon in Whitechapel. Mr. Coutts provided chin music and they danced a square set, Rosehannah and Missy partnering the Sevier brothers, Mr. Sevier standing up with Mrs. Coutts, and Eliol taking the female part with Joe Ganny. Later, Rosehannah and Missy escaped from the heat and smoke and lay in the deep snow outdoors, looking up at the moon and stars.

"I wish we could live like this all year," sighed Missy. "Sleep ten or twelve hours every night, out cutting wood or checking slips just long enough to work up an appetite, and then nothing but fun and games, cards and stories, to fill up the hours between meals and bedtime."

"I don't know," answered Rosehannah. "I think you'd get a bit tired of it after a while. Four months of it is probably enough." She began to sweep her legs and arms up and down to make a snow angel and Missy followed suit. "I'm glad I have Mahala's lessons to prepare. Teaching the Coutts children their letters is fun, but now that Mahala is older, I can read things with her that I'm also interested in. It makes me think."

"I never had a head for thinking the way you and Mahala do," said Missy, "but I like listening in when you're reading to her from that book about the knights and the Lady Rowena. That's a fine story. Imagine being the queen of the day and wearing wonderful clothes and having everyone do whatever you liked."

"I think I admire Rebecca better than Rowena," admitted Rosehannah. "She's got her feet on the ground, and her loyalty to her father gives him courage he otherwise wouldn't have."

"You're too high-minded for me, Rosie," laughed Missy as she climbed up out of the snow and gave her hand to the younger girl. "All I care about is the clothes. Look," she said, "I've messed up my snow angel so it looks like it has a rat's tail." Breaking a stick from a nearby tree, Missy leaned over the impression and drew two horns on the head and a barb on the inadvertent tail. "That's more like it," she pronounced. "The very image of me."

Rosehannah, thinking back to Harris's portrait of the spoiled young woman, took her friend by the hand. "I promise you, Missy, you haven't got it in you to be truly wicked." At that moment, Rosehannah's little cock, confused by the lamp light and the unexpected activity, gave a mighty crow, causing a howl of protest from inside the tilt. "Let's go in and see if the children slept through that. Eliol has promised me he'll do his imitation of Mrs. Raymond on wash day, once the little ones are out of the way." And leaving the snow angel and the snow devil to the moon and stars, they ducked back into the tiny tilt to rejoin the others.

The next morning it snowed again, and the morning after that, and every morning for a week. Time in the winterhouses passed slowly and cheerfully, with the men engaged at work in the woods, and all hands carrying on small chores inside—sewing, cooking, and lessons for the girls and women; carving, knitting twine and the production of small items of furniture, such as stools, for the men. Everyone took turns chopping firewood and carrying water from the small creek, which continued to flow despite the cold weather. Rabbits were plentiful and Rosehannah reduced the number of slips she set.

On Sundays, she laced on her snowshoes and climbed up and over the hill to the harbour to wash the mister's shirts, bake bread and cook him a meal that was slightly more elaborate than the simple ones he was becoming used to fixing for himself. The house was cold and Rosehannah did what she could to stop the drafts, hauling an old canvas sail from her father's twine loft to hang along one corner near the fireplace, but she was hoping the cold might drive Mr. Harris out to the woods with her, so she did not try too hard. Certainly, he looked miserable enough.

The snow, so deep in the woods that Rosehannah was never sure of the trail from one week to the next, was sparse on the shoreline. She would leave the tilt and climb up through the muffled silence of spruce and var groves, loosening her clothes as she warmed up from her efforts, until she arrived at the height of the land and looked down at the harbour and the thin slip of smoke from the one house that showed any sign of life. As she progressed down, the wind became more chilled and she would reverse the dressing process, replacing scarves and shawls, wrapping her face against the cold. Her snowshoes would strike rock and frozen clods of earth more often until she was forced to pull them off to save the webbing. By the time she reached the house, away from the protection of the trees, she was often walking on a path swept bare by the wind and salt spray.

Harris looked with curiosity and some longing at her snowshoes, but she did not offer to let him try them and he did not ask. In fact, he asked very little of her, as if he had taken a vow not to complain of the decision he had made and to which he obviously intended to adhere, but like a spiteful monk, was silent very loudly. Their conversations were rather one-sided, with Rosehannah telling him about the Coutts family, Mahala's lessons, the small triumphs and trials of Tulip and Jumper, and he occasionally asking direction in matters of domestic conduct. There was considerable tension between them towards the end of each of these visits, and Rosehannah was unsure if he was anxious for her departure, or dreading it.

Early in February, Mahala became fractious during one of her lessons, so Rosehannah put the slate and calculations away and took out her copy of *Ivanhoe* to read again the exciting passage in which the Black Sluggard comes to the rescue of the Disinherited Knight. Teacher and pupil curled up on the small cot, while Missy, the Coutts children and Eliol took possession of the large bed, where they listened for the third time to the account of the competition, the removal of the knight's helmet so that Rowena might crown him with the chaplet, the knight's subsequent swoon and the discovery of the lance wound in his side. Upon the last sentence of the chapter, Mahala burst into tears.

Rosehannah attempted to soothe the girl while Missy took the opposite tack, trying to tease her out of her fit of weeping by calling her a "big sook" and a "crybaby." It was Eliol who pointed out the bright patches of fever on her cheeks and the damp hair clinging to her forehead. The Coutts' children tumbled out into the snow to fetch Mrs. Sevier, and were indignant to discover they were refused re-admittance to the tilt when they returned with her. Eliol soon joined them in their vigil and made himself useful by scraping the frost from the one small window and setting a snow block to reflect the light into the interior of the dark little hut.

Inside, Missy busied herself lighting the two small oil lamps and stoking up the fire, while Mrs. Sevier and Rosehannah questioned the child. When they tried to remove her limp little doll from under her arm, Mahala wept harder and insisted it was only the dolly that stopped the pain. Mrs. Sevier had the girl out of her dress and underclothes in seconds—"like peltin' a beater" as Missy put it to Eliol later—and turning her to the light, lifted her arm to disclose an ugly gathering that was sending harsh red streaks down the inside of her arm and across her chest.

"She must have chafed it, pulling the wood in on the sledge," Mrs. Sevier told the younger women. "We'll make up a plaster and try to draw it out." The mother seemed concerned, but not unduly so. In the course of raising six children, two of whom she had buried, she had seen a great many crises considerably worse than this.

Rosehannah, who had caught her breath when she saw the raw swelling, looked pale and frightened in the flickering light of the extra lamp. "I think I should get the mister. He'll know what to do."

"Sure, what good will he be?" asked Mrs. Sevier, not unkindly. "He's got neither chick nor child of his own—he'd not know if a youngster was fit to eat, never mind how to fix her up. We'll get the plaster made up and see how she is in the morning."

"I s'pose you gave all your bread scraps to them two chickens," observed Missy. "I'll go get some bread from Mrs. Coutts. Maybe she has some mustard to mix with it." She handed the blowing pipe to Rosehannah, who was looking sicker even than Mahala. By the time she returned with the bread, her young friend had regained her composure and was soaking a square of flannel in a basin of hot water to make up the plaster.

"Here," she announced, handing the basin to Missy, "I'm going after the mister. He told me he was apprenticed once to a doctor and he knows how to make up pills and things."

"Rosehannah, deary, it's good of you to be so concerned, but the day is half gone." Mrs. Sevier seemed more unsettled by Rosehannah's sudden decision than she was by her youngest child's malady.

"That old divil will never make it through," declared Missy. "He'll be bogged in the snow before he's half way up the hill."

"He's not old, he's not a devil, and he'll make it if I have to haul him by the collar," declared Rosehannah, pulling on her skin boots and coat. "I should be back not long after dark. If we're late, put some old fat or something on the fire, so we can smell our way here. If it begins to snow, have your brothers drag some boughs through to mark this end of the trail."

"Lovey, are you sure you wouldn't rather wait 'til the morning? Or we could send one of the men." Mrs. Sevier had cradled Mahala in her arms with the poultice beneath her oxter and the child was now dozing fitfully as Rosehannah fitted a pair of fur cuffs over her hands. Rosehannah didn't answer, just darted a swift, frightened look at Mahala and let herself out the low tilt door.

She made the journey to the harbour in record time and let herself into the house without knocking, startling Mr. Harris, who was heating up a kettle of salt pork and beans for his supper. Part of her mind registered the fact that the room was untidy, the table covered in crumbs and unwashed dishes, and Mr. Harris was wearing his outdoor clothes indoors in an attempt to keep warm. The other half simply registered relief that she had arrived and could now bring him back with her.

"You're needed at the winterhouses, Mr. Harris. Mahala is ill." Dropping her mitts on the floor, she moved the kettle off the fire and began to spread the coals to let them die down. "You will need any medicine kit you have. I'll get your supper on the table while you pack up."

"What's wrong with her?" Harris's voice sounded rusty and unused, and he looked a little dazed at the speed with which Rosehannah was moving.

"She has a carbuncle or some swelling under her arm, and it is spreading through her. She has a fever. Mrs. Sevier has a plaster on it, but I don't think..." Rosehannah's voice broke at this, and the tension and exertion of the previous two hours flooded over her. "When Mama got ill, it was just the same. She had a growth on her breast just there," she sobbed slightly as she laid her hand to the side of her own breast. "Please hurry. I could not bear it if something should happen to Mahala."

"Of course, I'll get my things." Harris scrambled up the steps of the loft to scravel through his trunk, while Rosehannah did likewise in the little linney that served as her bedroom. She came out with a pair of snowshoes clasped in her hands, just as he reached the kitchen again.

"You'll need these once we get up into the snow. They were Mama's. I have no skin boots for you—I gave my old ones to Mahala when I grew out of them. Papa took his with him."

Harris said nothing, just shoveled the cold beans down as quickly as he could, while Rosehannah raked the coals from the fire into a bucket and dumped them outside into a small drift of snow. He had bundled his medical gear into two small packages, which he now fitted down into the pockets of his greatcoat, and he wrapped a scarf over his head and tied it under his chin. The gloves he drew onto his hands were worn full of holes from chopping wood and Rosehannah felt a pang of guilt for having left him so ill-provided. Time to make amends after Mahala was seen to.

The sky was darkening as they made their way up the hill and Harris questioned the wisdom of setting out so late, but Rosehannah was in no mood to discuss any delay, so he just sailed along in her wake. Halfway up the path, they stopped and Rosehannah recovered her snowshoes from the drift of snow where she had left them. Kneeling, she helped him step onto the pair she had been carrying and strapped them onto his feet using strips of cloth she had hastily torn from a table runner that had been packed into her trunk.

"Don't move for a few moments, Mr. Harris. There's a trick to this, and I'll show you as soon as I've got my own rackets on." Rosehannah expertly looped the toes of her skin boots into their laces, and delicately swung around to face him. "Look at how I walk," she ordered, and lifted her foot in an exaggerated dumbshow to demonstrate how he was to move. "If your legs are too close together, or your steps are too small, you will tread on yourself and fall. Spread your legs apart a little and glide one racket over the other." She turned and walked slowly and carefully away from him, then turned and loped back with ease.

Harris spread his arms as if he were about to fly and stepped off the bare path into the snow that led into the trees. "Not too bad," he said, and promptly jerked to a halt, as he planted one snowshoe on top of the other.

"Don't lift your knees too high or you'll wear yourself out. Just slide the right foot forward and then the next, that's it." Rosehannah urged him slowly along, walking backwards and uphill effortlessly on her own red-tassled skinnyrackets, while he plodded forward awkwardly on his blue-tassled ones. "Papa got these from a man down in Labrador three years ago," Rosehannah told him, as she coaxed him along through the first patch of dark woods. "A pair for each of us. They are a great improvement on the pot-lids we had been using. Someone your height should have a slightly bigger pair, to accommodate the weight, but these will do and the smaller they are, the easier to get used to."

Rosehannah resisted the urge to hurry him along, recalling her father's patience when he first taught her to use snowshoes. "You'll have very sore legs tomorrow, but it is still easier than trying to wade through the snow. You can't tell unless you know the path, but we are probably walking on top of five feet of snow in places."

When they came to areas that had been swept bare of snow by the wind, Rosehannah insisted on his taking off the snowshoes and walking, although it meant she had to fumble with knots and strapping with bare and frozen fingers, kneeling at his feet and working in the near dark. He could see in the dim light that, on her own journey out to the harbour, she had avoided the bare patches and stayed in the snow.

They stepped into the last stand of tuckamore before heading down into the cove where the winterhouses were tucked away and found the Sevier brothers waiting for them with a small sledge. Harris was tired and soaked with sweat by then and did not protest when the two sturdy young men lifted him bodily and placed him on the dray. Rosehannah turned wordlessly and bolted down the path in the moonlight, flying over the snow as if she were a hare instead of a human. The Seviers' wooden pot-lids were not as clever as the rackets but they served well enough to impress Harris, who, until this night, had found the snow an impenetrable impediment to movement.

The moon shone brightly on the snow as they came down into the small cove, but Harris was still surprised when they arrived at the first tilt as it was almost invisible, half buried in a drift. Rosehannah was waiting to relieve him of his rackets, after which the Sevier boys heaved him up onto his feet and tumbled him in through the door of the hot little house. Eliol reached forward and tipped the mister's chin down towards his breastbone just in time to keep him from hitting his head on the low lintel, then stepped out into the cold and pulled the door behind him, leaving Harris and the women in possession of the place.

The smell was what he first noticed—wood smoke and spruce boughs, mint and mustard, chickens and wet wool, the odour of sweat and stale tobacco, the scent of companionship and trust. It seemed as if he had smelled no one and nothing for months, not even himself, although he was sure he was as ripe as any of the others in this small box of humanity, and it brought on a wave of longing, the wish that he was part of this stew of living creatures.

My dear Brina,

I have been considering the problem of Jacob Harris in Newfoundland. Do you suppose he had an interest in nature? There is a great deal of it here—icebergs, wildflowers and animals, scenic vistas, whales, seabird colonies and more. I am sending you, under separate cover, a copy of Newfoundland Studies, *which contains the diary of* Philip Henry Gosse *for the years 1827-1835. Gosse was an educated young man who came out to Newfoundland from Poole to work for the firm of Slade and Elson at Carbonear. He would have been somewhat younger than Harris but might have been engaged in the same kind of work. He eventually wrote some forty books on religious and scientific subjects, suggesting that even a person of philosophic bent could find things of interest in this country.*

The weather is improving somewhat, so I am beginning to plan my trip to Trinity and environs. Shibby has the chickenpox and is miserable, so I am miserable for her. Judith and Harry are in the middle of exams, so I am designated nurse. We have watched the children's video of Madeline *("twelve little girls in straight lines") three times (because of the hospital scene) and* Chicken Run *twice (because of the chickens). I have had a hard time convincing her that you don't get chicken pox from chickens. We have used up all the baking soda in the house (in the bath) so I cannot even make soda bread for supper, but we are having a very nice stew with a pastry top. Judith has allowed Shibby three poxes (is that the plural of pox?) on her belly to scratch as long as she doesn't touch any of the other ones, in the hope that it will limit the damage, and if they scar, she will never want her belly-button pierced. I am doubtful this would stop her, judging by what I see around town these days.*

I'm sounding like a geezer now, aren't I? That's the last straw. I've turned into a geezer and didn't even realize it. What a rotten, miserable, ruinous way to end a miserable, ruinous, rotten week.

Yours sincerely,
Cranky Old John

"Make your home a regular meeting place for the scholars."
Yose ben Yoezer of Tzereidah, Ethics of the Fathers

*H*arris sat on a snow bank and pulled at his pipe, watching the smoke dissipate in the damp air. Rosehannah had cut fir boughs to make him a comfortable and dry couch just outside the door, and had shooed him into the open air along with the chickens, so that she could give the tiny tilt a good cleaning. From a nearby branch, Tulip and Jumper eyed him suspiciously. He had, just for badness, thrown a snowball at the cock and knocked him off his branch, earning the enmity of both chickens for the duration of the day.

His five days in the winterhouse had passed quickly, and he no longer thought constantly of returning to the harbour, although he had not yet consciously decided to stay. Mahala's ailment had turned out to be nothing worse than a very ugly boil, which he had lanced and drained within minutes of his arrival, but his own excruciating leg-pains had been sufficient to maroon him for several days.

The cramps had ambushed him in his sleep, sending him screaming and tumbling from his small cot onto the floor of the rough hut and frightening both Mahala and the chickens into fits of bawling. Mrs. Sevier had retired to her own tilt for the night, leaving Missy and Rosehannah to mind the child, so it was these two who leaped from their blankets to knead and massage the knots out of his calves. It had taken only a few minutes for the initial pains to subside, but they were the longest minutes of his life.

"I'm so sorry," Rosehannah repeated urgently, over and over, as she and Missy pounded and squeezed his calves. "It's the rackets caused this. You use muscles you're not used to, and I should have warned you, but I was hoping the walking in between would be enough to prevent it." Harris had only roared in reply and writhed on the cold floor.

Missy Sevier's strong fingers had tracked livid bruises up and down his legs, but the cramps had subsided, leaving him sore and aching. Since then, the two nursemaids had knelt and rubbed his lower legs with seal oil every few hours throughout each night, and during the day, the Sevier brothers had come to walk him on the path between their two tilts. He was recovered enough to hobble along on his own, which had contributed to Rosehannah's decision to exile him to the elements for part of the morning.

Now, almost prone upon his bed of evergreen boughs, Harris was aware of the silence. When he strained to listen, he could detect Rosehannah rattling around in the cabin behind him, and there was the *chock, chock* of someone at the Coutts' tilt splitting wood for the fire, but otherwise, the world seemed muffled in wool. Behind his head, the tops of the hills were wreathed in a soft fog, but below, it was just cold enough to keep the snow from melting.

The snow was omnipresent. It lay in huge soft drifts between the trees and over the tilts, it coated the branches of the trees and weighted them towards the ground, it hung in the air and smothered the noise of the sea beyond the woods. There was little sun on this grey, moderate day, and no wind at all, but Harris was warm from the inside out. Everything Rosehannah had said about the snow was true—it protected, comforted, sealed every crack, blanketing the house and sparing the whole little village from the ravages of the winter. He understood, finally, why the livyers retreated into the woods when the snow came.

In fact, Harris understood a great deal that he had not grasped prior to his retreat into the woods. The Sevier brothers, whom he had previously thought dull, sullen young men, more like two oxen than like two healthy male humans, had metamorphosed into such strapping and lively lads that he had hardly recognized them when they came to fetch him for the first of his walks.

"Handle him gently," Rosehannah had warned them when they appeared, red-faced and beaming, at the door the morning after he had arrived. "Not too much at first. And no tricks."

"He'll be like the prize filly, showin' his paces," joked Robert, the younger of the two.

"Two dancin' masters and the one prize pupil," added Thomas, the elder.

130

They had hauled Harris onto his aching legs and bundled him into his coat in the flick of an eye, and before he knew it, he was outside, being half-led and half-carried down the beaten path between one tilt and another. The brothers linked their arms under his on either side of him and he found himself lifted up so that he barely touched the ground.

"Not too much weight, mister," warned Thomas, "not 'til you're used to walking a bit, just step like you're walking on air and let us take the weight of ye."

The brothers had kept up a rapid, mocking, exchange between the two of them, punctuated by spontaneous bursts of chin-music, as they dandled their cargo along, stopping at their own tilt to give Mrs. Sevier a look at the doctor-turned-patient.

"You'll be right as rain in a day or two, Mr. Harris," Mrs. Sevier had assured him, and her taciturn husband had grunted his agreement behind her. "Sure, when we heard the screeching and the howls coming from Rosehannah's tilt last night, we knew right away what it was. The first time Father here went out on rackets, it was a month before he could get through the night without having the fits. I had to pack his legs in warm stones so's I could get a few hours sleep."

A gruff rasp from her husband prompted her to continue. "That's right, my lovey. You got no trouble now, do you? Just take it easy for the first day or two after the snows come. Now them two boys, they was born wearin' pot lids." This was an image even Harris did not wish to pursue, and before he could think of a suitable reply, the puppet masters had him turned around and were air-walking him back to Rosehannah and his waiting cot.

Later that evening, when Missy took Mahala over to visit with their mother, Harris commented on the extraordinary change in the Sevier boys.

"They aren't changed, Mr. Harris," came Rosehannah's reply, "they're rested. You only saw them during the fishing season, when they were working eighteen hours a day. What you saw was exhaustion, sheer, dog-weary fatigue. The men and boys are all like that for about five months of the year, and half-exhausted for another three or four. It's only when they've been in the woods for a bit that they come alive. As they get older, they'll learn to pace themselves a bit better, take a spell now and again. They have to, or they'll burst their hearts from the effort."

"And the women?" he asked.

"We're born in harness," Rosehannah answered, smiling to take the sting out of her reply. "Besides, the cook never goes hungry. But if you wonder why the women around here spoil their sons when they're little, it's because they know that it's their only chance for a bit of fun. If a boy can split wood or haul water, childhood's over, and it's nothing but chop and haul until they finally wear out. Mr. Garland said to Mama one time that poverty makes you stupid, but I think it just makes you tired. Not that we think of ourselves as poor—you don't, when everyone else is in the same position."

Rosehannah lifted the kettle up onto the crook and picked up the blowing pipe to send a thin stream of air into the centre of the fire. Harris studied her face in the firelight. Her dark eyes were somewhat hooded, and her nose was a little too full to be fashionable, but she had a calm intelligence that shone through her youth. She was going to be a handsome old woman one day. Harris winced a little as he tried to settle his aching legs more comfortably on the cot.

"Do you think of yourself as one of them, Rosehannah? You could escape from this, you know. You said yourself, you could pick a good husband, and no doubt Mrs. Garland could put you in the way of some fine young men."

"I do and I don't, Mr. Harris. The people of Ireland's Eye are the only family I've got left, and you don't turn your back on your family."

"Not even if your family turns their backs on you?"

She gave him a quick sideways glance. "You have a point. I know you think I'm repeating what my parents said too often, but my mama once told me that you should never treat those close to you worse than you'd treat a stranger you just met. She was talking about good manners, speaking politely and such, but I think the rule holds true in the larger sense. If you'd forgive a stranger who had offended you and apologized, you should extend the same courtesy to a son—or a nephew."

"Your mother sounds like she was a very kind and good woman, Rosehannah. I shall never tell you not to quote her again." The two fell into a companionable silence after that brief exchange, so that when Missy came bursting through the door with her usual raucous laugh, it felt as if a spell had been broken.

Joe Ganny and Eliol had avoided the mister for the first few days, but Eliol was too sociable to stay away for long, and where Eliol went, Ganny eventually followed. He arrived in his servant's wake with an old handkerchief in his pocket, from which he tumbled a set of crudely made chess pieces. The handkerchief had been marked off in squares and was smoothed out on Mahala's slate to provide a game board. The two men were soon immersed in their game, and Ganny was sufficiently good to distract Harris from his aching legs. Eliol sat by one of the two lamps, mending socks, while Rosehannah stitched together two scraps of brocade left from his vest to make a bag to carry the chess set.

When Mahala grew tired of being ignored, she began to beg for a story, moping and whining in a most uncharacteristic way until Eliol coaxed her into a better mood. Harris, who was only half aware of the conversation going on over his shoulder, suddenly pieced together the fact that the particular story Mahala was being refused was about three brothers from a village called Helm who compete for a pair of golden shoes. When he turned and looked at Rosehannah, she quickly hid her embarrassment in her pannikin of tea. To hush the child, she agreed to read a chapter from *Ivanhoe*, and the chess game was abandoned as Ganny soon lost his concentration and became immersed in the story.

When Rosehannah closed the book, shy Mr. Ganny took a deep breath, as if he had been holding it for the duration of the reading. "It's a wonderful thing to be able to read," he admitted ruefully. "I wish I had the knack of it."

"Well, Mr. Ganny, it's not as difficult as some would like you to think," said Rosehannah, shifting Mahala's head from her lap and sliding off the cot to reach for the slate, which was no longer in use. Watch this," she continued, as she reached into her apron pocket for a lump of soft chalk:

Make three-fourths of a cross and a circle complete,
And let two semi-circles on a perpendicular meet.
Next add a triangle that stands on two feet,
Then two semi-circles and a circle complete.

As she chanted her rhyme, Rosehannah drew the letters on the slate, and then read them off. "T-O-B-A-C-C-O. Tobacco!"

"Is that what it says?" asked Mr. Ganny, grasping the slate and looking up at Rosehannah as eagerly as a child. "Say the rhyme again so I can follow while you do it."

Rosehannah chanted her rhyme out again, while Ganny drew the letters in the air over the slate. He then repeated the little ditty, just to be sure he had got it right, before turning to Eliol. "That's not so hard, lovey. It would be wonderful if we could learn our letters before the twins do." Eliol's mouth opened in protest, but for once he was speechless. "I'll practice these ones, Rosie, and then I'll be back for more. Maybe you could teach me to draw out my name before the winter's over."

"I'm sure I can, Mr. Ganny. Eliol says you are so clever you can put a..." she hesitated, trying to avoid repeating what Eliol had actually said. "You can put an egg in a hen," Rosehannah finished triumphantly. "Wait, I'll mark them on a bit of bark." Tearing a strip off a birch billet Eliol was about to lay on the fire, she took her darning needle and scratched the letters onto the surface.

When the men had left and supper was over, Mahala went to see what was holding Missy up. Harris seized the opportunity to quiz Rosehannah about the peculiar relationship between their previous guests. He was not usually inclined to pry into the lives of others, but he had enjoyed his afternoon and his curiosity was piqued. "Is it true that they say Eliol is the father of the twins?"

"It's true that they say it," replied Rosehannah, who was surprised at the mister's question. "I don't believe it's true that he is, however."

"Why do you think that?"

"Eliol is not inclined to women, Mama said, and he is devoted to Mr. Ganny; he would do nothing that might make a fool of him, though he is more than happy to play the fool himself."

"Well, Ganny is fool enough to treat his servant as if he were his wife, fussing over him and calling him 'lovey,'" replied Harris, his distaste evident in his voice. Rosehannah received this in silence. "Well, don't you think so?" She avoided his eye but was too polite not to answer.

"The 'lovey' thing means nothing. There's an Irishman in Trinity who calls all his servants his 'darlings' all the time: it's just a word." Rosehannah clamped her mouth shut.

"You're working at not saying something, Miss Rosehannah. Spit it out." Harris glared at her in a way she had not seen in many months. He had started this uncomfortable conversation and was now committed to finishing it.

"You said Mr. Joe treats his servant like his wife. Do you know what they say about you?" She rushed on, not waiting for a reply. "That you treat your wife like your servant." She dropped her tin cup on the floor, spilling tea into the rough boards, and was down on her knees mopping it up before she nervously began her retreat. "I know I'm not really living as your wife, but they don't. Or at least not the ones over in Traytown, though I'm sure some guess. That's why Mrs. Sevier won't have Missy and Mahala back in their own tilt as long as you are here. They are my chaperones. People believe anything can happen in the winterhouses, though it seems to me people are just as likely to misbehave wherever they are, if they've a mind to."

"Oh, Rosehannah." Harris's exasperation was palpable. "I'm sorry my presence puts you into such an awkward situation, but it wasn't my doing or my desire. If there's some way I can undo what's been done, you've only to say."

"All I meant was that how things seem from the outside isn't always the way things are," replied Rosehannah miserably. "Whatever Mr. Ganny and Eliol have worked out between themselves, I believe they are both kind and good men and I don't care to know otherwise." She looked up at him from where she knelt on the floor, and for a moment he saw the child she had been when he arrived.

Harris thought about this particular conversation as he sat smoking on his snow bank. It was certainly the most disturbing exchange he'd had since coming to the winterhouses, and he wished in retrospect he had not broached the subject. However, the awkwardness he felt had dissipated as soon as the two Sevier girls had arrived for the night. It was clear from the gloomy silence that had greeted them as they ducked in through the door that something untoward had passed between the mister and Rosehannah, yet they both ignored it and, within moments, it was as if it had never happened, as if the camaraderie they pretended existed really did.

This ability to select out what to hear or see and what to ignore produced an illusion of privacy that was shared by all the winterhouse people. At night, when they were lying in their beds, he could hear the two older girls talking in low voices, and it was as private as if he were not there. So complete was this illusion that Harris was never tempted for a moment to break that barrier, to comment on any of their conversation. If he had to use the urine bucket, they could hear him get out of bed, could not fail to notice the hiss and splash of him emptying his bladder, but even Mahala would give not the slightest indication that anything awkward was taking place not three feet from her nose.

His assumption that the settlers of the colony were a rude, rough lot was tempered by this experience, for there was something exquisitely polite about the way they kept one another's secrets, and protected one another's feelings. Missy might cry into her pillow over her long legs and her cropped hair, but nobody would be unkind enough to mention it, or to use the knowledge against her in the broad light of day. On reflection, Harris thought this must be not only helpful, but absolutely essential to life in the colony. To be trapped on a small island with forty other human souls would be intolerable if one could not at least sometimes act as if one had true privacy. Perhaps this was what allowed Mrs. Ganny to continue happily in her peculiar marital arrangement.

April 22, 05

Dear Brina,

I had no idea you were a bird watcher. I am so glad to hear it. It is true that I am somewhat obsessed with chickens, but I know enough about wild birds to appreciate their appeal, and to put you in the way of a few really thrilling close encounters, should you ever be in my neighbourhood.

I have been doing a bit of rudimentary research on Jeffrey and Street, since they are the only real lead we have, and I find that the business had split into two separate firms in 1789. Thomas Street's business ended when his last surviving son drowned on a voyage from St. John's to Poole in 1809, and I've no idea what happened to John Jeffrey, as he isn't in any of the Newfoundland reference books I've checked. This suggests that he didn't come out to the island, or if he did, it wasn't for long enough to have an impact. This brings us back to Lester Garland. Lester died in 1802, but Garland married Lester's daughter and, by 1813, had full control of the business.

Garland never came to Newfoundland, but his sons did. His son John was one of his agents here, until he left and went to work for twelve years with the London firm of Hart, Garland and Robinson, before moving back to Poole in 1821. Now, aside from the fact that your own family name comes into this saga, we have also a "factoid" (horrible word) that I wish to propose and it is that Garland is the connection between Newfoundland and the Jewish community in London.

Consider the following: one of the Harts was in partnership with John Garland. Lemon Hart, the famous rum merchant, had considerable business in Newfoundland related to the fish-for-rum trade. Simon Solomon, the postmaster, had a son, William, whose middle name was Leamon or Lemon, spelled both ways. There was also a John Lemon in business in Trinity in the 1760s, when Lester Garland was first establishing itself in that town. Over in Bonne Bay, there is a silver communion cup with the stamp of Napthali Hart on it, possibly having arrived there by a circuitous, but plausible, route from Trinity through Labrador, where Lester Garland and Co. had mercantile holdings.

Assuming there was a business or social connection between John Garland and the Jewish community in London, what could have been more normal than for John Garland, who had been to Newfoundland, to

137

sign a guarantee for Jacob Harris and send him out to Trinity as a favour to one of the Harts?

Take the family tree and give it a good shake, my dear. You might discover that your Newfoundland roots predate mine.

Fondest regards,

John

P.S. *About the chicken soup, it is* supposed *to turn to jelly when it is cold. That's the difference between real chicken stock and that fake stuff from an envelope. Don't be discouraged. Even Shibby can make chicken soup, although her matzah balls tend to be a bit on the tough side (I slip them to Culhoon, who will eat anything). Probably all your ancestors had servants, while mine were the ones doing the serving, which is why I can cook and you cannot.*

"The reward is proportionate to the suffering."

Ben Hay-Hay, Ethics of the Fathers

"Rabbits again, I'm afraid," Rosehannah announced at midday, when Harris was allowed to come indoors for his dinner. The tiny house had been tidied and scrubbed within an inch of its life, so he brushed the snow carefully from his boots before he limped in to shed his coat and sit to the table.

"You've made a fine loaf of bread, though," he said, in an attempt to mitigate his obvious disappointment. His hopes in the commissariat line had been frequently blighted since leaving Mrs. Hart's tender ministrations, so rabbit four days in a row wasn't an unbearable tragedy.

"The barm is working well because of the soft weather," Rosehannah conceded. "Some winters, it would be so cold that Mama had to sleep with the jug tucked down in the bed between us."

"Good heavens, that must have made for some uneasy nights," Harris replied, tackling the rabbit stew with a surprisingly good appetite.

"I'll see if the Seviers got any grouse in their slips," Rosehannah continued. "It will make a change, anyway."

"If you aren't too tired, you could always go over to the harbour and pick up some meat and a few potatoes." Harris used a large slice of bread to mop up the gravy in his dish and was thinking of second helpings, when he realized that the girl was studiously ignoring him. "Did I just say something wrong?" he asked, irritation flaring up instantly.

"Well, not wrong, exactly," she explained reluctantly. "It's just that we can't be eating salt beef while everyone else is still eating rabbit." She gestured towards the pot with her spoon. "I didn't catch these rabbits. I haven't been out to check my slips in days because I didn't like to leave you when you couldn't walk. The others have been feeding us all week. They've given us the best they could."

"For pity sake, Rosehannah, I can't be expected to know these things. You have to tell me straight out. If it's time we made a contribution, then you had only to say so. Go home and get whatever you need to produce a good feed for the whole lot, and don't be tightfisted about it. And you can bring me back a clean shirt and extra stockings while you're about it." He reached for the pot and used a heel of bread to blot the remaining gravy from the sides.

Rosehannah's face lit up at the prospect of being able to provide a treat to her neighbours. "I'll take Missy with me to help, and I'll tell Mahala to fetch and carry for you while I'm gone. There's beans in soak for supper, tell her. She can mind the fire for you too." She was out the door, on her way to fetch the Sevier girls, without finishing her rabbit; Harris was absentmindedly eating what she had left, when she flung the door open again. "Think what else you might like me to bring back. Maybe something to amuse you until you're properly back on your feet." Then she was gone again.

The two older girls had left for the harbour immediately and arrived back at the winterhouses just after dark. Their skirts were soaked almost to the waist, and they were both flushed and breathless from their hasty journey over the Nob.

"Give us a drop of tea, Mahala girl, we're parched," demanded Missy, as she swung her burden off her shoulders.

"My blowing pipe! What are you doing to it?" Rosehannah wailed at Harris, who was comfortably ensconced on the small cot and working assiduously away with an awl to produce holes down the length of the brass tube Rosehannah had laid claim to some months before. Harris placed his fingertips over the holes, lifted the pipe to his lips and produced a flutter of soft notes.

"Not quite right yet," he explained, "but it's coming along."

"But I used that for the fire," complained the girl. "There wasn't another one like it in all of Newfoundland." Another flutter of notes was all the reply she got.

"Isn't it lovely," beamed Mahala. "Nobody round here's got a whistle like that."

"Nobody round here had a blowing pipe either," grumbled Rosehannah, depositing her parcel on the table with a dissatisfied bump.

"Cross patch, draw the latch," taunted Harris amiably. "I'll make you another. Mahala, put a drop of molasses in her tea; sweeten her up a bit."

"The mister's going to teach me to play on it," announced Mahala. "And I sang him the whole of 'The Golden Vanity' and he says he will play it with me, once he's got the whistle properly tuned."

"You let the beans dry out, didn't you," Rosehannah said accusingly, after examining the pot on the table.

"Now who's the green-eyed monster here?" laughed Missy. Rosehannah opened her mouth to object, but instead clamped her lips shut and began to undo the bundle she had brought back with her.

"Clean clothes, Mr. Harris," she announced, placing the folded things on the bottom of his cot. "And I thought you could use these. I didn't know you'd be amusing yourself by making toys for Mahala." She defiantly handed over his box of paints and what he assumed was the stretched canvas wrapped in a bit of cloth. Harris stopped fiddling with his whistle long enough to uncover the canvas, which he hung on a nail overhead.

"What happened to her face?" asked Mahala, gazing up at the painting. Where there had once been a devilishly pretty young woman's head, there was now a white blot of paint.

"I soured on it," explained the mister. "It wasn't the kind of face one could live with for long." He worked the awl around in one of the holes of the pipe, and tried it out again. "Getting better," he announced. "Perhaps I shall do your portrait, Mahala."

"Will you make me wear this dress," she asked, looking down at her rather ragged shift and pinafore, "or can I have the dress the lady is wearing. I'd much rather her dress. It's very pretty."

"Perhaps her dress is too mature for you, Mahala. I may have to find a more grown-up model if I'm to save the dress." He glanced over at Rosehannah who was assiduously avoiding his eye. "Now, sing the first verse of your song again, and I'll try playing it with you, while Missy and Rosehannah eat their suppers."

Perhaps it was the prospect of meat and potatoes, or it may have been the sound of the pipe carrying out into the night, but the tilt was soon filled with all the occupants of the other three houses. Mahala sang 'The Golden Vanity' three times in total, and each time Harris added a little more decoration to his accompaniment, until Eliol declared it was better than anything he'd heard on stage in London. Mr. and Mrs. Coutts contributed a rather dreary shipwreck ballad that ran for twenty-six verses. The Sevier boys, Thomas and Robert, danced on a plate and Joe Ganny told a very funny story about a duck hunt that went awry. All the time, Rosehannah sat very quietly in a corner of the larger bed, doing her best not to look cross.

"Who's next to amuse the company?" demanded Harris. "Missy, what can you do?"

"Well, I can't sing, I'll tell you that flat out," declared Missy. "And I'm not one to dance, either, as I've banged my head on the ceiling too often just trying. But I can make pictures without paint, and that's more than you can do," she laughed. Pulling a string from her pocket, she tied the two ends together and proceeded to manipulate the loop into a cat's cradle, a garden rake, and a rabbit coming out of a hole. Then, turning so that neither Mahala nor Rosehannah could see what she was doing, she twisted and looped the string into a shape that left Mrs. Coutts and Joe Ganny blushing and the others all laughing and hooting with shock.

"Your mother will have a few words to say about *that* when she gets you alone," Harris said, smiling.

"Who do you think I learned it from," shot back Missy, tucking the string back into her pocket and ignoring Mrs. Sevier's vociferous and entirely unconvincing denials. "Rosehannah's turn next," she added, and pulled Mahala away from her friend, who had been using the child to shield her from the attention of the room. Harris had never heard Rosehannah sing and fully expected her to refuse, but much to his surprise, she climbed off the bed and took her place in the middle of the room. She stood for a moment, thinking and calming herself, and then sang in a plain but pleasant voice.

As I walked out one May morning,
One morning, oh so early,
I spied a fair and a comely lass,
'Twas charming blue-eyed Mary.

Twelve verses later, Mary sailed off o'er the main to be a captain's wife, much to the satisfaction of the entire audience. When the company broke up, it was long into the night and Mahala was soundly asleep. Rosehannah doled out the salt meat and a few precious potatoes to each household, and dropped the remainder of the beef into a pot of water to soak for their own dinner the next day. Missy had draped an old bit of sailcloth as a curtain over their bed, and had climbed in with Mahala. She now handed her still damp skirt to Rosehannah, who spread it out over the bench to dry before slipping her own dress off. Harris watched her put out the lamp through almost closed eyes and when he had heard her settle into bed next to the two Sevier girls, he lifted his whistle to his lips, and in the comfort of the dark, he played a soft, slow air, full of foreign-sounding notes, a tune so replete with longing that it was not just Missy who cried herself to sleep that night.

May 8, 05

Dear Brina,

I'm glad you enjoyed the CD. Newfoundland folk music isn't to everyone's taste, but I thought the a cappella approach might appeal to your sense of history, as well as your Jewish ear. (Or do they use instruments at your synagogue? Tali and I attended a Reform synagogue in the U.S. once and we almost fell off our seats when they began playing an organ at the Saturday morning service.) The singer, Anita Best, is a national treasure, and I'm delighted you listened to her by the light of sixty-four shabbat/birthday candles—makes quite a conflagration, doesn't it. Does this mean you will be retiring from teaching next year? Notice that I don't write just "retiring," but "retiring from teaching." Academics, like writers, never completely retire, but go on until they drop in their tracks. I miss my students sometimes but I don't miss the drudgery of marking papers, which during my last years in collar became almost intolerably burdensome because of the increased class sizes.

I have continued reading around our subject and I found a reference in a book about the two John Peytons that may give us some insight about Harris. Apparently, Lester Garland owned the salmon fishing rights to Dog Bay Brook in Gander Bay, and in 1817, sold these rights to two former servants. The author writes that "Both men were illiterate and confusion arose in their trading transactions, so they requested an educated "English youngster" to keep matters straight." A boy named John Bussie ("youngster" or "bedlamer" is what they called teenagers) was sent out by Garland to fill the post and later settled in the area.

Harris was educated, we know that. He spoke Yiddish, German, English, and possibly French. He likely played the flute. He was apprenticed for a time to a watchmaker, possibly as a way into the diamond and precious metals business. I know a little about the watchmaking trade from my research on the postmaster, and I can add that he would have been familiar with nautical instruments, and possibly pharmacology (postmaster Solomon sold supplies for ships' medicine chests), and he could probably do basic draftsmanship and technical drawing. He would have been, if anything, overeducated for such a position, but a very handy fellow to have around in a pinch.

My guess is that he would not have been posted too far away from home base. I don't think he would have been sent farther north than Catalina, nor farther east than Random Island, and not south at all, as it is across a large bay that is tricky for small boats. I am enclosing a map of that section of the coast. Use your instincts on this one. See if there is any name that catches your eye.

On a more personal note, my step-son Harry is going to be in England at the end of the month, doing some work at the Scott Polar Research Institute in Cambridge. He plans to get up to London for a couple of days and was wondering if he could call on you. I'm giving away a secret here, but Leah and Shibby have constructed a mobile for you from bits and pieces they found on the beach and Judith thinks it is too fragile to trust to the mail, so Harry has been seconded as courier. Wait until you see it—I think you will understand why we are all anxious that it arrive intact.

My history proceeds apace. I am currently doing a survey of the graveyard, which sounds morbid but is actually a very pleasant way to spend a couple of afternoons. My Hebrew transcription is improving. Prior to this week, I have only ever gone into the graveyard for funerals and with Harry for the cemetery service prior to Yom Kippur, but this week, I find myself stopping at Tali's grave and telling her about you and Jacob Harris and the children. Very silly, I know, and I don't think I'll make a habit of it, but it has been helpful, rather like thinking out loud in front of my students.

I do hope you can find time for Harry's visit.

Fondest regards,

John

"More menservants, more thievery. More possessions, more worries."
Hillel, Ethics of the Fathers

"Where do you want this, inside or outside?" Selby had ducked in through the doorway unannounced. He had a bundle of birch bark in one hand and a skinned haunch of some large animal over one shoulder. Only Rosehannah's unnatural stillness and calm gave Harris any indication that she was startled by this sudden appearance.

"Have you brought meat to the others?" she asked, with no more greeting or salutation than he had offered her.

"A shoulder each to the Coutts and Ganny tilts, and the other haunch to the Seviers. I brung you the tongue and liver, too." He held the bark bundle out to her and a large drop of blood splashed down onto the floor. This seemed to release Rosehannah from her rigid stance, and she quickly grabbed a tin basin and held it out to receive the gory gift.

"Thank you, Selby. Put the haunch on the roof for the time being and I'll deal with this first." In the moments he was outside, the girl quickly turned to Harris and whispered into his startled ear. "Act like everything's fine. He's a welcome guest here." By the time Selby had stepped back into the tilt, Rosehannah was undoing the package of meat. "This looks lovely, Selby. Papa is very fond of caribou tongue. It's a pity he's not here to share it with us."

"He's probably got plenty over in Rise's Harbour. The woods is maggoty with 'em this year." Selby dropped down onto a bench with the merest nod of acknowledgement towards Harris. "I'm cut loose from Garland, got my own boat now. I'm lookin' for a bit of help with the swiles. I got a net to put out in the tickle between the Indian Islands, but I need another man to help me set it."

"What are the shares?" Rosehannah asked.

"Three for one, that's only fair. It's my boat and my net."

"Two for one would probably get you the two Sevier boys. That will be safer all round and you'll probably get more seals because they can take turns watching." Rosehannah glanced over at the mister. "What do you think, Mr. Harris?"

"I expect you are probably right in this matter," said Harris, who had no idea what they were talking about.

Selby grunted agreement. "I'll go talk to them after supper. How many you got in this tilt? I'll be needing a place for the night."

"Only the two Sevier girls and us. There's a bag of moss up in the rafters—you can bed down on that. I have no extra blankets but you can sleep under your coat and get up close to the fire." As she was speaking, Rosehannah was washing the tongue, which she then placed in the kettle with peppercorns, salt, vinegar and a few bay leaves that she had been saving for just such an occasion.

"That's a lovely chimbley," said Selby, and looked around admiringly at the small tilt. "You got a snug little place here, Rosie. I stayed in a tilt over on Random and I almost choked on the smoke." He went over to the roost that was set into the back wall and gave the hen a poke with a thick, blunt finger, eliciting a scream from the cock, who didn't care to see his property being abused.

"Leave them be, Selby. I'm hoping to get a few eggs before March is out and she won't oblige if you frighten her like that." Rosehannah sounded tired of their visitor already. "I'll fry up some of this liver for supper and we can have the tongue for dinner tomorrow. You're in for a treat, Mr. Harris. Fresh deer meat is one of the things that keeps some of our fishermen from giving up on this place and going home again."

The meal was ready in very short order, despite Rosehannah's veiled remarks about how much quicker she could have done it if she had the services of a blowing pipe, and Harris ate almost as much of the organ meat as Selby did, and with a lot less grunting and slurping.

"Haven't got a drop of the good stuff to wash this down, do you Rosie?" Selby was peering round the cabin, but even with the cruise lamp lit, it was far too dark for him to discern the brandy jug that Rosehannah had surreptitiously nudged into a corner while he was teasing the hen.

"Not a drop, Selby. I suggest you try Mr. Coutts. No doubt he's got a belly full of caribou meat by this time and he might be feeling more sociable than Methodist. You should go with him, Mr. Harris. Joe Ganny will likely go visiting there and you can have a game of chess."

"You should come, mister," urged Selby, much to Harris's surprise. "If old Coutts ain't feeling too ronk, we might even get a game of cards on the go."

Harris had said very little up to this point and was taking his lead from Rosehannah, but he was still taken aback to find Selby treating him like a long lost friend, when at their last meeting, he had threatened the man with the sharp edge of an axe. He started to protest, but seeing the look in Rosehannah's eye he demurred and before the dishes were off the table, the two men were out the door and on their way through a starlit night to the winterhouse of Mr. and Mrs. Coutts.

Their return wasn't quite such a straight line as the crow flies, and twice Selby had to pluck Harris from the snow when he strayed from the beaten path, but they made it safely back to what Harris, on this night at least, was thinking of as "home." Missy, Mahala and Rosehannah were all in bed, behind their tightly drawn curtain, and a large sail-bag of sphagnum moss was waiting invitingly for Selby in the glow of the dying embers of the fire.

At dawn, Harris woke with a cracking headache and the urgent need to urinate, but a quiet murmur of conversation on the other side of the room warned him to lie still. Missy Sevier's comfortable snore from behind the curtain told him it was Rosehannah who was talking to Selby, and for once he strained to listen where he was not wanted.

"By the look of it, you ain't really married to the mister, Rosie, and I'm my own man now, so I thought I'd just come and ask you the once." Selby's baritone was easier to discern than Rosehannah's indistinct reply. Harris discreetly turned his ear from the pillow to try to catch the answer.

"...and I appreciate your offer, but I don't think we'd dodge along too well after the first while. Papa always said I hadn't much of a sense of humour, you know, and I think you'd need that in a woman more than the book reading and such. Besides, I'm only fifteen."

"Big enough to bleed, big enough to butcher, I always say," and Selby laughed at his own wit.

"There, that's exactly what I mean. I don't think that's a bit funny, and you'd be fed up with me always scowling at you every time you made a coarse joke." Rosehannah's voice took on an urgency then, and Harris no longer had to strain to hear. "Selby, have you given any thought to Missy Sevier? She's clever, you know, she can do anything with her hands, and lots of the men won't look at her because she's so tall. I think if you let me talk to her first, I might be able to convince her to consider a proposal from you."

"I haven't clapped eyes on Missy since last year. She still got those big long legs, I suppose?"

"Yes, Selby, she does. She has wonderful legs, grand for climbing hills and hauling water."

"It might be kind of interesting to climb aboard of someone you can look in the eye without lyin' down," answered Selby thoughtfully. "Tell you what, you kind of spy her out for me, and if you think she's game, just tip me the wink over breakfast." Harris could hear Selby get to his feet. "I got to piss, and check on the boat. I'll try and get a chance to talk to her before we go after the swiles."

The door was hardly closed before Harris was on his feet. "You aren't really going to marry her off to that pig, are you?"

"Why not? She's longing to get married, and he's the only one I've ever heard her express any interest in." Both Rosehannah and the mister had forgotten to lower their voices during this exchange, and they looked guiltily towards the curtain, when the snoring suddenly stopped. Missy's spiked head with its picket-fence smile poked out.

"You two talking about me?"

"She wants you to marry that pig, Selby." Harris was indignant.

"Sure, why not? He's a lovely man."

"He's a thief, Missy. You know that, don't you?" said Rosehannah, who suddenly seemed to be taking the other side of the debate. "He's a real skeet."

"But he's awful tall, and he's a hard worker when he wants to be."

"And he drinks," said Harris, whose aching head was a guilty reminder of his own participation in that particular pastime.

"But he likes your long legs," admitted Rosehannah, who was only too conscious of her own talismanic contribution to the courtship—a paper slip with "a fine leg for a skin boot" written on it, sewed into the cap that Missy was even now hauling on to cover her cropped hair.

"He'd need to be kept well in line, Missy. You'd never be able to take your eyes off him for a second." Harris could see which way the wind was blowing and was preparing to capitulate.

"He's coarse and rude," said Rosehannah. "Maybe he'd even beat you," she added darkly.

"I'm coarse and rude as well," pouted Missy, "and if he beat me, I'd beat him back."

"He owns his own boat," conceded Harris, "and he's a dab hand at playing cards."

"You didn't play cards with him, did you?" Rosehannah was shocked. She'd hoped Harris had put all that behind him.

"No, no, of course not. I played chess with Mr. Ganny, but I watched him playing with Eliol and the Couttses, and he did better than I'd have expected."

"All I knows," said Missy, "is that, if I'm goin' to be courted, I wants to be wearing a better dress than this one. Wake up, Mahala, we're going over to Mam's." She began pulling her dress on over her shift at the same time that she was poking her little sister, while Harris turned away to give the two of them a little privacy.

Once the Seviers were out the door, Harris waded in. "I can't believe it. You just sat there and let that brute rattle on as if he'd every right to court you."

"And what exactly was I supposed to do, Mr. Harris? Tell him he was an ignorant lout who wasn't fit to clean my boots? I've got nobody, I own nothing, and I eat through the courtesy of Mr. Garland, who doesn't want to see you drowned or starved or murdered by the likes of Selby before your first winter is out. I don't need Selby as an enemy. I'll be safe from him once he's under Missy's thumb, and while it's true he's a lout, there are worse men out there ready to take me or her, by force if necessary."

"Surely not. This may be a colony but the Governor wouldn't allow such a thing."

"The Governor is in St. John's and doesn't know that Rosehannah Quint and Missy Sevier exist. If some sailor off a ship or a livyer from up the coast decides to take himself a country wife, the Governor will have nothing to say about it. Selby has a vile tongue, but his attitude is not unusual. 'Old enough to…' Well, I don't need to repeat it. You must have heard him; you seem to have heard everything else."

"And a damn good thing, too. As long as you're under my protection, I'll not have you being courted by the likes of him."

"Am I under your protection, Mr. Harris?" The defensive anger Rosehannah had projected up to this point seeped away, and she looked at Harris helplessly. "I've never been quite clear what my standing is with you. Are you my master, my guardian, what?"

"I've no idea, Rosehannah, I'm sorry. I don't know the rules out here; everything seems to work differently. Sometimes it seems to work better, and other times it's worse. All I know is that I thought I understood Gentiles and now I know I don't. I thought you were different from us, and now I'm not so sure. But let's make a bargain. You keep me from falling into the nearest bog-hole or being eaten by a bear, and I'll keep you safe from the Selbys of this particular part of the world. I don't know what the devil we were doing with him under our roof in the first place."

Rosehannah noted his use of "our" to refer to "her" tilt, but ignored it. "He came with a gift of meat and an offer of work. He was trying to mend fences with the whole community. Even if I hadn't needed him, the Seviers or the Coutts, or Mr. Ganny and Eliol might have, and I had no right to turn him away. He wouldn't have gone, even if I had, so I was just accepting what I couldn't stop, trying to turn it to advantage. He's a lout, not a monster."

"I suppose you're right. I just hope Missy knows what she's letting herself in for."

Dear Brina,

I was quite delighted with the report on your first attempt at intuitive scholarship, though I don't think you should make a habit of resorting to séances, even just for fun. Channeling Rahel Levin, using the leftover stubs of your birthday candles, was probably so close to witchcraft that it would get you excommunicated, even from a Reform synagogue. You have got the spirit of it right, though, even if your results don't hold up to sober second thought.

Ivanhoe is, indeed, a striking name, even in a country noted for its striking names. No doubt you noticed, in the same bay, Baker's Loaf, Dildo, Little Heart's Ease, Shuffle Board, Old Shop, Rantem and Ireland's Eye, which is the name of the island Ivanhoe is on, as well as the name of the main settlement. Unfortunately, although the novel Ivanhoe *was published in 1819, and it does indeed contain the first positive depiction of Jews in English literature, the town was not named for the novel. Ireland's Eye was the first fishing station on that island, and the two smaller communities developed as winter quarters—Old Tilt and Traytown. The name of the former changed from Old Tilt (a tilt being a cabin or shack) to Ivanhoe in 1917, on the recommendation of Rev. C.M. Stickings, in honour of a large family by the name of Ivany who lived there.*

The name Ivanhoe may not be significant but that's not to say Ireland's Eye isn't a good candidate as the station assigned our man Harris. It's the right distance from Trinity (about twenty kilometers by boat), it was small enough that a green man could manage it without doing too much damage if he messed up, and it had a strictly C. of E. population, so it would have been free of the sectarianism that later caused trouble in communities such as Carbonear and Harbour Grace. Besides, could the ghost of Rahel Levin be wrong?

I confess, I have my own associations with the name Ivanhoe that leads me to treat Harris's presence there as a premise. When my father was a boy, his mother taught his older half-brother to write shorthand by dictating to him from Ivanhoe. *Each morning, he would write out a number of pages as she read it to him, and each evening, he would read it back to my father and his sister. That was around 1908 or 1910. My uncle got a job as a stenographer for the legislature as a result of this skill, and the income eventually helped send my father to school to become a teacher. That, in turn, led me to become a teacher too, and it probably had something to do with my family's positive attitude towards Jews.*

So we will look to Ivanhoe, or Ireland's Eye, and see if we can come up with some more substantial link than that one of your birthday candles ignited the spine ribbon of a volume of Ivanhoe *during your experiment. You are lucky your salon lady didn't burn the place down, just to drive her point home. But in the meantime, I do not think we should rule out other fishing stations, just in case.*

Harry is in England as I write this, and will be seeing you in a day or so. I have no doubt that you will like him, as he has such a sunny disposition and is a great favourite with everyone who comes in contact with him. He does not carry the Harris genes, so I can take no credit for that, but I feel very pleased that he is to be my first human contact with you, as it will predispose you to like the rest of us should you ever come to visit.

Fondest regards,

John

"There is nothing more becoming a person than silence."
Rabbi Shimon ben Gamliel, Ethics of the Fathers

A small white feather floated down on a current of cold air from a chink in the back wall and Harris swatted it away. Rosehannah rose from her stool by the fire and plucked it from the air. The two chickens were moulting and the flurry of loose feathers was a source of some irritation for at least one member of the household. The girl pulled a handful of moss from the bag lodged in the rafters and, using a wooden wedge and a round beach stone, chinched up the hole.

"It's going to be a fine day, Mr. Harris. Do you think your snowshoeing skills are up to a walk over to see how the swiling is going?" Harris took a certain pride in his recent mastery of the skinnyrackets and Rosehannah was confident that he would rise to the challenge.

"Anything to get out of here for a few hours," Harris replied, and put aside the piece of wood he was working on. His carving skills had improved considerably during the weeks he had spent at the winterhouse, and he had progressed from crafting netting needles on to shaping toy animals for Mahala. He was currently attempting to produce a matched pair of candlesticks, which Rosehannah believed were to be a wedding gift for Missy Sevier. "Can you find something nice to eat to bring with us?"

"Everything I give you to eat is nice, Mr. Harris. What you want is something different, and yes, I think I can find you a bit of that pickled tongue, just as long as you realize it will be the last of it." Selby's gift of caribou meat had been stretched out through several weeks, and Harris had developed an appreciation for how useful it was to have a strong, energetic hunter as part of their small community. He was not so fond of the seal meat Selby brought, perhaps because of its dark colour, but anything fresh was welcome and Harris found that a lot of the small physical complaints which had bothered him through the winter were relieved by the change in diet. He bundled into his coat, while Rosehannah packed provisions into a nunny bag that she slung over her shoulder.

The pair stepped out into the sunshine, looped their feet into their rackets and started up the hill behind the tilt, Harris leading the way. "It's getting soft, I believe," observed Rosehannah. "This may be the last chance we have for a randy. Once the snow starts to melt, it will be too difficult to go through the woods for a time."

"It seemed odd to me, when I first arrived here, that people always referred to the wilderness as 'the woods' instead of 'the forest,' but I can see that you do need a different name for these evergreen forests—they are not at all like a real forest." Harris was getting into his stride now and Rosehannah had to work at keeping up with him.

"What's a real forest?" asked Rosehannah, who was too glad to be out in the fresh air to take offence at his dismissal of her beloved woods.

"A real forest is oak, deciduous trees, trails and paths that pass under the branches rather than through them. This stuff is harder to get through than a hedgerow."

"That's tuckamore, Mr. Harris, not woods. But the woods are not much easier to penetrate." They had skirted a large patch of low vegetation at the top of the hill, stunted firs and spruce, and were about to head down the other side towards the sea again after stopping to catch their breath. "Isn't it beautiful?" Rosehannah was bright-eyed with pleasure as she scanned the horizon.

"It is, but in a rather sinister way, don't you think?" Harris looked out over the same landscape but viewed it through less affectionate eyes. "It's so dark and dense. It goes on forever, and it's all the same. There's no variety in it at all, just endless evergreens."

"That's not really true, Mr. Harris. The pines don't look at all like the spruce or fir, and even those two trees are quite different from one another. Look," she added, plucking a sprig of needles from one tree and handing it to him, "this one has flat leaves, and is a brighter green." Then snapping another sprig from a tree that to Harris looked exactly the same, she pulled the needles out and rolled them between her fingers before tipping them into the palm of his hand. "Can you feel the difference?"

"These ones are round," he admitted.

"And smell them. They smell different," Rosehannah urged. Harris lifted the two sprigs to his nose but, in the cold air, could smell nothing at all. "The fir has a resin—what some call 'snotty var.'" She took the twig and carefully prodded a blister on the trunk of the tree, collecting up a generous drop of the gum which she held to his nose.

"Is this the stuff I get all over my hands when I'm carrying in the firewood?"

"And all over your clothes." In the woods, Rosehannah wore old dresses that had belonged to her mother and had coaxed Harris into switching back into her father's cast-offs after he had virtually ruined his own trousers. "But you can use this for all sorts of things. Robert Sevier cut his foot badly with an axe one year so Mama had to sew it up. Mrs. Sevier smeared turpentine like this all over it and you can't even see a scar now. And the spruce, that's what we call 'the green doctor.' You can make beer from the new tips, and it's a wonderfully potent tonic."

"So, where I see a million hectares of useless woods, you see a medicine chest." Harris headed down the hill, with Rosehannah in his wake.

"More than a medicine chest—I see heat and houses, furniture and bedding. And it's all for free, you just have to reach out your hand and take it. See this?" Rosehannah had stopped and was examining a twig sticking up through the snow. "This is withrod. You can tell from how straight it is, and from the grey bark and the rusty deer ears on the top." She tickled the top with her fingertip and Harris could see two long, narrow leaf buds ready to sprout.

"This gad is so flexible you can tie a knot in it, yet it's strong enough that it can be used to make baskets or cradles. When the spring comes, you can scrape the peel off with a dull knife and then it takes a dye beautifully. The men use it for barrel hoops and oar locks, for a dozen different things. It has a lovely flower, and it develops fruit that dries on the bough—wild raisin we call it—that will keep all through the winter." Rosehannah stood and gazed admiringly at the single straight shoot sticking up through the snow.

"If I could see through your eyes, Rosehannah, I could live and die a happy man here on Ireland's Eye," Harris observed in an ironic voice.

"You don't need my eyes, Mr. Harris, you just need to open your own, learn to see what you are looking at. You are an educated man, you know different languages—surely you had to study them." Rosehannah looked up to see how he would receive this rebuke, and he scowled at her deliberately.

"You know, Rosehannah, when I first came here, I thought you were a very shy and fearful little girl, qualities I find quite attractive in children, but you remind me more and more of a particularly bossy and judgmental nursemaid I was entrusted to back in my own childhood. Merely thinking about her makes my backside sting," he added, rubbing that tender part of his anatomy.

"I'm sorry, Mr. Harris, I..." She stopped for a moment, suddenly annoyed beyond toleration. "No, I'm not sorry. I've had enough of your poisonous opinions about this place. You complain of the weather, the housing, the food, you say the people are ignorant and little more than slaves, you mock our accents, and you disrespect our traditions. For pity's sake, you don't even like the trees, because they aren't like the trees you are used to. Well, get used to them or go back where you came from. These are the trees we have, and we like them." And to their mutual astonishment, Rosehannah leaned over and pushed him roughly back into the snow, a considerable feat given that he was wearing snowshoes. Harris howled in surprise.

"Oh, I'm so sorry. Really, I *am* sorry this time," she insisted, and reached out to haul him to his feet. Instead of accepting her apology and her hand, Harris pulled her down and, with the well-practiced moves of a former boy terror, rubbed her face briskly in the snow before disengaging himself and sorting out the tangle of snowshoes and lacing that threatened to unite them in a cold tomb.

"The food wasn't damaged, was it?" Harris asked solicitously, after they had regained their feet and brushed the snow out of the folds of their clothes.

"Not as much as my nose," answered Rosehannah, with mock sulkiness. "Serve you right if the bread is squashed."

"You started it."

"I did not."

"But it's true, what I said. You did seem to be a very shy and fearful child when I arrived, and now you are quite different." Harris took the nunny bag from her shoulder and hefted it onto his own back.

"I suppose that's from not having Mama around to rely on," answered Rosehannah. "And teaching Mahala makes me feel different, too. I think that if I'm to tell her what's right and what's wrong, I have to tell myself first, which requires that I think about things instead of just accepting whatever pops into my head. Oh, look! Turrs!" Out over the water, a small flock of birds beat its way through the sky. From below, they heard the retort of a gun.

"I'll bet that's Thomas. He's a great one with a gun," said Rosehannah, and she hurried forward, immediately overtaking Harris, who was not so quick going downhill as he was when climbing.

At the bottom of the hill, they pulled off their snowshoes and quickly located Thomas, who was copying across the pans of ice just offshore, retrieving a bird from the water with a weighted line of hooks. A bulging game bag rested on the rocks, and he hopped ashore and placed his catch with the others. "Turrs for our dinner," he called cheerfully, as they came up on him.

"How is the sealing going?" asked Rosehannah.

"Not too bad, but the ice keeps moving in and out, so we have to be ready to take up the net at any moment for fear of having it tore to bits." He motioned out towards the offshore islands, where they could see Robert rowing the boat in their direction. "We anchor her on the far island, and then we drag her across the lead so's the swiles swim right into it as they try to pass between 'em." Small pans of ice floated around the bay, and, even as they watched, these began to drift towards the passage between the outcrops of land.

"Selby handles it from the land and we pull her from the boat. It's hard work, but harps is thirteen shillings each this year, and bedlamers seven." Thomas put his gun and the game bag safely into the large lean-to that served them for shelter, and prepared to climb into the small skiff, as soon as his brother touched shore. "Tide's turned," he observed. "Time to get back to work."

"Let me have a go," said Harris suddenly, and stepped towards the oncoming boat.

"Mister wants to try his hand at swilin'," Thomas called to his brother.

"Then he'd better step lively," Robert retorted. "Tide don't wait for no man." Thomas pushed his brother off almost before Harris was in over the thwarts, and turned to Rosehannah with a grin.

"Don't suppose you got a loaf of bread in that nunny bag, do you, Rosie? It'd go right good with a bowl of turrs an' gravy."

"I not only have bread, I've got a nice lump of fatback, so we can skin those birds instead of plucking them and save ourselves a lot of work." Rosehannah moved towards the makeshift camp, prepared to make a more substantial dinner than the cold tongue she had intended for them.

She was rendering down the fat when she heard Thomas's cry of "God Almighty," and looked up just in time to see a rocking boat with one man in it, where a moment before there had been two. Within seconds, she and Thomas were on the shore, watching helplessly as Robert fought to pull the net up into the boat.

"What happened?" she demanded, pulling fearfully on Thomas's sleeve.

"I don't know. They were working at pulling in the net, and all of a sudden, there was a heave in the water and the mister just got yanked out and over the side. Maybe they struck a whale or something."

Out on the water, they could see net and man surface momentarily before being pulled under again. Robert's anguished cries reached them and the two clutched one another as they saw him fight to draw the net up again. On the far island, Selby was pulling in length after length of the twine, drawing the net, the boat and the two men into shallower water. Even from that distance, it looked like an untenable effort, but after several agonizing minutes, he dropped the head ropes and waded into the water to pull the trapped man up into the air. It took Robert's splitting knife to cut Harris free and deposit him into the bottom of the boat.

"What's he doing?" Rosehannah begged of Thomas. "Why isn't he bringing him back?"

"I've no idea, maid. Maybe Selby's hurt hisself."

"They'll need to be dried. I'll get more wood on the fire."

"That's if they're alive," replied Thomas ominously. There was no sign of life from the bottom of the boat, and Selby had collapsed into a heap on the shoreline.

Rosehannah turned away from the scene of the accident, and concentrated on getting a roaring fire going in front of the bough-whiffen. "Dear God, let him be alive," she murmured and then amended it to "Let them both be alive." When she heard the scrape of the boat on the rocks, she ran down to the shore.

"That was the biggest old dog hood I've ever seen, must be over 800 pounds," gasped Robert, as he and his brother heaved the mister out of the boat and dragged him up to the camp.

"Is he alive?" Rosehannah could not tell from looking at him.

"Oh, he's alive all right, but I'm not so sure about Selby. I think he must have strained his heart or something; he can't even speak." They dumped the mister unceremoniously on the bed of spruce boughs. "Bring your gun, Thomas, that seal ain't dead yet, and I'm not letting it drown me, nor you either."

The Seviers headed back to the boat, while Rosehannah searched the camp for extra clothes for Harris. There weren't any, so with some difficulty, she stripped him of his wet things and wrapped him in the blankets. He was clearly in shock, but except for vomiting up about a gallon of sea water, he seemed not to be injured.

She heard several gun shots and, by the time the Seviers were back with Selby, she had the kettle boiling and the turrs in the pot. Robert had given Selby his coat and Thomas had contributed cuffs and a cap, but Selby looked worse than wet. They eased him down next to Harris, and then looked to Rosehannah for help.

"What can we do for you, Selby," she asked, and began working his soaking boots off his feet. His first attempt to answer her came out as little more than a faint whisper.

"Hurts," he admitted. "I think I've pulled something in my chest."

"You might have injured your heart or something. I don't think you should move too much until we know."

"Not much chance of that," he whispered weakly, and smiled at the irony. "How's your man doing?"

"I'm about to find out." Rosehannah turned her attention to Harris. "Mr. Harris, Selby needs your help." Harris turned his head away from her and didn't respond. "Mr. Harris, you've had a very bad time of it, but you're all right now, and Selby needs you. He's hurt himself pulling you from the water and I don't know what to do." Slowly, Harris turned his eyes towards her.

"I've lived my whole life with nothing worse than a splinter in my finger until I came here, and now all of nature is out to get me." Harris rolled over slowly and curled into the blankets.

"Oh, for pity's sake, think of someone else for once," Rosehannah said impatiently, kicking him in the rump. "Selby saved your life, and now he's in trouble and if you're so stupid and selfish that you won't do what you can for him, then perhaps we ought to throw you back in the water." Rosehannah astonished herself with her invective but continued. "That's what we do to useless, lazy, self-involved, uncooperative men around here. We drop them through the ice or lose them in the woods, or arrange for a convenient accident with a falling tree. Now for goodness sake, stir yourself to see to the poor man or you'll be drying your own clothes and cooking your own dinner."

"Now, there's a feed of tongues for you," said Thomas, who was busy consuming his share of the cold caribou tongue, while waiting for the turrs to be cooked.

"Rosehannah, if you're going to make threats, you must increase the gradation as you go along. It's no use telling a man that you're going to arrange to have him murdered, and then up the ante by refusing to cook his dinner." Harris sat up, shivering, and tightened the blankets around himself. "Let's have a look at him."

Robert had, by this time, got Selby out of his wet clothes and covered with the remaining blanket. Rosehannah turned her attentions modestly toward the pot of turrs.

"Three cracked ribs, I think," Harris announced. "Painful but not fatal, so long as he doesn't move about and puncture his lung. Have we anything to make a bandage of? It will be less painful if I strap him up."

"I'll cut up my shift," said Rosehannah, and immediately disappeared behind a convenient tree.

"Just the skirt should do. Can you cut it off at the waist?" Rosehannah didn't answer but the men heard a tearing sound and, moments later, the girl emerged with a length of white linen in her hands. "Give me your knife, Robert. I'll notch it and you can tear it into bandaging."

By the time Harris had Selby's ribs bound, some of his clothes were dry, though a little singed from the fire. The Seviers got him dressed and lay him carefully down on the floor of the lean-to.

"What's so funny," asked Rosehannah, as she heard Selby snort with laughter and wince with the pain it caused.

"Well, I was just thinking, I always wanted to get inside your skirts. Didn't know I'd have to fish the mister from the ocean to do it."

Rosehannah glared at the men. "Don't even think of smiling. If that little jest makes its way back to the winterhouses, I'll cut your liver out and then I'll tell Missy why I did it."

"Now you've got the hang of it. Follow up the threat of disembowelment with something worse." Harris, like Selby, fancied himself quite the wit. Rosehannah was not impressed.

Dear Brina,

You are right, there is something eerie yet beautiful about the mobile. I knew you would see it. The execution is crude, but the way the light comes through the bird skull and the various coloured seaweeds, and the odd confluence of shapes that makes the transition from sky to sea and fish to feather so natural, is extraordinary. Judith saw it at once, also. One of those girls is gifted, but I'm not sure which of them it is as they did the whole thing together. Judith told me later that she hung the mobile and took a whole roll of film of it before she packed it up to go with Harry. A reciprocal gift wasn't necessary, but the children are thoroughly enjoying the Philip Pullman books you sent.

Thank you for the photograph of you and Harry at Cheyne Walk. You both look so extraordinarily pleased with yourselves that I was positively jealous. Judith said Harry called you a "kindred spirit," which in case you aren't up on your Can Lit, is a phrase borrowed from Anne of Green Gables. I gather the girls included a photo of themselves with me and Culhoon, so now we both know what the other looks like and you can stop imagining that I'm four-foot-nine and bald. I have quite a lot of hair, in fact, just not as much as Culhoon. And most of mine stays on my head, while his goes everywhere it shouldn't.

That silver halo of yours is magnificent. Tali insisted upon dying her hair the moment the first strand of grey appeared, so I never did get to see what she would have looked like au naturel. Harry says you told him you've been white-haired since you were seventeen. What good luck indeed, for it absolutely suits you.

I wrote my most recent column for the Downhome about winter-houses, and worked in an appeal for information about Ivanhoe. Newfoundlanders have been semi-nomadic people for centuries, but the only real scholarly work on the subject is by Philip E.L. Smith, a retired anthropologist from U. d'M. I don't know the man, but I have been in touch with him by mail and he sent me several of his articles. I am enclosing a copy of "Transhuman Europeans Overseas: The Newfoundland Case."

My property here in Beachy Cove was probably originally the site of winter quarters for Portugal Cove. It was known as Henry's Gardens, and it is tucked back from the sea in the crook of Beachy Head. The usual process was to build your fishing room by the water, using lumber from the trees in the immediate area, and after it was all cut over, move back inland for the winter. A winterhouse might last from one to five years, possibly longer if the wood was harvested carefully, and then it would be abandoned or sometimes converted into a farm, which is what happened here.

The settlement of Ireland's Eye is on the outside of the island itself, and would be exposed to the wind and weather all winter; while Old Tilt, or Ivanhoe, would have been a bit more protected, being farther back from the bay, into Smith Sound. There would have been more wood available at Thoroughfare, also, which is just a short distance across the tickle (which is called "The" Thoroughfare, just to confuse you), and in fact, there were no less than two sawmills in Ivanhoe in 1941 when the population was just 97 souls. The main supplier at Thoroughfare closed up in 1960, and over the next six years, the entire population of the island moved on and resettled elsewhere. The island is now abandoned, except for a few summer cabins and a small herd of goats, I'm told.

Last night, my old blue hen died in her bed. I went to open the hatch and change the water this morning, and she was just flopped over with her chin on the edge of the nesting box. She had laid an egg the previous day, as she had almost every day for years, so I wasn't expecting her to go quite so quickly. I think she was the best layer and the best mother hen I ever had. She would adopt an alligator if it happened to be born within the boundaries of my fences.

We are having a thunder storm here at the moment, so I think I'd better print this off and shut down before the computer crashes. Country electricity is not as reliable as town.

Affectionately,
John

P.S. I realize I am anthropomorphizing. Hens don't have chins.

"Knowledge not increased is knowledge decreased."
Hillel, Ethics of the Fathers

"Mr. Harris, wake up." Harris groaned and tried to push Rosehannah's urgent hands away. His head ached and a wave of nausea swept over him. "Please, sir, wake up. Mahala has been sick and Missy is in trouble too." Rosehannah was pulling the stifling blankets away from him and trying to prop him upright on his cot. Harris fought to remember the night before. Had he been drinking? There wasn't enough liquor on the entire island to give him a headache like this one. He disentangled his legs from the bedding and tried to stand.

"Light a lamp while I look at her," Harris said. His tongue felt thick and dry.

"I tried to. It won't catch." Through a fog of pain, he could hear panic in the girl's voice.

"And the fire?" It was their habit to let the fire die down at night, but there were always enough embers in the morning to start it up again in moments.

"I stirred it. There's almost no flankers. The rinds don't catch." Rosehannah was steadying him with her shoulder as he tried to stand.

"Get the door open. We need air in here." Harris was confused, but clearly there was some reason other than drink or illness why the whole household was suddenly ill.

"I can't open it. I think it's drifted over with snow." To allow a little more room in the small tilt, Harris had changed the leather hinges of the door so that it would open outward, an improvement that Rosehannah had tolerated with considerable reservation. It would seem that particular chicken had come home to roost. "What is happening, Mr. Harris?"

"I think we are smothering. We have to get out of here." Harris looked around the room for his axe, wondering if he could chop or pry their way out as Rosehannah had done when he was trapped in the smoke house. Rosehannah's mind must have been moving in the same direction, as she answered his unspoken thoughts.

"The walls are too substantial to break easily, and I don't think we can get out that way in time to save ourselves." She leaned him against the chimney, grabbed her father's old jacket, and pulled a stool over to the closet where the chickens lived.

"Forget about the birds, Rose. This is serious." Harris felt a surge of irritation increase the ache in his head.

"It's a way out," she answered, and lifting the bit of netting that usually kept the chickens enclosed, she laid the jacket over the dirty browse and tossed first the cock and then the hen out into a corner of the room. Sliding open the hatch at the back of the linney, she encountered a wall of snow. "Hand me the broom," she ordered Harris from the confinement of the coop. It was the work of a moment to push the wall of snow away and a sharp blast of cold, fresh air swept into the fuggy tilt. Backing temporarily out of the confined space, she rolled up the jacket, pushed it through the hole into the snow, and a moment later Harris saw her heels disappear through the hatch. Briefly, her small, pale face blocked out the patch of light. "I need rackets. They're up in the beams."

The cold air increased Harris's headache twofold, but he felt capable of thought again, and he quickly passed the snowshoes through the coop to Rosehannah before turning his attention to the two remaining girls. Mahala was whimpering pathetically in a pool of vomit in the big bed, so he lifted her and dumped her onto the blankets of his own cot. Missy lay, barely breathing, and did not respond to the sharp slaps he administered to her cheeks. He tried to lift her up but she was as least as big as he, and in his own weakened state, her dead weight defeated him. Taking her by the wrists, he dragged her onto the floor and towards the faint current of chilled air that came in through the chicken hatch. Exhausted, he allowed his knees to fold under him and fell back against the wall.

Harris was unsure how long it took for Rosehannah to return, but when she was again by his side, he was cold enough to appreciate the blanket she was tucking around him. Mahala was sitting with Missy's head in her lap, too sick to cry, and Harris could hear movement on the roof of the house.

A small avalanche of snow tumbled down into the fireplace, and the chill breeze picked up strength, clearing the stale, poisonous air out of the tilt. Selby's coarse voice came tunefully down the funnel at them:

I wish I had a few more bricks
To build my chimbley higher—
A cat got up on my old roof
And pissed down in the fire.

"Mr. Harris, how are my girls?" Mrs. Sevier's anxious head poked into the chicken coop from outside. Harris looked to Rosehannah for an answer.

"She's alive," Rosehannah whispered. "Thank God for that."

"They're fine, Mrs. Sevier," Harris called back, as convincingly as he could. "Right as rain, just a bit of a headache."

"The men are at the front, digging you out. The whole house is covered in a snowdrift except for a hollow at the back here." The light shone through the hole again for a moment as Mrs. Sevier consulted her husband, and then she continued, "I'm going to prepare hot food and bedding at our house. They will haul you all over by sledge as soon as they have freed the door." The light shone into the dim tilt once again and Harris allowed his head to slide back down onto the floor.

The unnatural warmth of the night had now dissipated and the three invalids lay shivering on the floor of the house. Rosehannah, who appeared to be unaffected by the near suffocation, did what she could to make them comfortable. The chickens, which had perched on the beams above them, defecated neatly onto Harris's foot but he was too tired and ill to object. He managed instead to laugh at his own bad luck and Rosehannah's discomfort at their choice of a target.

The next day, with nothing worse than residual headaches and a lot of dirty laundry to show for the experience, Harris was able to make some sense of what had happened. Apparently, the snow had begun early in the evening and in the space of the night there had been a fall of almost three feet onto the island. The wind had not been particularly strong. Usually, it swept snow away from the houses into the sea, but on this occasion, it had come from the main island, so most of the houses were drifted in. Their tilt had been particularly susceptible and, at some point in the night, the snow had entirely covered it, except for a small area in back where the chickens' linney caused it to eddy away.

Rosehannah had woken briefly during the night, feeling over-heated as the snow blocked up the usual drafts in the house, and had removed a small plug of moss from the wall near her head to allow a thin current of cold air to penetrate the stifling, enclosed bed she shared with the other two girls. This chink coincided with the hollow in the drift by the linney, and as a result she had a steady source of fresh air all night, and this saved them.

At the Seviers, the three afflicted were bedded down to sleep off their illness, while the men shoveled snow off the roofs of the tilts and created channels to draw off the water when the drifts began to melt. Mrs. Sevier washed the bedding as best she could, given the limitations of the winterhouse, and Rosehannah cooked rabbit soup and occasionally read aloud from *Ivanhoe* for the ben-efit of Mahala, who was the least affected of the three. Harris fell asleep to the incantations of the Saxon Ulrica burning to death on the turrets, and woke to the passage where Isaac of York dares to estimate the ransom that should be paid for the arrogant Prior.

Mrs. Sevier, too, listened to the story as she lay stroking the sleeping form of her elder daughter. When Isaac was told that he needed less money because he no longer had a child to provide for, she clucked her tongue indignantly, and when he lamented that the Christians know not how the child of his bosom is entwined with the strings of his heart—"O Rebecca! Laughter of my beloved Rachel! were each leaf on that tree a zecchin, and each zecchin mine own, all that mass of wealth would I give to know whether thou art alive"— she burst into tears and pulled Mahala to her bosom. Harris and Rosehannah returned to their tilt alone that evening, left to manage their own behaviour again, and the mem-bers of the Sevier family were reunited under one roof.

As they tramped the short distance between the tilts on their snowshoes, Harris gazed around in wonder at the transformed landscape. Huge, soft drifts of snow buried or disguised all the familiar shapes around them—the wood stack looked like a white Viking ship, the bushes had disappeared and the trees were reduced to mere shrubs. Only the steep cuts in the snow towards the doors and the windows of the tilts gave any indication that these new contours were temporary. The silence was profound.

Rosehannah, who had been leading the way, stopped and looked up into the dark sky and began to whistle softly. Harris followed her gaze upward, expecting nothing more than the usual glorious show of stars, and was startled to see a sheet of light, like a curtain, waver above their heads. The luminescent bars of green tipped with red appeared to dip and hesitate before swooping low and rising back again.

"It's the aurora," she explained, laughing softly. "Papa says they come when you whistle, but they are skittish, like my chickens." They stood and watched the lights flicker and pulse, and Harris pursed his lips to whistle but found he was afraid to. After some minutes, the lights faded and dimmed and the stars once again possessed the sky. "Do you know any of the constellations, Mr. Harris? I know only the dipper, and how to find the North Star from it." Rosehannah raised her arm and traced the outline of Ursa Major.

"I know a few," he admitted. 'There's Cassiopia—a big W— and Orion is there, towards the harbour. You can see the three stars of the belt just above the hill. In a little while, it will have risen and you will be able to make out the lower end of the hourglass. His bow is towards our right." Rosehannah studied the sky assiduously and then turned to him with a smile.

"I think I see the stars of the belt. I shall try to find it again tomorrow night, when it is higher. I wish I knew as much as you, but I don't suppose I ever will."

"You have practical knowledge, Rosehannah, more than I do. I know how to make navigational instruments, but not how to use them. If we were lost out on the ocean, your knowledge of the

North Star would be worth all my knowledge of metal-working and watchmaking, music and languages put together." She smiled at that and the reflection of the snow gave her small face a blue, ethereal look, like an exotic ghost. "Do you realize that you have saved my life three times now? Tomorrow I shall try to paint your likeness, and we shall see if I can do you justice."

"And we'll see if I can do justice to that pretty dress your head-less demon was wearing," Rosehannah replied with a laugh, and turning, she led the way down into their winterhouse.

Dear Brina,

This morning I went to the shul *for a* bar mitzvah. *We had to wait about fifteen minutes for a minyan to get started (no, they don't count me, but the community is so small that the presence of another warm body is appreciated) and in the course of conversation, a rather amusing story emerged. I cannot use it in my history but it will go very nicely in my "Book of Scandal," a manuscript that I enjoy planning but will never write.*

At the lunch after the bar mitzvah, I heard Harry casually telling someone that he was expecting a friend to visit from England at the end of the month. I hardly paid any attention until I noticed Shibby and Leah giggling and covering their mouths, and then the cat was out of the bag. I don't much like surprises, but in this case, I might have managed to put a good face on it. Better still is to know ahead of time, as I do now, that you are planning a visit. That way, I can do a little housekeeping before you arrive.

I hasten to assure you that it isn't my house that needs attention (I'm tidy enough for most people, I think) but the hen house needs scrubbing down. The hay accumulates to about a foot in depth during the winter, and then in spring, I dig it all out and deposit it as far from the house as I can haul it, but I put off scrubbing the perches and nesting boxes until the first clutch of eggs are hatched. This year, the hens went broody too soon, when it was still far too cold for babies, so I took the eggs away. Now, when I'd love to have a few little ones around to amuse you, they decline to reproduce.

Harry says you are attending some kind of gathering at Yale in honour of your late husband, a symposium and festschrift for what would have been his ninetieth birthday. I had no idea he was so much older than you. Your life must have been very constrained in his last years.

If you have the opportunity while you are in New Haven, look for a portrait of Rabbi Haim Carigal in the library, and if there is a postcard or reproduction of it, I would very much appreciate a copy. Carigal came to St. John's in November of 1773, after his ship was blown off course by a storm on the way from Rhode Island. A letter to his patron in Newport reads, in part:

We have arrived here after 49 days of travel, for the first ten days of which we had to endure very many torments and contrary winds so that we hardly believed to come out of it alive...I would have preferred to be cook in your kitchen if I had any inkling ahead of time about what would happen. I was ill for 30 days, I had a heavy fever, a kind of epidemic, and I could not get up. Even the chickens were affected by the epidemic, died and had to be thrown into the ocean, as they could not be eaten. As well, water became very scarce and how members of the crew almost died because of lack of water made me very sad. The Heavenly Majesty came to my aid in due time so that I can only be amazed at this miracle.

Let us hope your voyage is shorter and easier. I am finding it very hard to focus on my work this week—I will scrub the hen house instead. A three-day visit is not very long—we will have to stuff as many birds of both the domesticated and wild variety into it as possible.

Yours,
John

"Do not regard yourself as an evil person."
Rabbi Shimon, Ethics of the Fathers

*H*arris lay in the dark, too tired to get up and light the fire Eliol had laid for them, but too alert to sleep. Rosehannah had not had the advantage of a full day of napping, and she had tumbled quickly into her cold, lonely bed, wishing Missy and Mahala were there with her, but unaccustomed solitude had not prevented her from curling into a tight ball and plunging almost immediately into a deep sleep. Harris, however, was never far from melancholia and the chilly dark of the tilt after the dim warmth of the Seviers' cabin had tipped him into a state of pensive sadness.

He had never felt at home anywhere in his life, so he was not surprised that he felt like an outsider in this backward wilderness. Much was made in art and literature of the wandering Jew, the perennial outsider, doomed to homelessness and loneliness for the duration of his long, cheerless existence, but Harris had never seen much of that in real life. In Berlin, in London even, he had felt that all the other Jews around him were like ants in a colony, living together, working together, swarming on and over one another, thinking collectively. Only he was on the outside.

His uncle, who apparently had regarded him with genuine affection, he had insulted and rejected. He had resented his cousins for their legitimate place in the inner circle of familial devotion, and only realized their value when they were lost to him. His relationships with his teachers had been cautious, careful, distant. Only old Mrs. Hart had ever managed to pierce his armour to insert a small sliver of reciprocated love under his skin. And yet, here, on the rim of the world, his strangeness and aloneness seemed appropriate, normal. All this small group were of such disparate backgrounds that they had to be strangers to one another, yet they knew one another so well, were so aware of the unwritten rules that allowed them to function and live as a community, that being different and foreign was normal.

Rosehannah, who might have been little more than a scullery maid in Plymouth, was here a teacher, a bookkeeper, a seamstress, a hunter. Joe Ganny, who had one of the most interesting minds Harris had encountered among the Gentile populations of Germany or England and its colony, felt no compunction about sitting with her, Mahala's slate on his knees, learning his alphabet.

A was an archer who shot at a frog,
B was a butcher and had a great dog.

Harris knew the whole alphabet, all the way to "Z was a zany, a poor harmless fool," from hearing Eliol recite it back to his master, who was in turn teaching his servant and friend what he was being taught. So much of the old country had been trans-ferred here, holus bolus, yet there were curious possibilities here also: the chance to remake yourself, to define who you were and what you would become.

Harris lay sleepless on his cot long into the night, thinking of these and other things, until dawn came creeping in through the tiny window and he fell soundly asleep.

The fire was lit and the bread set to rise when he finally woke. The first thing he noticed was that Rosehannah had draped the canvas curtain from her own bed over the front of the chickens' hutch, to keep the rooster in the dark and silent. It was a small gesture, but a thoughtful one, and he was newly aware that he benefited from many such gestures each and every day.

He pulled his outside clothes on and was momentarily stopped when he went to open the door, which someone—Joe Ganny or one of the Sevier men—had re-hung to open inward. Here again was proof of the care that was taken to accommodate him, a small job done immediately and without comment. He stepped out into the grey morning and blinked hard as a large, fat flake of snow settled wetly on his eyelid. "Big snow, little snow," Rosehannah had told him, meaning that large flakes augured a sparse snowfall, while small flakes, like those of two days previous, warned of a heavy blanketing.

Harris literally had to climb out of the doorway of the house to reach the outside air: the whole tilt was under a drift of snow. He found his snowshoes standing upright in the bank at the top, their blue tassels twisting gaily in the light breeze. A firm path had already been beaten between the winterhouses, and he knew better by now than to step from the path without his rackets for fear of plunging up to his chest in the soft drifts. He studied the path for a moment, distinguishing the tracks made by Rosehannah's skinnyrackets from the pot-lids of the Sevier boys, and then made his way into the nearby copse of spruce and fir to relieve himself before skirting around the clearing to Joe Ganny's.

"Mr. Harris." Joe Ganny's ready smile welcomed him, as he let himself into the small hut. Ganny sat on the bed, surrounded by drifts of birch shavings almost as tall as the drifts of snow outside the door. "How is your head today? Still moithered?"

"I'm feeling much better, thank you, Mr. Ganny," Harris answered and made himself at home on the bench by the fire. Ganny continued his whittling but first tossed his tobacco pouch over to Harris, an indication that he was happy to converse while he worked. "What are you making?" Harris inquired as he carved a tiny shaving of tobacco into his pipe bowl, which was already packed and ready to light.

"Birch brooms," came the answer, with no suggestion that the question was a foolish one, although a quick glance at the pile of brooms stowed in the rafters should have made the inquiry unnecessary. "Birch is a lovely wood, so clean and straight. It's a pleasure to handle it."

"I don't know too much about wood," demurred Harris, puffing gently on his clay pipe, the stem of which had been reduced to a two-inch stub as a result of his careless treatment.

"You'll learn, Mr. Harris. It all takes time." Mr. Ganny continued skillfully drawing the long strips of birch back from the handle of the broom, bending them towards the head which Eliol would later sew into place. "Birch is useful for making anything that is going to be subjected to a lot of stress—the legs of tables, the backs of chairs, or bedposts and other furnishings. It's strong but flexible, which is why it makes such a fine broom." Ganny pulled his crook-knife effortlessly through the wood, producing long, narrow slivers which gleamed pale in the dim light.

"Is it really worth your while, though?" Harris looked at the dozens of brooms which were filling the top peak of the tiny house. "Surely you don't get more than a penny a piece for them."

"I usually give them away," admitted Mr. Ganny, "and what I get in goodwill is worth considerably more than a penny. I'm good at making them—have been doing it since I was a boy—and I enjoy it. Mrs. Ganny gives them to all her friends, and in return they always have some small thing for her, a pot of jam or dried deer meat, perhaps a skein of wool, if they have goats. It keeps me occupied when the snow is too deep to work in the woods." Ganny laid his broom aside long enough to hook the kettle over the fire.

"So your labour is useful in preserving friendships. You put a lot of work into that, I think. I'm astonished at how well everyone seems to get on here, even people I would have thought had nothing in common." Harris put a handful of shavings on the fire to speed the boiling process.

"But we have a great deal in common, Mr. Harris—want and need and necessity, poverty, bad luck and illness, isolation, ignorance and ambition. The list is endless, and somewhere in that list, you can surely find something to connect even an educated man such as yourself, who can read the scripture in its original, and an illiterate old fisherman like myself." The older man gave one of his odd, sweet smiles at this.

"Of all the people in this little settlement, Ganny, I think we are the most different, yet the most companionable," Harris admitted. "How is the reading coming along?"

"I wish my mind were as nimble as my fingers, Mr. Harris, but all things considered, I am not unhappy with my progress. I can write all my letters, read them out singly and in small groups, and the other day, I sounded out a verse I had never seen or heard before." At this, he stood and pushed aside the pile of shavings at his feet to reach into a dark corner and fetch out an earthenware jug with a wooden stopper. Harris took it, turned it towards the light from the fire, and read aloud:

Use me much and break me not
For I am but an earthen pot.
As we sit by the fire to keep ourselves warm,
This pot of good liquor will do us no harm.

"You see, Mr. Harris, it is easy for you, but it took me all evening to work out those words so they made sense."

"Where did the pot come from?" asked Harris. "I don't think I've seen it before." He shook it and determined it was empty, though the fumes from the neck when he uncorked it suggested it had been drained only recently.

"Oh, I believe Selby had it tucked away somewhere in the woods. Once it was empty, he thought I might like the writing, though he didn't know what it said. I was very pleased that I managed to puzzle it out."

"And you didn't mind that Selby was hiding things from you, though he's sharing your food and your roof?"

"It's his nature, I think, to satisfy his own appetites first. What was important was that he was willing to expose himself to our disapproval by admitting he had the liquor put away for his own use, rather than deprive me of the opportunity to read the verse on the jug, which he knew would mean far more to me than a drink." Ganny poured tea for himself and Harris, and settled back with his broom. "It would have been much easier for him just to smash the jug and leave it in the woods."

Harris picked up a piece of worked wood that lay near the fire and held it up for Joe Ganny's inspection. "Not your work, I think, Mr. Ganny."

"No, Mr. Harris. As you have no doubt guessed, Selby has been amusing himself in a less useful way than by making brooms." The carving, made from a forked branch of spruce, was an armless woman in bark underclothes. The creature wore high-heeled slippers, had lopsided knots for breasts, and the natural fold in the fork was obscenely realistic. "Missy saw it and was greatly amused. I expect those two are well matched in some ways, and only hope she can control his tendency to expropriate everything that isn't nailed down."

"Well, I doubt that Rosehannah would find this to her taste," said Harris with conviction, and tossed the figure on the fire.

"No, Miss Rose does not care for such amusements, but then her mother was a much more cultured woman than Mrs. Sevier, who is a fine woman, too, in her way, but cut from different cloth." Ganny finished the birch broom he was making and laid it aside with some satisfaction. "Shall we go and see what's happening down by the water, Mr. Harris? I've been hearing crows racketing all morning and it's time I stretched my legs." Ganny stood and reached for his coat.

"I believe every man, woman and child here must go and look at the water a dozen times a day, as if some message were expected momentarily. What exactly is it you are looking for?" Harris ducked through the doorway, climbed to the top of the snow bank and twisted his feet into the strings of his snowshoes with a satisfying ease. Ganny was immediately behind him, equally agile on the sticks and boards of his roughly hewn pot-lids, and waited until they had both settled into their strides before he answered.

"The sea is not like the woods, Mr. Harris. Both provide us with the things we need to live, but the sea is not as predictable, so you must always be on the look out."

They made their way over the snowbanks and along the edge of the clearing towards the water, stopping occasionally to admire the extraordinary change in the landscape that the unusual snowfall had achieved. The slight flurry of huge snowflakes that had descended that morning had given the contours an indistinct, hazy look, ethereal and unreal. Snow lay lightly on the branches of every tree and bush that still showed above the drifts, like feathers dropped from the sky.

"It's lovely, I have to admit," Harris noted with grudging admiration. "That birch there, it looks like a cherry tree in bloom."

"I wouldn't know about that," Ganny replied. "I've never seen a true cherry tree, that I know of. But it puts me in mind of a chuckley plum in spring, and I can't imagine a cherry could be any more delicate or beautiful."

Ganny strode easily alongside Harris, and the two men made their way down towards the shore. Overhead, a white-pated eagle winged its way towards them, a fish in its claws. Pursuing it was a raven, and high above both were two crows, tiny in comparison to the bigger birds. The men stopped to watch the pursuit, and Joe Ganny laughed with delight when the raven caused the eagle to drop his catch. The raven was on the fish in seconds, tearing away at the flesh almost before it had landed on the rocks. They both laughed when the two crows, joined by several others, managed to drive the raven away from the prize with barely a mouthful.

"That grebe is like our merchant," Ganny said. "Most of the time he gets to keep whatever he catches in his claws, but sometimes one gets away from him, and us crows get to eat."

"So where does the raven fit in?" asked Harris.

"Why, he's the dealer," came Ganny's prompt reply. "He's able to wrest an occasional fish away from the grebe. That's the trouble with Selby—he isn't satisfied with his share, but he hasn't enough weight or tenacity to get fish from the grebes of this world, or even from the ravens. Instead, he turns on his fellow crows and makes off with whatever he can. If Missy can't straighten him out, he's going to disappear over the side of a punt one dark day."

"So, do you think there's room in your world for someone like me? Or am I too much like Selby, concerned only with what I can get for myself?"

"A man must follow his nature, Mr. Harris, and I believe it's my nature to love everyone who will let me. It is your nature to love only those who are persistent enough to break through your natural reserve. There's a living to be made here, if it's handled the right way, but you have to stop fighting the place first."

Both men stood silently on the shore, looking out over the lazy swell of ocean below. The surface looked greasy and grey, like a congealing pot of beef broth, its half-frozen condition suppressing and modifying the usual lop and lift of waves. Sky and water were an unbroken, featureless drab blot, lacking even a horizon, so it was with surprise approaching fear that they saw a trap skiff come sailing silently towards them out of the snow-filled element.

July 6, 05

Brina, my dear,

What a perfectly wonderful time you had, "even if I sez it, that shouldn't." Such a narrow window of opportunity, and then the capelin struck just as your plane landed. I was worried that you would find going straight from the airport to Bay Bulls a bit more than you could cope with, and certainly hadn't intended to subject you to an additional side-trip to Middle Cove to see the scull, but it all worked out wonderfully.

The girls and I have since had a chance to look up the jellyfish that came in such numbers around the boat in Bay Bulls, and Leah and Shibby said to tell you that the ugly orange ones were lion's mane jellies, and the pale, beautiful ones were moon jellies. You mustn't mind that they both ignored the puffins—they have seen them many times before, but they had never seen such hoards of jellyfish. I thought you were going to throw yourself out of the boat and swim ashore when we finally got close to the islands. I have since had a talk with one of the bird biologists at the university and he thinks it is possible we might get you a permit to assist him in a banding operation if you come back again next spring before the chicks are hatched.

I apologize again for Culhoon's abominable behaviour. He can usually eat anything, but Essays on the Enlightenment in Eighteenth-Century Prussia *would defeat even the most iron-clad stomach. It's just unfortunate that he chose to return it to your luggage after attempting to digest it. If you stay with me instead of Harry next time you visit (and I'm sure you will want to come back, if only for the birds), you can avoid the hound entirely.*

Whether you can avoid the attentions of Leah and Shibby is another thing. I doubt I could fend them off for any length of time. I thought we were going to be closely chaperoned the entire duration of your visit. The birthday party that lured them away long enough for our trip to Cape St. Mary's was fortuitous. No, do not apologize for having spent four hours straight with your eyes glued to your binoculars—that is why I brought you there and why I brought a book and a substantial lunch for myself, although I confess, the smell of five million gallons of partially digested chowder going down the gullets of the young gannets would put a horse off his oats.

182

The combat boots were quite fetching. I was not entirely surprised to find you had served in the Israeli Defense Force, but I was impressed that you had actually fought in the Seven Day War. I won't ask if you were decorated— Tali always said everyone who fought in that war was a hero. Our young Arivim volunteers come here straight out of the army, usually, and what I want to know is how on earth they manage to break down an M-16 without chipping the polish on their two-inch nails—another one of Judith's Questions that Plague the Universe.

I'm sorry we didn't get out to Trinity, but the first week of July is a perfect time for birds and a perfectly dreadful time for tourists. We wouldn't have had a chance to talk to anyone useful and the drive is considerable, perhaps three or four hours.

There is a slight bit of progress on the Jacob Harris file, however. I had a call from a woman who is a home-care giver for an elderly lady in New Bonaventure, which is about half-way between Trinity and Ireland's Eye. Apparently this Mrs. Pitcher suffers from macular degeneration and is almost blind, so she has the home-care woman read to her, and they finally got around to reading my column in the Downhome *with the appeal for information about Ivanhoe in it. Mrs. Pitcher's parents were James and Rebecca Watton of Ireland's Eye, and they were married in Trinity on November 27th, 1917 by Rev. Stickings. After the ceremony, Stickings told them they had left Old Tilt but would return home to Ivanhoe, as the name of the community was to change at midnight that night.*

I tried to get Mrs. Pitcher herself on the line, but apparently she doesn't care for the telephone, a sentiment with which I'm in complete agreement, although I may have to give up that particular affectation in the immediate future. In any case, I intend to travel out to Trinity to talk to her. I think it will be a fruitful visit, even if it doesn't lead to any more Harris information.

Brina, do you think we might try talking on the telephone occasionally? I am a luddite, I know, and I want nothing to do with cellphones, blackberries, digital cameras, or any of those other expensive and time-wasting toys, but I would occasionally like to hear your voice. When I found out that Harry and Judith and the children had all spoken to you a mere twenty-four hours after you left Torbay Airport, I was positively green with jealousy. I realized that I don't even have your phone number.

I also realized that I have not been entirely forthcoming with you about my own history. Tali was not my first wife. I was married early, at twenty years of age, to a childhood sweetheart who died of sudden kidney failure while pregnant with our first child. The baby did not survive either. I was twenty-three years old at the time, teaching in a small community on the west coast, and I suffered what I suppose you would call a nervous breakdown in the months that followed. It was not simply depression but something far worse. I don't remember very much of what happened, except that my mother came and brought me home, and my brother supported us both until I was able to function again. I went back to university, got a master's degree, and then won a fellowship and went on to do my doctorate. I am an inquisitive person but I do not have a scholarly bent, so my pursuit of a Ph.D. was an odd choice. I think it was a way of avoiding going back into a classroom full of children.

My recovery took a very long time, and I think it was not until I married Tali, after eighteen years of being alone, that I truly felt balanced and certain of myself again. She was an extremely centered person, as was Harry even at a young age, and by watching and learning from them I became happy and contented once again. Only a very few old friends are aware of my first marriage, and how disastrously it ended; I do not share the information with anyone who does not need to have it.

There is a great deal of talk about closure in the popular media these days, but there was no closure in this matter for me, except to put it away into the deepest, darkest gloryhole I could find in my head and forget it as best I could. I believe this is the first time I have ever been able to tell anyone about it without feeling threatened with a tidal wave of emotions, even after forty-five years. Each April, at the Yom Hashoah service, one of our old Holocaust survivors recounts the story of his or her ordeal, and almost always they break down and weep as if it were yesterday and the loss fresh and raw. It reminded me so much of my own deep wound that I gave up trying to attend the service. Closure for me means close the door, don't think about it, don't talk about it, don't go there. Her name was Rose. We would have had a son. I wish I had told you sooner.

God bless,

John

"The begrudging eye, the evil impulse and hatred of one's fellow human beings will ruin a person's life."

Rabbi Yehoshua, Ethics of the Fathers

"He's not sleeping in here," whispered Rosehannah. She had barely glanced at the Yankee trader, but gave the small boy with him a thorough looking over before sitting him on a stool by the fire and handing him a large wedge of bread smeared with caribou fat. "He's crawling. He'll infest the lot of us. He shouldn't even be in the house." Harris appeared not to hear her, so she moved back to the fire and began banging pots, as if daring a louse or flea to jump across the room onto her. When the boy had finished the piece of bread, she poured him a pannikin of tea with a lethal dose of molasses in it—far more than she would ever have allowed even Mahala—and watched as he glutched it down.

"Well now, mister, you'll have sailed over from Random, no doubt." Joe Ganny's manner towards the trader was affable and relaxed, but the very fact that he had not deferred the opening gambit to Harris was a puzzle and Rosehannah avoided looking at Harris who seemed to be trying to make himself as inconspicuous as possible.

"I ran aground on the shoal near Grindstone Head," the stranger admitted bitterly. "We sailed into a snow squall and couldn't see a damned thing except that there was water under the keel and the next thing you know, we're grounded. When the tide came back up again, we tried winching her off and lost both our anchors. When the tide went down, we tried prying her off, and the bottom must have been rotted out of her because, the next thing I know, there's a bloody big hole in the side and the tide coming up again."

"That's a bit of bad luck," Ganny admitted. "You came up pretty early, though. The weather isn't very reliable at this time of year."

"Trying to get a jump start on the rest of them. I heard this was a good time to pick up a few furs, before the merchants gear up again." The trader looked as miserable as he sounded. "A couple of fellows from Flowers Cove came by and offered to lend me their skiff in exchange for a keg of brandy and some tobacco. Said I had to take the boy with me to keep an eye on their property. So I left my own two fellows to mind mine, which is sitting on the shore until I figure out what to do."

Rosehannah, who had been heating up the remains of a pot of seal meat, looked up sharply. "Did you have no clothes on board that trading vessel? No ready-mades? This boy is half naked." The dull-eyed child was leaning towards the pot and scratching the sores on his arms that showed through his rags. Rosehannah picked up a stick and inched him carefully back onto his stool. "Stay put and you'll get something to eat. If you move off that stool, you'll find yourself out the door."

"I suppose I could find him a shirt," conceded the trader. "Maybe you have an old coat or something you could let him have. He's really not my responsibility, you know." Rosehannah dished up a plate full of the steaming black meat and added another wedge of bread for the promised shirt. It made her itch just to look at the child. "So have any of you had any luck with the furs this winter?" The Yankee looked to Joe Ganny hopefully.

Ganny's answer, slow to come at the best of times, was ambushed by the arrival of Selby, Eliol and the Sevier boys, some mysterious instinct having informed them that there was entertainment in the vicinity. Rosehannah put more water to boil to add to the tea, and Harris busied himself with his stub of a pipe until the four newcomers had all found places to perch.

Once they were settled, Ganny veered back to the topic at hand. "There's not much in the way of furs about here, just rabbits and seals and such, and I assume you'd be wanting something a bit richer," he began, "but it wouldn't make no mind even if there was, because we're all signed up with Lester Garland, out of Trinity."

"You trading?" asked Selby, interrupting with interest. When he and the Seviers had heard from Eliol there was a skiff on the beach, they had assumed it was another fisherman like themselves. A trader was a different kettle of fish entirely.

"Most of my stuff is back at Grindstone Head, but I've got some things with me, tobacco and spirits, a few nice bits of frippery for the ladies." He glanced at Rosehannah, who was rummaging through a sea chest trying to find something to give the boy to wear, since she had every intention of getting him out of the tilt before his infested head nodded down towards any of her pillows and blankets. She was indifferent to the trader's enticement, but Selby was clearly hooked.

"We all have accounts with Mr. Garland's man, over in the harbour," Ganny reiterated.

"I don't," Selby declared. "Not now, I don't. What's more, I got two of the finest otter skins you'll find on this coast just sitting there, all cleaned and dried and ready to go." He was on his feet, and the trader quickly stuffed the last bite of bread into his mouth and made to duck through the door. "You wait here," he said to the boy, but the child was on his heels before he had finished speaking. Rosehannah handed the urchin a pair of her own darned stockings and a threadbare rectangle of cloth as he passed her and she let out a sigh of relief when the door closed behind him.

"C'mon, boys, let's see what he's got," declared Robert Sevier, and the three piled out of the tilt into the brightening afternoon, leaving Ganny, Harris and Rosehannah behind.

Rosehannah picked up the empty plates and tin cups, and glanced over at Harris. "What's this all about, Mr. Harris?" Joe Ganny said nothing but waited to see if Harris would enlighten them. There was a dark, growing anger in the man that disturbed them both. Abruptly, Harris headed for the door, and they both scrambled to follow him.

The trader's borrowed skiff sat in the water, tied by a long rope to a tree well back from the shoreline. The boy was perched in the bow. He was wearing Rosehannah's stockings on his hands, having turned them into mitts by the simple procedure of poking thumb holes through the thin fibers, and the square cloth was wrapped around his ears and tied beneath his chin. A cheap cotton shirt was pulled down over all, reaching his knees.

Selby had maneuvered his own punt between the shingle and the skiff and was bent eagerly towards the gunnel of the latter as the Yankee laid out items from his bundles for inspection. The otter furs gleamed in the weak afternoon light, and the trader casually pulled them from Selby's boat into his own, dropping them into the arms of the boy who promptly buried his face in the soft hair. The Seviers and Couttses stood in a clump on the shore, watching the deal with eager anticipation, while Rosehannah and Joe Ganny watched Harris.

It took only minutes for Selby to make his selection, and then he was so anxious to show off his purchases that he stepped out of the punt and waded to shore, oblivious of the water soaking through his boots.

"See here, Missy, a wedding present for ya." Missy almost danced her way to the water's edge.

"I have to get on before I lose the light," the trader shouted out. "Just untie that line for me, will you?" The bundles were retied and stowed safely under a sail even before Missy had looked to see the gifts her man had gotten for her. Thomas Sevier strode towards the tree and quickly untied the knots, but before he could cast the line towards the skiff, Harris had taken the rope from him and pulled the boat a little closer towards shore.

"Let's see what you've got there, Missy," Harris said quietly, still holding on to the rope, despite a shout of protest from the trader.

Selby triumphantly held up a tin kettle, divided into two separate compartments. "You can boil a partridge in one and your tea in the other, both at the same time." He proffered the utensil for inspection and admiration. Harris ran a finger quickly along the seam where the handle was attached to the band around the semi-circular pots, and turned to Missy, who was holding a cheap, shiny blouse stiff with resin up against her breast. Even from a distance, Rosehannah could see how shoddy the stitching was.

"Mind if I have a few words with him on your behalf, Selby?" Harris was uncharacteristically deferential, and Selby shrugged in surprised agreement. Looking towards the skiff, Harris tugged it a few feet closer to the shore. *"Shemen zich in dein veiten haldz!"* He spoke quietly, but his words caused the trader to freeze where he was. Harris gave another small, angry tug at the rope he was holding, almost taking the trader off his feet. The Yankee steadied himself on the gunnel of the boat and reached into his pocket.

Slowly he pulled out a string of a dozen brass buttons, which he tossed to Harris who caught them but did not release the rope. The hand dipped into the pocket again and a silver thimble cage and a small, engraved perfume bottle were added to the buttons. Missy, who had caught the gleam of silver in the light, was whooping with delight, and Harris reluctantly flung the rope out to the skiff, which the boy hastily pushed away from the shore. *"A chazer bleibt a chaser,"* he shouted after the retreating trader.

Missy snatched the trinkets from Harris's hand and, if he had not turned and abruptly headed back towards the tilt, he might have been the recipient of one of Missy's exuberant and rib-cracking hugs. "That was one dandy bit of trading, mister," she called at his back. "You'll be kep' on!"

By the time Joe Ganny and Rosehannah had reached the tilt, Harris had slipped from anger to black gloom. They found him sitting in a corner, playing a deeply melancholic tune on his whistle. Rosehannah waited until the tune wound down but, before she got a chance to speak, the hen, which had been huddled in the back of the coop all afternoon, gave a bawk and flew out onto the floor, looking for water. Rosehannah poured an inch from the water jug into a bowl and laid it on the floor well away from Harris. The afternoon was fading into evening and all three sat quietly, watching the hen dip her beak and lift her head to allow the water to run down her thirsty throat.

"I have a riddle for you, Mr. Ganny," Rosehannah said quietly. "See if you can guess it:

In marble walls as white as milk,
Lined with a skin as soft as silk,
Within a fountain crystal clear,

A golden apple doth appear.
No doors are there to this stronghold,
Yet thieves break in to steal the gold."

Rosehannah glanced over towards the coop.

"You won't find the answer in there quite yet, Miss Rose,"
Ganny answered with a smile. "But I'll wager you a new laid egg
you will before many more days go by. Now, see if you can guess
my riddle:

Four legs up as cold as stone
Two legs down flesh and bone,
The head of the living in the mouth of the dead,
Tell me the riddle or I'll send you to bed."

"Four legs up," mused Rosehannah. "A table on its back? A
chair being carried into the next room?" Harris once again
began to doodle on his whistle, while the older man and the girl
quietly dismantled the riddle, the murmur of their voices slowly
dissipating the low spirits that had seized Harris after the cheating trader's visit. Rosehannah, with a lot of help from Joe Ganny,
had worked out the answer (a man carrying a bark pot on his
head) and they were all three sitting contentedly in the duckish
light of evening when Selby quietly made his way into the tilt.

"The others are on their way over, Rosie, hoping you'll finish
off your book. I just wanted to tell the mister thank you. A man
got a right not to be made a fool of in front of his wife."

"Your business is fishing, Selby, the mister's business is trading. That's why Mr. Garland hired him." Rosehannah's comment
seemed to cheer the fisherman up, and he was puffed back to his
usual self-contented size by the time the Seviers and the Couttses
had made their way into the tilt.

Mrs. Coutts, usually so silent that Harris had actually wondered if she was mute, spoke for the group this night. "We
thought that, as Collar Day is coming on soon, you might want to
finish up the story."

July 23, 05

Dear Brina,

My hens and I have been under hawk attack all afternoon, but fortunately have all come though it unscathed. A Northern Goshawk turned up at about four o'clock and pursued my poor birds through the trees and bushes for several hours. My little bantam cock was wonderfully brave and deserves a medal. When the hawk would get in among the branches of the spruce after a hen, little Maccabee would go on the attack just long enough to confuse it, all the time letting out the most blood-curdling screams to alert me that I was needed. Three times I came within a foot or two of the hawk, and believe me, I did a bit of screaming of my own, not to mention stone-throwing, arm-waving and cursing.

Just at sunset, long after they would normally have been indoors and on the roost, the first of the hens began to bawl out for the cock, who zigzagged over to her, and accompanied her back to the hen house. When I saw him go for the second one, I realized he was going to have to do it for all nine hens, so I took over. It was really quite remarkable—each hen, in turn, set up a racket to get my attention, and then when I reached its side, it lit out for home close in next to my legs, exactly as the first two had for Maccabee.

I got a good look at the hawk with the binoculars, and wished you were here, as I believe you would have appreciated it much more than I did. I just wanted it to go away. I think it was immature, judging by the colouring, but it was really quite big, all of twenty-four inches in length, I'd say. I think I will keep the hens in their pen for the next few days. I have stretched a capelin net over the top, which should help.

I have been to New Bonaventure to visit Mrs. Pitcher. She's an interesting old girl, alternately pious and wicked, all genteel nicety one moment and vulgar and funny the next. Her parents came from Ireland's Eye, but she grew up in Kearley's Harbour, which is now abandoned also.

She told me an interesting story about how the Ivanys came to settle in Ivanhoe. Apparently, John Ivany, who is generally acknowledged as Ivanhoe's first resident, came from Skimmer Cove, but he was an unruly individual and, in retaliation for some particularly dangerous bit of misbehaviour, he was tied to the bottom of a punt and let adrift down Smith Sound, coming ashore on the west end of Ireland's Eye. This would have been in the late 1860s. He settled there, and called it Old Tilt because of the remains of a winterhouse he found on the shore. It eventually came to be called Ivany's Hole, a hole being a small cove or a collapsed sea cave (there is a Drummers Hole near Beachy Cove. Hibb's Hole has recently been gentrified to Hibb's Cove). From Ivany's Hole, I suppose, Rev. Stickings got the idea for the somewhat more polite "Ivanhoe," but when I suggested that to Mrs. Pitcher, she got quite cute with me and said only "P'raps he did, p'raps he didn't."

I have the distinct impression that Mrs. Pitcher is holding out on me, and I'm not sure why. She made it quite clear that she expected me to come back and visit her again, and said she might have some things to show me, a marriage certificate and a few other bits and pieces. I suppose this would be her parents' marriage certificate from 1917. She also suggested that, since I write for the Downhome, I can get her a free subscription so she won't have to wait to get her home-care worker's copy.

I'd probably make more progress if I were to spend my time reading microfilm at the Centre for Newfoundland Studies, but this is more fun. On the way out to Trinity Bight, I spent an evening with a friend, who is a fisheries inspector at Hickman's Harbour, and, on the way back, I stayed over with a friend who has a painting studio in Champney's East, so it was a grand excursion.

I will let Mrs. Pitcher simmer for a few weeks before I attempt to contact her again. She's not the only one who can play hard-to-get.

I very much appreciated your kind words about Rose. I suppose she is the reason I was overly cautious about asking about your own marriage. I confess, I was startled to realize how very eminent and how extremely elderly your husband had been, and I didn't wish to seem gratuitously curious or prying. However, I understand now why you chose to withdraw into the world of study and teaching—no war is good, but yours seems to have been particularly painful.

The girls send their love, and that dirty smudge at the bottom of the page is a nose-print from Culhoon, who has managed to chew the corners off every other piece of blank paper in the house, making it impossible for them to go through the printer. I shall soon be reduced to sending you letters written on birch bark or cedar shingles.

Love,
John

"Morning sleep, midday wine, children's prattle, loafing in the meeting places of the vulgar—all these things will ruin a person's life."
Rabbi Dosa ben Harcinas, Ethics of the Fathers

pring, when it finally came, crept in like a fog, so slowly and inexorably that Harris barely noticed it until it was all around him. The snow gently settled and the surface took on a stippled, sugary appearance, like a badly made meringue. Harris found that the surface of the path between the winterhouses, which had been hard-packed and reliable, occasionally gave way under the pressure of his feet, bringing him to a jolting halt a few inches lower than he expected to be.

The insects, which were to be found winter and summer around any rotten log or under any damp rock, seemed suddenly to have multiplied and could be seen crawling up the legs of the chairs, tumbling from the walls of the tilt, congregating in corners and even making their way into boots and trousers while their legitimate occupants slept. These creatures, so inoffensive that even Harris was not repulsed by them and watched with interest when the two little Coutts boys rolled them on their backs to see the gymnastics required to right themselves, began to appear somewhat sinister due to their sheer number. As their population increased, Harris developed an aversion for all things that had more than two legs, and looked forward to the day these interlopers would abandon the house for the greater opportunities afforded outdoors.

One noon day, he returned from a game of chess with Joe Ganny to find Rosehannah, Mahala Sevier and Mrs. Coutts sitting quietly at the table, eyes focused on the dark opening of the cupboard-like chicken roost. Rosehannah raised a finger to her lips as he opened the door, and though he shut it as quietly as possible, the slight movement elicited a long series of protesting noises from the nerve-wracked hen huddled at the back of the hutch. He drank the tea he was served in silence, noting with amused superiority the tension in the faces of the three females in the hen's vicinity, but was almost as relieved as they were when the bird finally produced an egg. The egg was admired all round, and more tea was drunk in its honour, before the small ovoid package was put away in a safe place, hopefully to be joined by several others before being shared out among the younger members of the winterhouses on Easter Sunday.

Although the sudden, quick melt the livyers anticipated had mercifully not happened, the mossy chinching between the studs of the tilt was soon saturated and the repeated *drip drip* of water lulled them to sleep at night and often drove them from their soggy bedding in the morning. The long silence of the depth of winter was broken more often now by the cries of crows and sea-gulls, the trickle of the nearby creek, the occasional muffled crash of waves from the nearby ocean, and the cockcrow of the little bantam rooster, who greeted each hour as if it were sunrise.

Rosehannah spent most of her time trying to stem the leaks in the roof and walls of the tilt, and the rest drying their sodden clothes and bedding. Harris, in response to pleading from a visi-bly distressed Eliol, spent most of his mornings visiting Joe Ganny, who was suffering from rheumatism in his feet such that he was almost unable to walk until Harris prescribed footbaths made with shavings of tobacco from his own meager supply. The two men smoked thin strips of withrod bark that Rosehannah had put by for just such an eventuality, and diverted themselves with longer and more complex games of chess.

Early one rare sunny morning, Rosehannah found the mister reclining on a layer of spruce branches on top of a large boulder, pulling on his pipe stump just enough to keep a faint ribbon of smoke twisting up into the steaming air. "You look like you were born and bred here, Mr. Harris, laid out in the sun like a fish on a flake. I suppose you thought winter was never going to end." Harris smiled, and tipped the old sealskin hat he was wearing over one eye.

"I was sure it wasn't." He hunched down into his overcoat and tucked his fingers back into his armpits.

"They say the sun increases by half a cock's step from St. Bridget's Day on, and judging by our own little fellow, he's in full stride by now," Rosehannah continued companionably. "But don't be disappointed if we get another round of snow. 'Sheila's Brush,' the Irish call it. Papa said he had known it to snow in June, though that was before I was born."

"So this good weather is just *a lek un a shmek?* What you call 'a lick and a promise'?"

"Maybe, maybe not. I don't think there's any such thing as good weather or bad weather, just weather. Mr. Ganny would say this is a *civil* day."

"Well, I'm all for civility, despite my rustic appearance. And I think this is a very civil time for a nap, so if you can think of a way to keep that cock from crowing for the next half hour, I would be most appreciative." And propping his pipe stem in a convenient hollow of rock, Harris tipped his cap over his other eye and lay back on his spruce-bough bed. The huge sweep of rock seemed to hold the sun in a way that was particularly comforting and invit- ing. After several minutes, and without removing his cap from his eyes, he added, "You haven't gone away."

"No, Mr. Harris, I haven't." Rosehannah's voice reflected more satisfaction than sorrow.

"And why have you decided I am not to have a very civil nap on this very civil morning?" Harris enquired from under the cap.

"You did say, sir, that I was to tell you if anything of a civil nature was wanted or needed to be done, and that you would oblige in the most civil way once you were informed."

"And what could be wanted or needed, Miss Rosehannah, that cannot wait a civil half hour on this very civil day," asked Harris, unfolding one arm and raising one finger to his forehead, where it pushed back his cap from his forehead by about one inch, revealing one eye with one drooping lid.

"A floor is wanted, Mr. Harris. Have you been in the Seviers' tilt in the last week?"

"I have not," he responded with mock weariness, and sat up as if he had not slept in a year. In anticipation of his marriage, Selby had more or less taken up residence with his future wife's family, giving Harris clear access to the much pleasanter company of Joe

Ganny. The mister had subsequently avoided the teeming chaos of the Sevier tilt.

"It is full of water. In fact, it bears a distinct resemblance to Round Harbour as we speak. They are planning to planch it this morning, which means they must empty it out of all furniture, clothing and gear, dig six or eight inches of mud from the floor to allow for the loss of head room, and then butt the squared logs in before nightfall. If they fail to complete the job, we will have Selby and Missy in with us tonight and, from what I hear, there is not much sleeping being done in the Seviers' tilt these nights." Rosehannah waited calmly for his response, which came with a sigh of resignation.

"And what contribution to this Herculean effort is required from us, might I ask?" Harris unfolded himself from the warm rock, as if he were being forcibly ejected from a feather bed.

"Dinner at noon for ten, supper for ten at nightfall, with tea and lunches in between, and perhaps a hand getting the logs into place. I can do the meals or the logs, whichever you prefer." Rosehannah patiently awaited capitulation, which came almost immediately.

"Very well. Since you put it that way, I suppose I can allow you to have the easier job indoors. But I was just getting used to a life of leisure and was thinking we might simply stay in winter quarters all summer." Harris stretched in anticipation of a long day of work and suddenly noticed on Rosehannah's face a wry smile such as he had seen in his own mirror more than once. "The idea amuses you, Rosehannah?"

"Yes, Mr. Harris, it does. As one is amused by the outrageous wishes of a two-year-old who wants you to pluck the moon from the night sky. I shall fetch you your heavy gloves and Papa's old jacket." She turned and headed towards their tilt, tossing over her shoulder the old phrase, "Out dogs and in dieters!" in a remarkably cheerful voice.

"You're enjoying this in anticipation, aren't you Rosehannah? Admit it. You like working hard."

"You are right, Mr. Harris. And the only thing I enjoy more is watching you work even harder." She laughed and stepped lightly along the path that was now showing small patches of earth in anticipation of the new season. Harris shook his head at the realization that she thought she was getting off lightly by being asked to produce enough food to feed a small army, with nothing more than a crook and a bake-pot to assist her. His aunt would have fainted at such a request, and even the redoubtable Mrs. Hart would have required the services of at least two servants before tackling such a chore.

By the time he got to the Seviers' tilt, about half their belongings were in the open air, balanced on a makeshift foundation of longers and spruce boughs. The rest were being passed in bundles from the open door, and as the mountain grew, Harris marveled at the pile of material that had accumulated over the winter. Besides the clothes, cooking pots and bedding, there were half-knit nets, spoons and brooms and other small wooden items that had been carved by the men in the dim light of the evening fire, old dresses being turned into aprons, worn aprons being embroidered to serve as handkerchiefs, a small collection of toys and amusements than had been fashioned and given to Mahala at various times by the adults—toys which served to amuse the maker as much as the recipient—a variety of odds and ends including sea shells, variegated burls of wood, seed pods and cones, dried rabbit skins, and other mysterious, nameless bits of nature that had caught the eye of one of the seven inhabitants of the tilt.

The job of butting in the logs was not quite as simple as Harris had expected, in part because the slurry of mud that constituted the cabin floor not only had to be dug out into buckets, but transported back onto the hillside to an area marked out for a garden. The frost in the ground was the least of the planchers' problems—the rocks that had to be dug up and worried out through the narrow door were infinitely troublesome. The need to maneuver inside the cramped tilt made a difficult job even harder, and after having his eye blacked by Robert Sevier's elbow, Selby employed some fine, old Anglo-Saxon expressions. Mr. Ganny envied Harris, who could take refuge in language that expressed his frustration but, being foreign, offended no one.

Dinner was taken out-of-doors, as the weather was still fine and the men were well heated by their exertions, and as the day wore on, a large lunch was snatched from the hands of Missy and Mahala whenever the recipients were able to stop to catch their breaths. By dark, the floor was in and the contents of the tilt, with the exception of the bedding, was piled in a heap at one end to await sorting and stowing in the morning. The women and children had been fed by this time, and the men all piled into what they insisted on calling Harris's tilt for a late-night supper.

Once their hunger was satisfied, Rosehannah discreetly fetched out the jug containing the last of the fortified wine, taking care to begin pouring it out as far away from Selby as possible so that when it came to his turn, there was just enough left to fill his pannikin by about two-fingers' depth.

August 18, 05

Dear Brina,

Curiouser and curiouser. As I told you on the phone, Mrs. Pitcher had a veritable treasure trove of artifacts from Ivanhoe, and I have since been able to negotiate their purchase. She was so mysterious and canny about the whole thing that I was initially convinced she didn't actually own the stuff, but as far as I can determine, she came by it honestly and has every right to sell it. The cost isn't great, as the candlesticks are the only really saleable items in the box, but the provenance of the items makes the whole collection interesting.

I have called in every favour I'm owed on this. I got a written assessment of value from the man who writes the furniture and collectables column for the magazine ($360, which was less than Mrs. Pitcher hoped for, but more than she deserved), and several other people are helping me stabilize the other items, as they have been rotting in a barn for the best part of a century and are ready to fall apart in my hands.

For the record, here is a list of what Mrs. Pitcher sold me:

1) A pair of hand-carved wooden candlesticks, 350 mm high, Jacobean in design, with brass finials apparently adapted from a couple of drawer knobs by someone with training in metalwork.

2) A handwritten marriage certificate for one Jacob Harris of London and Rosehannah Quint, 1820, copy enclosed.

3) A document, apparently in German, copy enclosed.

4) A small canvas, perhaps 150 x 200 cm., evidently a portrait of some kind, impossible to copy until the material has been "relaxed" and unrolled.

5) A collar from a woman's dress, brocade.

6) A first edition of Ivanhoe, *crudely bound in the same brocade as the collar.*

The marriage certificate and the German document are very damaged and the copies I've included here are not good, but I have given the originals to my neighbour, Mrs. Brown, who looks after my hens for me when I am away, and she is going to see if she can do better. She works at a local copy shop and, by resetting the scanners, she may be able to bring out the lettering so that it is possible to read them more easily.

The marriage certificate is not as bad (perhaps not as old) as the other paper. As best I can read it, it says "This is to certify that Jacob Harris, late of the city of London, now of Trinity Bay NewfLand (sic) and Rosehannah Quint of Ireland's Eye, Trinity Bay, Newfoundland, were married on the twenty first day of October, 1820 no [regular?] minister of the Church of England living within the limits of fifty miles and, the said Jacob Harris being the representative of Lester Garland and Co., the ceremony was witnessed by us, Capt. William Ryder, of the schooner William and Mary and X (Nicholas Quint, his mark)."

I will photograph the collar and book, and the painting also if I can open it out without damaging it further. As to whether this Jacob Harris is your man, I have no doubt, but neither do I have evidence to prove it.

Later:

I am sending on Mrs. Brown's best attempt to copy the Ivanhoe documents. The painting is slowly opening up, and it is a head and shoulders portrait of a young girl. The dealer I had look at it (the chazzan from the synagogue) says it is a fairly crude painting, not without charm but the work of an amateur. The surface paint is lifting in places and Ernie says he thinks there is another picture underneath, possibly another portrait or an earlier version of the one we can see. He is of the opinion that if it were a family picture, it would be something to cherish, but as it is an anonymous portrait of questionable provenance, and damaged at that, it is not worth having restored.

The threads of the dress collar have rotted and it came apart in my hands as I was positioning it to be photographed. Slipped in between the brocade and the lining was a bit of onion-skin paper, on which was written (I'm fairly certain I am reading it correctly) "My father has married me off to a mad old man. I want to die." I am not a superstitious or sensitive type, but when I read that, I felt like someone had just walked on my grave.

I am going to go back out to see Mrs. Pitcher again. All she said was that she had inherited the box of things, and she believed they came from Ivanhoe, but I don't think she has told me all she knows. When I tried to question her further, she pretended not to be able to hear me. That is nonsense—she may be blind, but her hearing is as good as mine. I wish you could come with me. I have a feeling that your English accent and *your Israeli interrogation techniques would get us a lot further than the meandering open-ended questions I employ to elicit folk narratives.*

My history of the Newfoundland Jews is lurching along. It will not be the best book I ever wrote, but it begins to look like something that a local publisher might take on and that is the best I hope for now. I am entirely fed up with it. Perhaps I am projecting, but I suspect your book on the Salon Women of Berlin is equally burdensome. I can barely remember my retirement year, as that was when Tali was first diagnosed with cancer. Before the bad news came, however, I was straining at the bit, longing to be free of students and office hours and committee meetings and the interminable, loathsome, endless marking. I can imagine only too well how you are feeling.

You wrote last week about selling your flat in London and finding a place somewhere quieter. I couldn't live in St. John's, never mind London, but for someone like you who is used to city life, this is a very dramatic decision. The country isn't for everyone. Perhaps you should begin with a compromise—rent your flat out and try living in a small town or village for a year. If it works for you, then you might make it a permanent move. I am the last person in the world to discourage someone from seeking out the peace of the countryside, but this would be a very drastic change in your lifestyle and perhaps it might not suit.

I don't mean to sound discouraging. It is rather that I want it to work for you more than you can guess, and am concerned that my enthusiasm for the kind of life I have here should not lead you to do something you might regret. Take care of yourself. I will phone on Sunday afternoon, but if you are out and about, don't worry about getting home in time to take the call. I can leave a message, and I will send this letter by expedited mail so that you will receive it before the weekend.

All my best,
John

"Love work, hate positions of dominance, do not make yourself known to the authorities."

Shemayah, Ethics of the Fathers

"I have been thinking…" Rosehannah began, in a voice that sounded as if it hadn't been used in a long time.

Harris looked up from the bit of wood he was wrestling into shape. "Thinking is a dangerous occupation. I forbid it." He held the wood carving up to the light of the small window and grimaced at it in dissatisfaction. "Every time you start thinking, I end up working, and playing with this bit of spruce is so difficult that I don't dare imagine how hard work might be."

"Would you object to work if it was mostly play?" The idle hesitation had gone out of Rosehannah's voice, and Harris groaned in anticipation of what chore she might have in mind for him.

"Your idea of work and play is so skewed that I hardly dare use either word around you. You find amusement in the most brutal labour and, consequently, rename it play, and when it really is supposed to be play, you attack it with such ferocity that it is worse than work." He gingerly touched the bruised side of his cheek and recalled the snowball fight she had organized with the children two days previous, in which a particularly icy sphere—launched by none other than Rosehannah herself—had caught him squarely in the face.

"The snow is gone from the Nob, and there is an excellent patch of partridgeberries that I didn't get around to picking in the autumn just the other side of the slope. I thought we might have a walk, and perhaps go over to the house if the path is passable, to check up on the roof. There are often new leaks at this time of year and…"

"And you will have me up on a ladder, doing something about them, before we have drawn breath from wading through soggy snow banks up to our waists. If you insist upon thinking, then think again, young miss."

Harris stuck his knife into a beam in the ceiling and hunkered down into his bunk to contemplate the doodle-addle he was working on. Rosehannah said nothing but moved quietly about the room, humming softly under her breath.

"Stop thinking, I told you," Harris ordered. "Have you never heard of leisure?"

"I have stopped," answered Rosehannah mildly. "Before, I was thinking about picking berries and walking over to the harbour, and now I've stopped thinking about it and I'm getting ready to go."

"And who is going to make my dinner, if you are off picking berries?"

"I've made your dinner. It's right here in my bag, wrapped up in a bit of oiled cloth. I shall need the cloth for the berries, as they will be soft from the frost, so I hope you have a good appetite by dinner time." Rosehannah pulled Harris's skinny-whoppers down from their hook and checked them for holes before tossing them onto his bunk. "Which would you prefer to carry, the hatchet or the teakettle? The kettle is lighter but it bumps a good deal more. Perhaps you'd better wear Papa's old jacket, in case there are any chores to do at the house."

Harris groaned in defeat, pulled himself to his feet, and allowed Rosehannah to help him into his outdoor clothes. "It's going to be soaking wet, you know. We're going to be like a couple of drowned dogs by the time we get up there."

"Come, Mr. Harris, it's a lovely soft day out. A little water never hurt anyone."

"We're not made of sugar, Mama used to say," they both chorused at the same time, Rosehannah cheerfully and Harris with bitter mockery.

"Very good, Mr. Harris. You're learning," Rosehannah added with a smile, and had the two of them bundled up, burdened down with bags and bottles, and out in the weak spring sunshine before Harris could think up a suitable retort.

"It really is spring," Harris grudgingly admitted as they climbed the melting path up from the cove. "I suppose we should be thinking of moving back soon after all."

"I believe the schooner won't be here for another few weeks, but it would be nice to be squared away and ready for them, don't you think?" The tin kettle bounced gaily at Rosehannah's hip, and Harris couldn't help but notice that, although she had thinned out even more over the winter, her shape was taking on a pleasingly curved contour. "The mice will have been at everything and I want to gut it all out before the new supplies come. Do you think Mr. Garland will want you to stay on here now that you've shown you can manage so well in the woods?" There was a slight tightening of her voice as she posed that last question, though her face registered no anxiety.

"I've no idea," Harris answered abruptly, preoccupied as he was with negotiating the icy path.

"Here, ashes from the fire. It will get us over this bad spot." Rosehannah handed him a tin she had tucked inside her voluminous shawl, and he twisted it open and sprinkled the grit ahead of them. They made their way up the slippery path and pressed on toward the top of the hill where they collapsed, breathless and only moderately damp, onto the rounded granite of the Nob.

"I feel as if I've never seen the country from here before, yet I know logically I have." Harris smiled, and twisted around to look towards Rosehannah, who was lying flat on her back on the bare slab of rock. "It's not fair. I've spent the last twenty-four hours getting good and grouchy, and now it's gone. Utterly dissipated. I'd no idea fresh air and a fine view could be such a moderating force." He leaned back on his elbows, gazing around in the direction of Smith Sound and The Thoroughfare.

"Do you want to stay, Mr. Harris?"

"You should call me Jacob. My name is Jacob."

"But I like to call you Mr. Harris." He could hear the amusement in Rosehannah's voice.

"I know you do, which is why I want you to call me Jacob." His own voice smacked of satisfaction. He had been preternaturally aware for some time that she had a way of twisting the word "mister" so that it carried a range of emotion, from respect to out-and-out insult. It was going to amuse him to see if she could make his first name an instrument of such scope.

"As you wish. Do you want to stay, Jacob?"

His ear could detect not the least twinge of irony or mockery in her voice, so he inwardly declared a temporary truce. "I believe I do, Rosehannah. I have nowhere to go, nowhere that I would be welcome at any rate, and I have been curiously content here these past months. I almost said happy, and perhaps I should have." His voice shook slightly, and the girl sat up slowly, turning to face him. "Is this what it means to be happy, Rosie? It feels somewhat painful, I think."

"I suspect you are a little out of practice, Jacob. It will come a bit more easily with time." She lowered her eyes, as if to allow him the momentary privacy this unexpected surge of emotion required, and when she looked up again, her eyes gleamed with a wicked mockery. "Of course, it could just be that you refused your breakfast and it's past your dinner time. In which case, I pre-scribe an immediate alleviation of hunger through the applica-tion of bread and meat, taken internally."

"You've been reading too much of the *Waverley* author," Harris said, but his mouth had begun to salivate at the words "bread and meat" and a loud, angry rumble from his stomach startled them both into laughter. Rosehannah spread her shawl over the rock between them and dumped the contents of her bag onto it.

"Quickly, before it wakes up the rest of the zoo," she urged, pushing the half loaf of bread towards him.

"Rosehannah, it's a good thing you are such a practical soul. That growl would have earned me a blow from most of the women I've known in my life."

Rosehannah reached towards him and lightly touched the bruise on his cheek with one finger. "I believe I delivered my blow already, Jacob. And I apologize for it. It wasn't that I meant to hurt you, but sometimes I just get so wound up, and so…con-fused, I suppose." She gathered her skirts and stood. "I'm going to get some berries to put in with the meat—I'm longing for something fresh in my mouth."

Harris turned and looked after her as she headed for the harbour side of the Nob, not a little confused himself at that moment. He could feel the tiny warm spot on his cheek where she had touched him, and wondered what it would have felt like if she had laid her whole hand along his face. The idea was unthinkable, yet here he was, thinking it all the same. He had just taken his knife from its sheath when he heard Rosehannah give a sharp yelp of surprise and then call out to him. He was at her side in seconds, knife in hand, ready to slay a mountain lion or black bear or whatever monstrous animal had surprised her.

"Good heavens, Mr. Harris. I believe I now know what Robinson Crusoe felt like when he saw that footprint." Rosehannah's voice was slightly shaky, and if Harris had tried to speak, his own might have exhibited a similar quaver. They both looked down towards what they had expected to be an empty harbour, only to see a large schooner secured at the wharf. A line of smoke was making its way up into the air from the galley, and even as they stood in silence, a figure came on deck and emptied a bucket of slops over the side. "I suppose we had better go down and see what's what."

Neither of them moved, however, and they stood silently for several minutes. Finally, Harris cleared his throat. "Is that one of Garland's ships, Rosehannah?"

"Yes, Mr. Harris, I believe it is." Her chin dropped for a moment and then she lifted it as if facing a very chilly wind. "It's too early for delivering supplies. They've come for you, Jacob."

Dear Brina,

Are you saying that Harris's first wife divorced him because his letter became worthless? I've never heard of a Schutzbrief before, and can't find anything about it in our library, although the Encyclopedia Judaica does have some general discussion of the community in Berlin around 1800. If I understand you correctly, Jacob Harris had inherited a letter of protection outlining the terms of his permission to live legally in Berlin, and this Schutzbrief had considerable value but could not be transferred except to his eldest son, if he had one. The Encyclopedia refers to a royal edict of 1750, which extended residency rights, and says it remained in force until 1812, but you're suggesting is wasn't the rights but the restrictions on those rights which were rescinded at that time.

Either way, it would seem that Jacob's Schutzbrief became worthless as soon as there was a tightening or a loosening of the residence rights. If they were tightened, he and his wife would have lost their right to live in Berlin, in which case his usefulness would have ended, and if they were loosened, any or all of the letter's value as a bargaining chip in an arranged marriage would have disappeared. In either case, she would have pressed for a divorce. I've forgotten how old we decided he was when he arrived in Ireland's Eye in 1820. Twenty-eight or so? He would have been barely out of his teens when his letter became worthless and his wife dumped him.

I see an ironic parallel here. Did you know that residency in Newfoundland was initially banned and later restricted during the colonial period? The anti-settlement laws were more often than not simply ignored, but they certainly drove some of our ancestors to withdraw into the most remote, hidden coves and inlets they could find, for fear of British gunboats shelling their homes into oblivion. When the laws loosened up, Catholics were still forbidden to settle (they didn't mention Jews, probably because they didn't think of it), and when it finally became economically necessary to allow us to come out to the colony, to act as servants to the English, only one Catholic was allowed to reside in each Church of England house, and we were not allowed to have houses of our own.

J.R. Smallwood, the politician who brought Newfoundland into Confederation with Canada, considered himself and Newfoundlanders in *general to have a great deal in common with the Jews—persecuted, dispersed, stubborn and stiff-necked. During the twenties, when he was working as a journalist in New York, he courted a Jewish girl and even learned a little Yiddish in an attempt to pass as Jewish with her parents. When he finally met them, he was for the first and second-last time in his life struck dumb, which was the end of that particular romance.*

But he had a point about Newfoundlanders as the wandering Jews of North America. For one thing, we are a dispersed people—there were more of us in Boston and New York at one point than there were at home, more now in Fort McMurray and Toronto probably. We are alternately self-deprecating and convinced of our own natural superiority, we are the butt of jokes and prejudice, while also the target of considerable envy, and we are leaders in the business of comedy and literature. There is even an old joke about it: Why do some people think Jesus was a Newfoundlander? He had twelve drinking buddies, he didn't leave home 'til he was thirty-two, and his mother thought he was God. Come to think about it, it was probably originally a joke about the Irish, but it still fits.

There is a strong and understandable resentment here in the Jewish community against Jews who assimilated, yet you can hardly blame the ones who just gave up and blended in. There was no official acknowledgement that Jews even existed—if you were listed in the census, you had only two choices, Catholic or Protestant. When Simon Solomon came out to set up as a watchmaker in the 1790s, he appeared on the records as a Protestant, because he had to be one or the other and why choose to be a Catholic? To be a Catholic was to be a Christian without any of the benefits of citizenship—not allowed to vote, not allowed to hold public office, sneered at, and so on. There were few enough women to marry, regardless of your religion, and no Jewish women at all. So the Jewish settler could stay single until he died, or marry and have Christian children. Not much choice there.

You say Harris was married and divorced. Divorce was permitted among Jews, but did that make it legitimate, according to the laws of the state at that time? Presumably, the divorce was legal in Germany, but was it recognized in Britain? Could he have married again in England? And, if so, was that the reason he came out to Newfoundland, and was his Newfoundland marriage legitimate?

What if, through some trick of fate, it turned out that Jacob Harris was my progenitor? You say he apparently had no strong religious belief, so what if he simply slipped out of his non-observant Jewish skin and into that of a non-observant Anglican or a lapsed Catholic, and lived happily ever after as the patriarch of a long line of contented, but indifferent, Christian Harrises? Should I feel ashamed of him? I'm not sure where I'm going with this speculation, except that perhaps I'm questioning whether it is such a terrible thing to just let the old self go and begin fresh.

I'm off to Trinity Bight tomorrow and will let you know if I crack the old lady's code.

Affectionately,
John

"Be compliant with your seniors, be affable with your juniors, and greet every person with a cheerful manner."

Rabbi Yishmael, Ethics of the Fathers

"Well, Mr. Harris, I was about to start firing off the guns in an attempt to flush you out of the woods." Captain Ryder held out a hand to help Rosehannah aboard the *William and Mary*, which seemed to Harris to be the epitome of civilized luxury, after so many months in a sod and timber tilt. "Come below and have some tea. And, I daresay you wouldn't mind a bite to eat as well. Mrs. Garland sent along some cheese and a basket of apples, just to wean you off your winter rations."

Rosehannah was suddenly aware of how she must look and made a brief, ineffective attempt to beat the twigs and bark off her sodden, grimy clothes.

"We look a sight, Captain, and for that I apologize. We were out after a few partridgeberries when we spotted you."

"Not to worry, my dear. Spent my first season in Newfoundland in winter quarters, and I can promise I looked a good deal worse than either of you by the time spring came." Ryder ushered them down into his tiny cabin and busied himself letting down the chart table while they got settled. "I must say, you look like you've come through the winter rather well, both of you. How are the others?" He looked to Rosehannah and so it was she who answered him.

"All well, God bless them," she answered. "No deaths, and no births, although I shouldn't be surprised if there's a birth before the next winter is on us. Missy Sevier has taken leave of her senses and Selby is swallowing the anchor as soon as they can get into Trinity to see the parson."

"Well, well, there's a filly to give him a run for his money. And what about yourself, Harris?" Ryder turned towards Garland's man, an amused glint in his eye. "You look pretty fit for a gentleman who's just crawled out of a snowbank after six months of freezing weather."

"I found the snowbank surprisingly comfortable, Captain, if you don't count a near-drowning, an attempted asphyxiation, various crippling accidents and at least one unprovoked murderous attack." He touched his bruised cheek, and smiled cheerfully. "In fact, I've been colder in some of the best parlours of London, than I was in our little hut in the woods."

"Is there anything wrong back in Trinity, Captain Ryder? It's too early for supplies." Rosehannah leaned forward anxiously. "Mr. and Mrs. Garland are well? And the children?"

"Right as rain, Miss Rose. Or should I be calling you Mrs. Harris?" He stifled a smile.

"You have always called me Rosehannah, sir, and I have always called you Captain Ryder," answered Rosehannah firmly. "What brings you out to Ireland's Eye so early in the season?"

"I believe Mrs. Garland was worrying about how you and Mr. Harris were managing, and Mr. Garland, to put her mind at ease, thought it would be a good idea for me just to dodge along over here and see how things stood. I'm to take back all that extra inventory you have on hand. Mrs. Garland went over the list of stock you sent back and she says some of it will sell now around the larger centres. Needle cases and sugar cutters and such fripperies are all the rage with the Irish servant girls, who now have servants of their own."

"Having seen what the average woman accomplishes in the run of a day around here, I've no doubt those Irish girls have earned whatever little luxuries their husbands can afford to give them," Harris put in, anxious to intercept any indignant eruptions from his companion. "Rosehannah, perhaps you could open up the house and find us some decent clothes, while I let Captain Ryder's men into the storeroom. The extra inventory is all packed up, so it shouldn't take long to get it aboard." He stood as he spoke and gestured for Rosehannah to precede him up onto the deck. He didn't care for the look of suspicion on her face and wished for the thousandth time that she weren't so tetchy.

"And is that all you have to do here, Captain? Ensure we are alive and pick up the surplus inventory?" Rosehannah clung resolutely to the chart table.

"Well, Mr. Garland did ask me to deliver this packet to Mr. Harris." Ryder reluctantly reached inside his coat and from an inner pocket pulled a small bundle of documents, tied and well embellished with official-looking wax seals. Perhaps you could get the men started on the loading, Harris, and then have a look at it. I shall wait in case there is a reply, or perhaps you will want to come to Trinity yourself to deal with it."

"So, you know already what it is, Captain." Rosehannah was not asking a question.

"No, not exactly, Rose. But I believe Mr. Garland does and he instructed me to wait and see what Mr. Harris wished to do in the matter." He studied her face but was unable to read the slight change that had registered when he spoke.

"Hold onto the documents, Captain Ryder, if you will," said Harris cautiously. "I'll see to the loading and then come back for them."

"I'll air out clean clothes for you and pack your sea-chest, Jacob. Whatever it is, Mr. Garland clearly expects you in Trinity." Rosehannah made her way out of the cabin and onto the wharf before either man could respond, and by the time they were on deck, she was beating her way up the hill to the house.

"She's a fine, lively girl, isn't she, Mr. Harris. No shilly-shally about her. She's all decision and acceptance." Ryder did not look at Harris when he said this.

"I'll open the storeroom," was all Harris replied.

"Rosehannah?" Harris peered into the gloom of the upper room.

"Here, Jacob." Rosehannah was on her knees in the corner, setting the last of his belongings into his trunk. "There are a few things at the winterhouse. I'll pack them up and send them on to you when the schooner comes back. Mr. Garland can forward them, if you've left Trinity."

"Don't you want to know what this is all about?"

"Do you want me to know, Jacob?"

"Mrs. Hart has died. She left me a small legacy."

"I'm sorry, Jacob. For the loss, not for the legacy. I know you were fond of her." Rosehannah lowered the lid and then struggled to slide a rope under the sea chest. "You never did get around to fixing that lock. Perhaps Mr. Green can do it for you when you get to Trinity." Harris made his way into the small room, and leaned over to lift the end of the chest, so she could slide the rope under. "It's not as full as when you arrived. If I can't get your winterhouse things to you in time, you shall have to get some furs or something to fill it up when you go back to England or the contents will slide around."

"Forget the winterhouse. There's nothing there of any value." He closed his hand over her two, which were struggling to tighten the rope into a knot. "Rosehannah, you can't go back there. You must come with me to Trinity. If I leave Ireland's Eye, Garland will have to send someone else out and they'll want this house, and you can't live in that hut. It's one thing to make do for a few months, but a lifetime in a place like that, with an illiterate husband and half a dozen babies in as many years…"

"Whether a man can read and write is not what determines his fitness as a husband. Not out here." Her eyes filled with angry tears and she blinked hard. Abruptly, she stood, banging her head on the low beams of the roof. "Oh…fiddlesticks!" She lowered herself down onto the bare ropes of the bedstead and rubbed her scalp, while allowing two scant tears to trace a path down her face. "Any decent man would have taught me some proper swear words during a winter's sojourn in a tilt, and here I am with nothing but the same tired old euphemisms to fall back on, just when I could really use a good, sound fit of profanity."

"Rosie, I can't leave you here. I've sent one of Ryder's men over to tell Ganny and the others that we are both going in to Trinity and we'll be in touch about our belongings when the schooner comes back. If we can't come up with a better plan once we're there, then you can return, though I think you know very well that it won't work. You're too clever for a place this small. Your talents are wasted." Harris dropped wearily onto his sea chest. "Garland says I'm to bring you in. Mrs. Garland is expecting you. Go and get your things together."

Rosehannah remained hunched miserably on the low bed frame for a moment, her hands pressed against her hot cheeks, before replying. "One word. Give me one very bad word that I can say to myself when I'm upset and I'll go."

Harris thought for a moment. "*Pupik*! That's your word. *Pupik*! And you must never say it to another soul or I shall die of shame on your behalf."

"What does it mean?" Rosehannah looked up at him, all sign of tears now gone.

"It means…" He struggled. "You know, your thing in the middle, your…" He gestured helplessly and then poked himself in the belly.

"*Umbilicus?*" Rosehannah asked. "And that's a swear word?" She sounded skeptical.

"It is in Yiddish. It's a very bad swear word."

"*Pupik!*" said Rosehannah. "Oh, *pupik!*"

"Please," said Harris, wincing visibly. "Not in front of me. Not in front of anyone."

"Why is it a bad word? It isn't a bad word in English."

"The English are cold. They don't know about these things. Everyone else in the world knows that the umbilicus…the *pupik*," he whispered, "is the seat of wantonness in women, so it's even worse for a woman to say it than for a man."

Rosehannah studied him carefully for a moment, and then apparently saw in his face whatever it was she was looking for. "Very well. I'll go get packed. But I'm not promising to stay there. If I don't like it, I shall come straight home on the next boat." She rose, ducked out the door, and within minutes Harris could hear her packing.

"*Oi gevald!*" he groaned to himself. "Oh, *pupik!*" he whispered decisively, and smiled.

October 12, 05

Dear Brina,

I was right, Mrs. Pitcher was holding out on me. It took some coaxing, and a reminder that at eighty-seven years of age she should be making
her soul, but she finally spilled the beans on the Ivanhoe box.

Apparently, she knew all along that Ivanhoe was called after the
novel, not after the Ivany family. It was a little conceit the Rev. Stickings
adopted to bind his backsliding parishioners to him. The notion that it
was to honour the Ivany family came weeks after he had submitted the
name to the nomenclature board, and from his point of view, the similar-
ity between Ivany's Hole (which it never was) and Ivanhoe was just a
happy coincidence.

Remember John Ivany, the ruffian from Skimmers Cove who first settled in Old Tilt? Well, he found the "treasure box," as Mrs. Pitcher called
it, when he tore down the old tilt for which he had named the place. He
had been using the structure as a barn, but it had finally collapsed, and
under the eaves, in next to the chimney which was made of nail kegs
stacked and strapped together, was the box. I expect the heat and smoke of
the chimney leaking through was partly what kept the contents from rotting.

Well, he kept the find to himself, but began asking around Ireland's
Eye about who had inhabited the winterhouse, and it turned out that the
Toops had used it for quite a while. Mrs. Pitcher said it had actually been
built by a man named Quint, presumably Rosehannah's father who put his
X on her marriage certificate. He'd left for Ryder's Cove, and a fellow they
called Old England, one of John Garland's men, took in the Quint girl.
The two of them disappeared one night, and the Toops worried that they
might be accused of doing away with them, so they "put away" the things
they'd left behind. I imagine there were a great many more bits than these
few, but they would have been generic, odds and ends that anyone might
have owned. These were probably the only things that could positively be
identified as not belonging to the Toops.

Mrs. Pitcher says that the Toops wanted to keep the stuff, but John
Ivany insisted it be turned over to Rev. Stickling. Ivany was Mrs.
Pitcher's grandfather and, if he was as sly as she is, I expect it was the
other way around and it was the Toops who insisted on giving it to the
minister. In any case, Stickling got the box, including the book, which of

course gave him the idea for the name years later when he was asked to rec-
ommend a new name for Old Tilt, and then he gave it back to Mrs.
Pitcher's parents as a wedding present. They were too nervous about the
provenance to use the stuff, so back into the rafters it went until it finally
came down to Mrs. Pitcher, who sold it to me.

I doubt we will ever know any more about it than that. I have sent
the marriage certificate and the Schutzbrief *to the archive, along with the*
collar and a brief account of where they came from. I have kept the can-
dlesticks and am presently reading the copy of Ivanhoe *to Shibby and*
Leah.

My folk history of the Jews in Newfoundland has gone to the publisher.
I have dedicated it to Tali, because it was really her book, not mine. If I
ever write another book, it will be on one of my own areas of interest, not
one wished on me by someone else—maybe Plate Dancing in Greene's
Harbour, *or* Parody and Scatology in Dance Tune Mnemonics *or*
Depictions of Seabirds in Newfoundland Folk Art.

I have been packing up the boxes of books and papers I used while
researching the manuscript and am bringing them all to the synagogue for
the library. My workspace looks tidy and bare, as if I am about to go off
on a journey. I would, too, if I could think of where to go. When you fin-
ish with the launch of your own book, maybe we could run away together
to some place warm with lots of birds. I could cook for you while you work
on your life list.

Shibby has been looking over my shoulder, which she is absolutely for-
bidden to do, and says I am not to go anywhere until I finish reading
Ivanhoe. *Culhoon is whining at the door and threatening to have an*
accident, so I guess I can't run away just yet. I feel curiously empty. Do
you feel that way about letting your salon women loose into the world?

Please write as soon as you have time. I am rather lonely again, I
believe. It is a curious feeling after all this time and I'm not sure I like it.
Love,
John

P.S. I have just received the pre-publication copy of your book, and I
note that you gave Jacob Harris exactly three lines. He gets only two in
mine. Wherever he went, I hope he found happiness. When I come to

London for your book launch, I will be bringing his candlesticks with me—
I hope you will accept them.

    Yours, J.

"If I am not for me, who will be? If I am for myself alone, what am I? And if not now, when?"

Hillel, Ehtics of the Fathers

Rosehannah found Harris at the rail of the schooner. He turned and led her across the deck to an upturned puncheon, and then squatted companionably down beside her. She tucked away the stray wisps of hair that were escaping from under her shawl before speaking. "Have you decided what you are going to do once you are back in England?"

"I'm not sure it's necessary for me to go back to England. I've been thinking that if the legacy is enough for me to live a moderately dull and respectable life in London, it might just be enough for me to set up in a small way as a merchant somewhere here in the colony. If I move out of Garland's district, he might be happy enough to have a friendly competitor fill some of the gaps in his trading system, rather than risk having a more voracious opponent, or worse still, leave the way open for opportunists coming in from Boston."

"You could do well as a small trader—perhaps, with your connections, you might in time even expand out to be as big as Mr. Garland himself." The wind kept pulling bits of Rosehannah's hair and she battened down her shawl before speaking again. "You'd need some help—a youngster who can cipher or someone to keep an eye on things when you are away."

Harris didn't respond immediately, but looked up at her, as if measuring her words before speaking himself. "What about you, Rose? What are your plans?"

"I have decided that I am ready to be married, Mr. Harris," she answered decisively. "Mrs. Toop told me last autumn that when I get to Trinity, I can ask Mr. Garland to provide me an annulment to the ceremony Captain Ryder performed. I'm going to do that and then I shall ask Mrs. Garland if she can recommend me to a kind and steady man who would be willing to let me take a hand in making a living. It's a seller's market for wives around here, I'm told, and I won't sell myself cheap."

"And do you think Mrs. Garland will be able to find you such a husband? Back in London, I should have to put myself into the hands of professional match-maker if I were looking for a wife."

"Mrs. Garland is better than a professional—she makes marriages for the love of the game. She is said to be an artist in her own way, able to intuit out the most unlikely unions, and not a mismatch in all the years she's been at it."

"And you would trust her with your happiness?" Harris turned so as to block the wind which was whipping high colour into Rosehannah's usually pale face.

"No, Jacob, I would not. I trust my happiness to nobody but myself. But I do trust her to put me in the way of someone who would enter into marriage with good will and the best intentions. Nobody can ask more than that."

"That settles it then." Harris stood abruptly, and held a hand out to help Rosehannah up from her makeshift seat. They could smell the smoke of Trinity on the wind, and already the underlying stench of gurry, nightsoil and manure was wafting over the rail of the schooner. "If the woman is as good as you say, then I, too, shall appeal to her for assistance in finding a mate. If she can find someone to marry a stubborn, willful Irishwoman like you, she will have no trouble matching up a fine, upstanding Jew with a few coins in his pocket and an ace or two up his sleeve." He tucked Rosehannah's hand under his arm and held tight to the rail, while the schooner heaved and bucked its way into the wind, carrying the two of them closer by the moment into the bustling harbour.